III

for the

THRONE

I

THE TRIAL OF TEN

S. McPHERSON

*This book contains varying degrees of the following:
dub con, violence, and open-door scenes intended for an audience of
18+ Please read safely and responsibly.*

FIT FOR THE THRONE: THE TRIAL OF TEN

Book 1 in the Fit for the Throne series

Published by S. McPherson
ISBN: 978-1-9163026-5-5
Copyright © 2022 (Kindle Vella)
Copyright © 2023 (Paperback)
All rights reserved.

To learn more about the author visit:

Instagram:
https://www.instagram.com/smcphersonbooks/
Tiktok: https://www.tiktok.com/@s_mcpherson_books
Bookbub: https://www.bookbub.com/profile/s-mcpherson
Facebook: https://www.facebook.com/Smcphersonbooks

This book is dedicated to those who dream of distant worlds and the devious men who dwell there...

ENTER
the
TRIALS

1

The Stranger

Whoever said diamonds were a girl's best friend, had never tried tequila. Specifically, Tequila Sunrise. Saluting the bartender, I knocked back my sixth sugary cocktail and cackled at the club ceiling. Tonight, was going to be a good night.

My hips pumped in time with the music and, just for a moment, I could pretend. Pretend that the girls I giggled with in the bathroom were my best friends and that the men I grinded with on the dance floor were my lovers. I could pretend that when we rolled our eyes at the stumbling waitress, it was an inside joke we'd shared for years. I could pretend that when I left the club tonight, I'd be going home—a place to call my own—not some rickety cot in a bar's back office.

"Girl, you look thirsty!" Marcus hollered over the music.

I smirked. "For a drink or for a man?"

"I was talking about a drink but you know I'd never say no to a man, honey."

I laughed and planted a kiss on his glittery cheek. I'd known Marcus for approximately three hours, and he was quickly becoming my favorite person of the night.

He'd instantly fallen in love with my deep hazel eyes, the reddish brown of my russet skin, my thick, dark Afro puffs and my ability to drop it low with the best of them. I'd immediately swooned over his hard pecs streaked with a rainbow flag and his *You Only Live Once* attitude. Now we were inseparable.

He pushed another cocktail into my hand and I lifted the glass in a toast.

"To new friends."

"May we never end." He thunked his glass against mine.

I smiled through a twinge of sadness. It always ended once the beer goggles came off and the truth came out. But that was a later problem. Now, I wanted to get shitfaced and forget about my troubles. Not that I'd ever gotten tits-up drunk. A healthy buzz was as much as I could hope for, no matter how much I drank.

I took another hefty gulp of my drink and almost choked when I noticed *him*. A raven-haired god-of-a-man with eyes that seemed to glow. They were unusual; a strange blend of deep lilac and dark pink and were pinned on me.

"Holy hotness," I breathed.

"Who is that?"

"I wish I knew."

Although, by the looks of it, I was about to find out. The stranger prowled towards me with intent in every stride. Heads swiveled in his direction, drawn by his mere presence. Eyes widened and mouths dropped open. If he noticed, he didn't show it. He only had eyes for me, which was as flattering as it was ridiculous.

I practically swooned when he reached me. Almost pressed a hand to my forehead and fanned my bloody cheeks.

"Hello, little bud." His gravelly voice was a thing of sin—low, seductive and entirely disarming. "I've found you, at last."

I blinked; reeled in by his closeness and heady scent. Was this my lucky night or what?

I downed the rest of my drink and ran my tongue across my upper lip, tasting tequila, orange and my strawberry lip balm. "And what are you going to do about it?"

My hips swished as I moved closer, setting my glass down on one of the standing tables. It was possible I was suffering from a severe case of tequila goggles but if they made the guy look like him, I didn't care. He'd be gone in the morning anyway, like everyone else.

I pushed up onto my tiptoes and draped my arms around his shoulders. Even in my heels, he was almost a foot taller; a towering wall of hard muscle sheathed beneath sun-bronzed skin. *Yum.* I drank him in; the height of his angular cheekbones, the cut of his square jaw, the slight point to his ears, and the deep set of his pale pink eyes that were pulled into a frown.

"What are you doing?"

I snickered. "Dancing?"

The stranger's frown deepened, and a muscle ticked in his jaw. "I didn't come here to dance."

"No?" I asked with a sly grin. I was barely listening to him; mostly admiring the movement of his mouth and imagining how it would feel against mine. "What did you come for?"

"You."

Heat flushed my skin. I barely suppressed a shiver of desire.

"Is that so?" I angled my head towards him; lips parted in invitation.

The stranger scoffed. "I didn't come for that either. I'm here to take you to *De Cinque Istrovos*."

"Where?"

"The Five Isles. Home of the blessed; those with enchanted blood, like you."

I stepped back, fighting off a laugh. Damn, I should have known. The only way a guy like him would be interested in me was if he was completely wasted. And this guy apparently was.

Pity.

I scanned the crowd for Marcus. The stranger had a pretty face but if he wasn't going to let me sit on it, there was no point in hanging around.

"Thanks. Maybe later."

I shook my head and turned away only to slam into the stranger's chest. I reeled back.

What the heck? He'd moved with blinding speed.

"I don't have time for this, Varialla."

His husky voice drizzled over my name and my toes curled in my 3-inch stilettos. What I wouldn't give to hear him purr my name all night long.

"Wait…" I rocked back, fear seeping through my tipsy haze. "How do you know my name?"

The stranger grinned; a wicked thing hinged on arrogance and charm. "Like I said, I came here for you."

Before I could argue, he grabbed my arm and pulled me towards the exit.

"Get off me!" I cried, trying to pry free.

My eyes searched for anyone who might help, and my blood ran cold when I saw myself and the stranger on the dance floor. His hands were curled around my backside and my fingers were tangled in his hair as we moved in time to the beat, our hips pulsating. We looked like we were one second away from tearing each other's clothes off. But it wasn't us.

My knees buckled. What the hell was going on?

"You'll find the Fae are quite skilled at illusion," the stranger purred, as if he'd read my mind. "No one can see us. To everyone here, we're over there."

We stepped out of the club and onto Trenchwood street. My body shook but not from the evening cold.

The stranger—the *Fae?* —pulled me against him. "Wrap your legs around me."

"I'm not that drunk, asshole." Though I was beginning to think I was. Or worse, that someone had spiked my drink.

He chuckled darkly. Midnight blue wings scored with threads of violet surged from his back. If he hadn't been holding me, I would have fallen down.

"Have it your way." Fae-boy bent his knees then shot upwards into the inky black sky.

My gut lurched and the world spun. Wrapped in the stranger's arms, I hurtled towards the stars. My scream snatched away by the wind. My fingers dug into his bulging biceps. His wings—*wings*—beating rhythmically at his back.

The night shattered and daylight erupted. Black spots swam across my vision then faded into midday sun. Its heat seeped into my bones, the sky a brilliant shade of turquoise.

My heart raced as we descended. This wasn't happening. This *couldn't be* happening.

The second my feet struck the ground; I staggered out of the strangers hold and retched onto a white marble step. The tequila burned worse on the way up. I wasn't the type to puke after a few drinks but apparently, careening through the sky in the arms of a winged man would do it.

"Are you finished?" His tone was flat.

I groaned and crushed the heels of my hands into my eyes, hoping that when I reopened them, I'd be back at the club. Instead, I was still here with him, standing in an open-air arena. Everything from the pillars to the raised seating was carved from raw marble and in the center, was an expansive field of powdered sand.

I swallowed, tasting citrus and bile. Hands braced on my knees; I heaved a final time.

My sullen stranger snarled, "Were you always such a train wreck?"

I wiped my mouth on the back of my hand and sneered. "I was never even on the track."

He made a guttural sound. I glared up at him, noticing that his wings were, once again, concealed. Like he had some kind of retraction switch.

"Come on. We're late," he huffed then strode across the arena.

I stared after him, debating whether it was a good idea to follow. Although my choices were limited.

Praying to a God I hadn't really considered until now; I smoothed down the hem of my gold-sequined minidress and stalked after Fae-boy. I had to admit, the view wasn't bad. He'd removed his black leather trench coat with olive green lapels—that had somehow morphed around his wings—to reveal one hell of an ass. The kind that filled out his dark fitted trousers and made my knees go weak—well, weaker than they already were.

I snorted. Of all the times to be swooning over some guy, this was not it. Then again, it was better than facing this impossible reality.

We stepped beneath an archway and a familiar symbol carved into the stone, caught my eye. I stumbled to a stop, gawking at the four-petalled flower. Each petal was separated by a gap with a circle in its center.

"What's this?" I asked. And what was it doing here?

"It's *De Cinque Istrovos;* the Five Isles." He tapped the circle in the middle. "You're currently in the Isle of the Eternals."

My thoughts raced. It was no coincidence that it was here.

"And this, is the Eternal City."

I rushed to keep up as we left the arena and entered a place of emerald grounds, arching trees, cobblestoned footpaths and medieval fortresses.

People…or rather, beings…were everywhere. They read beneath trees, sprawled out in the grass, made things levitate with a wave of their hands, and ate ice-creams whilst sitting on tree swings. They laughed as if there was nothing amiss. Like it was perfectly normal to have a picnic with someone who had giant red wings or a drooping snout.

A half-woman, half-horse, pranced between them and sang of broken crowns as a harpist played. Her ample bust was bare and bouncing; her dark skin burnished by the high sun.

I gasped. "That's a centaur."

Fae-boy drawled, "And you thought you wouldn't know anything."

Ignoring him, I gaped around me. The possibility that my drink had been spiked seemed more and more likely.

"Stop gawking," he grumbled.

"Can you blame me? That's a centaur."

Fae-boy let out an exasperated sigh. "Centaurs live in the Outer Isles but those with exceptional talents are occasionally invited here to attend certain functions."

"Outer Isles? As in there are more beyond the main five?"

He stiffened, his jaw tight. "None that matter."

There was so much brimming beneath the surface of those words.

"Move," he grumbled and stalked off.

I scowled and followed after him. Strange glass-like orbs that occasionally flashed, hovered overhead. Before I could ask what they were, I was, again, distracted by the impossibly familiar symbol of the Five Isles. It was printed on a large purple flag that billowed in the entrance of a black granite fortress with grand turrets, purple spires, and arched glassless windows.

My breath caught and I pulled my iPhone from between my cleavage. If this was real, I needed photographic evidence. However, when I tapped the screen, static rippled across it.

Fae-boy's hand pressed into the small of my back, sending shivers up my spine.

"Put one foot in front of the other, Varialla," he murmured. "Now."

Tongue-tied, I obeyed. The touch of his fingers would have made me agree to anything. What was wrong with me?

"That's it," he drawled. "I knew you could do it."

I glared at him over my shoulder but said nothing. My heart rabbited in my chest. Fae-boy didn't lower his hand as he steered me down marble arched corridors and passed silver suits of armor. It was impossible to concentrate on anything else.

Eventually and thankfully, we came to an oakwood door engraved with golden sparrows. He moved around me, unlocking the door, and we stepped inside a beautiful bedroom, lit by daylight. Before I could take it all in, however, Fae-boy spun around and slammed me against the wall.

2

FOUL FAE-BOY

Terror tore down my spine; my eyes shot wide.

"Who are you?" Fae-boy growled.

"What?" I tried to wrench free, but he'd pinned my wrists to the wall at either side of my head.

"Drop the act. I sensed your power the second I entered the human realm and it's only gotten stronger since we arrived here."

"I don't know what you're talking about."

The pink hue of his eyes turned a violent shade of red. "Liar."

Swallowing my fear, I gritted my teeth and latched onto rage instead. I should be terrified but I'd learned long ago to bury it. Fear served no one and nothing.

"Let me go, Fae-boy."

His eyes narrowed and he leaned closer; forcing my head to tip back so I could meet his burning stare. My breath stalled. He really was gorgeous. The heat of his body pulled me in.

"I'm no ordinary Fae. I'm of the *Bravinore* race; direct descendant of the Fates." He watched me closely as if expecting to see recognition in my eyes, but I didn't have a clue what he was talking about. "I am Protector of the Realm."

I pushed forward, getting right up in his face—or as much as I could considering he towered over me. "You're an asshole."

He grinned. "I go by many names."

His gaze flicked to my mouth that I'd unwittingly brought closer to his and my heart skipped. Something shifted in his stare; darkened, and he dragged his thumbs along the inner side of my wrists. Hot sparks lit inside my skin. I barely resisted the urge to close my eyes.

"This is the only chance I'll give you, little bud." His breath shuddered across my lips as he bowed his head. I could practically taste him; sweet and intoxicating. "Who are you?"

"Varialla von Hastings."

"Did your mother give you that name?" He pressed closer, forcing my hips back into the wall.

I smothered a moan. His scent made me dizzy in the best and worst way.

Focus, Varialla.

"I never met the woman," I managed to say, my voice breathless. What was it about this guy?

"Then who named you?"

His thumbs continued to trace circles on my skin, and I almost arched into him. There was no denying, he was delusional, demanding and pig-headed but there was something about him that drew me in and had my pulse racing.

11

"The name Varialla was stitched onto the blanket I was found in and…" My voice trailed off. I'd never told anyone this. "I chose the name Von Hastings, when I was six years old." I looked down; irritated and embarrassed. "It felt like the kind of name someone important would have. Someone who mattered."

Someone who wasn't thrown out like yesterday's trash.

Steeling myself, I met his stare; waited for his mocking taunt.

He blinked at me. "Is this the part where I'm supposed to weep?"

"Forget it!" I uselessly tried to wrench free. Of course, he didn't care about my sob story. Why would he?

He chuckled as I squirmed which only infuriated me more.

"Settle down, little bud. You're creasing my shirt."

I snarled, "Why did you even bring me here, asshole? Take me home!"

His calloused thumb moved to the middle of my palm. His pressure intensified. Every cell in my body honed in on that point.

Fae-boy bared his teeth as he stepped closer. I temporarily forgot how to breathe.

"This is your home now."

The earth pitched. His words rang in my ears. Before I could ask him if he'd lost his bloody mind, fists pounded on the door. My heart clamored in my chest.

"Hello?" A lilting voice called.

Fae-boy finally stepped back; his eyes still locked on mine.

"Hello? You didn't run away, did you?"

A trill of laughter followed this remark.

"Hello?"

The door clicked open. Five women in flowy dresses fluttered into the room. There was something ethereal about them, an unnatural grace and beauty. Flowers or leaves dotted their hair and one had antlers growing from the crown of her head.

I blinked more times than I thought possible. My tongue stuck to the roof of my mouth.

The ladies screeched to a halt when they saw *him*.

"Exekiel V'alin," gasped the girl with the antlers, her skin the color of melted honey. She bowed. The others followed. "I hope we aren't interrupting." There was a sly curve to her smile and a suggestive glint in her eye.

"Not at all," Exekiel dipped his head, the picture of a perfect gentleman. I almost laughed. "I was just leaving."

He strode out of the room with five sets of wide eyes staring after him. When the door clicked shut, they spun to face me.

"Now I know why you didn't answer the door." Antler-girl waggled her brows at me. "I'm Eudora Thistle, wood-nymph and trusted stylist to the stars."

I scrubbed a hand down my face. I couldn't keep up. All I wanted to do was curl up and scream into a pillow. "Okay?"

Eudora cackled. "You have no idea what's going on, do you?" Before I could respond, she cried, "Girls, she has no idea what's going on."

Like bells, they fell into tinkling laughter.

Eudora strutted further into the room, and I finally took it in. It was like the chamber had been cut from my childhood fantasies. The type befitting the Von Hastings name. Everything was a shade of blue and gold. From the plush carpets and velvet drapes to the crystals cut into the beveled wall. The canopy that fell over a fourposter bed was a deep blue patterned with gold, and floor-to-ceiling windows led out onto a grand terrace.

"There are two ways one can communicate. With their mouth and with their body. To be a queen, you must command with both." Eudora stated. "Your mind must be sharp for the words out of your mouth and your ensemble must be fierce for the words you do not say. That's where we come in—your team of stylists throughout the Games."

I frowned. "Games?"

"The reason you're here." Eudora raised a brow. "Every century, a new heir is crowned; chosen to govern the Five Isles and beyond. Whoever wins the Games, wins the throne." She scooped up a purple padded envelope that rested on the bedside table. "It's all in your welcome pack."

She handed me the envelope. It had my name on it and the return address was the Bureau of Royal Games.

I peeled open the wax seal and emptied the contents onto the bed. There was an invitation to compete in the Royal Games, a travel brochure of the Five Isles, a pamphlet for something called, Fit for the Throne, and a flyer, detailing activities for the upcoming summer solstice.

Lastly, there was a translucent device almost as thin as a sheet of paper. When I tapped the symbol of the Five Isles in its center, the wires inside lit up and a holographic screen emerged, about the size of my hand.

I squeaked. "What's this?"

The nymphs laughed and Eudora pressed a hand to her mouth as if she couldn't stop.

"A phone," she snorted. "You really know nothing. We'll have to fill you in while you get ready."

My head snapped up. "For what?"

Although, I vaguely remembered Exekiel saying we were late.

"The Opening Ceremony."

The nymphs spun into action. They set up racks of glittering gowns with matching heels and laid out vials, powders and extravagant jewels.

Before I could argue, my clothes were stripped, and I was dragged into the bath chamber where they ushered me into what looked like a heated rock pool. In seconds, I was submerged in sweet-scented water with five naked females pawing at me. Not my typical Saturday night.

I yelped and swatted them as they scrubbed my skin, but they carried on regardless.

"The first thing you should know, is that Fit for the Throne is the name of the show you'll be competing in to take the throne." Eudora explained. "And every step of your journey will be documented in real-time."

My blood went cold despite the warmth of the water.

"Competing?" I gasped. "I don't want to compete."

The nymphs laughed again. Apparently, I was hilarious.

"That isn't your choice." Eudora snorted as she scrubbed at my fingernails. "Once your name has been selected, the only way out of the Games is to play them. And you must play to win or die trying." She moved onto my arms. "And don't even think about running. It would be considered an insult to the Crown and is punishable by death."

My stomach dropped. Whether I stayed or left, my life was at risk.

Oblivious, Eudora went on. Something about reality shows, orb-vision, and eternal glory. It all went by in a blur.

Eventually, I was ready. My hair had been slicked upwards into a high ponytail where my tight Afro curls plumed from the center, and I wore a striking gown. The color was a gradient of turquoise run-through with golden threads. The top: a fitted bodice that accentuated my bust, had delicate off-the-shoulder sleeves that fell to mid-thigh.

Eudora whistled. "_Qhithalas,_ we're good."

I didn't know whether to be insulted or flattered at the blatant awe on the woman's face.

The nymph bowed her head; antlers glinting in the amber light. "You certainly look the part, Varialla. May you go with the brave and the blessed."

I'd never been on a horse and carriage, yet now, I was on a chariot pulled by a Pegasus, a white horse with silver wings. I held on for dear life as a herd of them galloped through the Eternal City towards a domed building with images projected onto its black glass surface.

Mine was among them. It was a photo taken earlier today, although it felt like a lifetime ago. My eyes were wide and hair wild.

Underneath, it read:
Varialla von Hastings

Cast: *Partially unknown*

Origin: *Undisclosed*

It was a slight distinction between the words but blatantly clear. My cast—whatever that was—was unknown but my origin; wherever I came from was being kept a secret. The question was from who?

Another image followed of a woman who looked to be around the same age as me—early to mid-twenties—with braided hair, grey eyes and toffee-brown skin. She was the most human-looking person I'd seen so far.

Hers read:

Lucinda Ironclaw

Cast: *Witch*

Origin: *Wiccan's Wharf*

The other equally curious contestants left their chariots and I reluctantly followed. We entered the building—a grand structure with walls and floors carved from sapphire and emerald glass. Those strange orbs that occasionally flashed floated overhead. Thanks to Eudora, I now knew they were cameras recording my every move.

We were met by a line of nymphs and *satyrs*. My mouth dropped open. I'd expected to see more magical beings eventually but wasn't prepared for the half-man, half-goat creatures.

"Welcome, Initiates," cried a nymph with leaves in her hair. "To keep things organized, we're going to split you into four groups of twenty-five in the order your name was drawn from the Conduit."

I quickly did the math. There were a hundred contestants competing in the show. With that many, I should be able to slip away once the Games began…right?

"As I'm sure you all know, if your name was drawn in the top ten, it is a great honor, and you'll definitely have the public's eye."

The nymphs and satyrs began reeling off names, indicating who should go and stand where.

"Number one; Exekiel V'alin."

My heart leapt when he strode out in fitted black trousers and a wine-red tailcoat embroidered with threads of silver. His powerful wings were once again, on display, arcing through the enchanted fabric.

He was stunning. Crafted by angels and carved onto my heart. I jerked back from the thought. What the hell? Had I become a fainting lady from some classic romance novel? I was clearly losing my mind.

"Number two; Vivienne Foraglade."

A beautiful brunette with pale skin and large white wings strutted up beside Exekiel. They made a striking pair and the girl smiled at him seductively.

I couldn't help the irrational twinge of envy. As if I had some claim to the overbearing Protector of the Realm.

Something clattered behind me, and I turned to see a satyr apologizing to a Fae-Male as the plastic cup of water he'd held tumbled across the tiles.

"What the gorge is wrong with you?" The Fae spat. His tone harsh and blue eyes bright. He gripped the satyr's collar lifting him in the air, so his little goat legs kicked.

My brows shot up.

"You got water on my shoes, you little shit."

Those around him snickered as if his reaction was justified. As if this was normal.

"Useless Outer Isle scum." He released the satyr, dropping him in a puddle of water. "Clean it up."

Anger bit into my bones. Who the hell did this asshole think he was? Old hurts rose in my chest as I remembered my second foster family. They hadn't wanted a daughter; they'd wanted a servant that they got paid to keep. I knew what it was like to be rejected, used; cast aside.

"Varialla von Hastings." The nymph snapped impatiently. It was clear by her tone and the way she tapped her foot that it wasn't the first time she'd called my name. "Number five."

Every head swung in my direction. Shock was heavy in the air; none more so than mine. Did she say, five? I'd hoped to remain under the radar, find some way to evade the Games and make my way back to reality. Now, I was going to be under the microscope at number flipping five out of a hundred names drawn from the Conduit—whatever the heck that was.

Numbly, I made my way over to the nymph—the incident with the satyr *almost* forgotten. Someone bumped into me as I passed, and I felt the press of parchment in the palm of my hand. I looked up but too many contestants were shuffling around to grasp who'd given it to me.

Frowning, I unfolded the sheet and read:

Their blood is on your brow, and I will drown you in it.

3

OPENING CEREMONY

Things were off to a terrific start. In the space of a few hours, I'd been manhandled, ridiculed, witnessed serious injustice to a satyr, and now, held a death threat in my hands. Letting out a breath, I tucked the note into my cleavage as we were led out onto a stage.

My heart thundered in my chest. How the hell was I going to get out of here?

I couldn't make out anything beyond the glare of flashing lights and the roar of thunderous applause. Screens ran along the back of the stage replicating what I'd seen on the outside of the building, the players' names and images.

Ahead, two rows of red cushioned chairs were center stage, and a satyr in a frilly shirt waited on a raised platform. His skin was a lighter shade of brown than his fur. Two thick goat horns curved from his head and an orange goatee sprouted from his pointed chin.

I followed in a daze as the players moved towards the seats. My thoughts locked on the note; on what it could mean. And who had written it? I had no way of knowing. No way of making sense of it. Suddenly, forfeiting the Games and risking my life to escape, seemed worth it.

Everyone filed into their seats—each chair numbered. Reluctantly, I sat in the front row on number five.

"Good evening, enchanters. Welcome to Fit for the Throne!" the satyr shouted. The crowd howled. "The realm's favorite reality show has returned, and I, Goather, will be your host for the season."

He paced his narrow podium, his hooves clopping. "Over the next year, it will be my honor and privilege to mentor these players. To see them through challenges like they've never known, as, together we uncover who among them is…"

As one, players and audience bellowed, "Fit for the throne!"

I stayed silent; nerves brittle and about to snap. Did he say a year?

"As always, we have a few questions from the audience and will start with player number one—the first name drawn from the Conduit, and a fan favorite."

Goather spun towards Exekiel who leaned casually in his seat.

"I know I speak for everyone when we say what an honor it is to finally have you up on this stage."

The crowd erupted.

Exekiel grinned. "The honor is mine."

"Our question is, why do you think the Conduit chose you now and not the times before?"

Exekiel scratched his chiseled chin. "Hard to say. However, the Conduit does everything in its time, and it doesn't make mistakes."

Forgetting the microphone they'd clipped to my bodice, I snorted. The sound echoed through the auditorium, and everyone turned to me.

Crap.

"You don't agree?" Goather's eyes glinted. "You think the Conduit makes mistakes?"

I scoffed; arms folded across my chest. "I don't even know what the Conduit is."

Applause and laughter followed this.

Goather unleashed a toothy grin. "Isn't she adorable?"

My nostrils flared. *Condescending twat.*

I usually liked being the center of attention but this wasn't the dance floor of some dark club. This was a bad dream that I couldn't seem to wake up from.

As soon as I got off this stage, I was going to find someone with half a brain to take me home. For once, I couldn't wait to return to my cot in the back office of the Crowne and Lion.

Goather turned back to Exekiel. "Of course, sometimes the Conduit must wait for the mate to be ready as well."

Mate? I almost snorted again but caught myself.

"Perhaps that's why it waited until now to choose you."

Exekiel dipped his head. "Anything's possible."

Goather leaned in close, as if whispering a secret though he held a microphone to his lips. "And, who among these players, do you think could be your mate?"

"Me," Vivienne cackled from her number two seat.

I tensed.

Goather beamed. "Are you two together?"

"Not officially." Vivienne said with a mischievous smirk.

Again, something sharper than envy twisted in my gut. I didn't even know why I cared. *I didn't care.* Still, I watched Exekiel from beneath my lashes, desperately trying to gauge his reaction. As always, he gave nothing away.

Goather chuckled then moved onto the next players.

Eventually, he said, "Varialla von Hastings." The viewers fell unnaturally silent. "Our mystery from beyond the veil."

I braced myself; quietly thankful that I didn't suffer from stage fright. Although, chatting with a satyr while surrounded by Fae, elves and other supernatural beings, was still extremely disturbing.

"As you can imagine, there were many questions for you. However, this one came up more than others." Goather paused, clearly for dramatic effect. "What's your favorite song?"

The audience burst out laughing.

I frowned. "Depends on my mood?"

"I'm sure it does."

The laughter increased. My frown deepened. There was clearly a joke I'd somehow missed.

I scanned the other contestants who snickered and eyed me suspiciously. Then my gaze locked with familiar grey eyes. It was the witch from the image; Lucinda Ironclaw. She shrugged and rolled her eyes. The gesture set me mildly at ease. It wasn't much but it felt like a show of solidarity.

"After party" were just the words, I needed to hear. I eagerly followed the others as we were led offstage and taken to a majestic hall. Candle chandeliers flickered overhead; their flames reflected in the pearlescent marble flooring and grand pillars. A band of goblins played on a small stage and inanimate objects seemed to take on a life of their own.

Tall tables, suspended in mid-air, zipped across the room whenever they were needed. Bottles of wine wove between the guests, filling goblets that could be plucked from the air, and, of course, glass-like camera-orbs drifted over the people.

When a chalice appeared beside me, I graciously took it and swallowed a deep mouthful.

Centaurs came next, with trays of canapes perched on their backs. I pounced on an egg roll and almost wept. Other than a pitcher of water and some welcome biscuits that had been left on my dresser, I hadn't eaten anything since the club and time was starting to blur. How long had it been since then? Since the world made sense.

The centaur moved on. I rushed after him and almost careened into a moving table. Leaping aside, I slammed straight into someone's back.

"Sorry," I breathed then looked up to find Exekiel glaring down at me.

Holy hotness! I couldn't stop my gaze from roving the expanse of his muscled physique. When my eyes drifted South, all I could think was: Eggplant emoji. *Dear sweet, enlarged eggplant emoji.* What was he packing down there? Why couldn't I look away?

Catching myself, I tore my gaze back upwards only to meet the curve of his sinful smirk. It was like he knew exactly what I'd been looking at and exactly what I'd been thinking.

"Like what you see, little bud?"

My face flamed. Desperate to change the subject, I snapped, "Why do you keep calling me that?"

He grinned and swirled a goblet in his hand. His stare trailed over me; slow and lingering. "Because you haven't blossomed yet."

It was a simple answer, but my body burned—my knees shook. It was infuriating that he had this effect on me; that he pulled me in even when I wanted to run away.

Exekiel leaned in and I trembled when his soft lips brushed my ear. "I can't wait to see you open."

He disappeared into the crowd like smoke.

I let out a breath. It was definitely time to go.

"Making a play for number one?" I swiveled to find Vivienne prowling towards me. "It's a smart move. It's also *my* move."

I spluttered. "Excuse me? I'm n—"

"You should guard your mind better around the Fae if you plan on lying." Vivienne cut in. "I know you tried to kiss Exekiel the minute you met him."

I didn't know how she knew that but refusing to let her see that she got to me, I leveled her with a look. "Have you seen him?"

Her eyes narrowed and the girls that trailed her, stepped forward, their smiles sinister.

"I'd be careful if I was you. Seems like you have more than enough enemies already."

I sucked crumbs of egg roll from my fingers and shrugged. "Then what's a few more?"

My tone was steady, but I couldn't help wondering if the enemy Vivienne was talking about was the one who'd slipped me the note.

Her rouged lips pursed. "Do you like to dance, Varialla? I think you do. I think you should. *Dance.*"

The word ripped through me like a command. Before I knew what was happening, my body moved to the music.

My hips jerked. My arms went up in the air. I gaped wide-eyed at Vivienne and her cronies who laughed into their hands.

No matter how much I tried, I couldn't stop. The presence of something foreign slithered through my mind and dug its claws in.

Dance. Dance.

And dance I did. Not in time to the rhythmic beat that the band played, but completely at odds, as if I was having a seizure. Goather approached but he simply watched; his eyes bright—no doubt calculating how this would amp up the show's ratings.

All around me, contestants turned and laughed. Some went as far as to point and whip out their phones. I wanted to scream but kept it caged inside my mind. I'd vowed long ago, that I would never be vulnerable again and I wasn't about to start now in a sea of snakes.

Instead, heart racing, I turned to the band and shouted, "Play something faster."

The goblins gawked at me. They weren't even playing anymore.

"Come on," I urged feeling that cold press of power again. "Play something faster."

I forced a smile though I knew it was unhinged. However, to my delight, the band played. It was fast, thriving and brilliant.

My body twisted, my feet stamped and hips swished perfectly to the wild beat. Suddenly, I didn't look erratic. I looked and felt like a goddess born of song.

I threw my head back and let my curls sway. The command was still upon me—still pressed me to dance faster, harder, but these bitches didn't know I had a flair for frolicking.

Flashing orbs circled me from tip to toe. I kept up the ruse. I could be a party girl when I wanted to be, after all. Soon, the sharp press of magic slipped from my skin and I was back in control. My stare went to Vivienne who scowled from the shadows. I threw her, my best up-yours smile as the other players dove into a dance of their own.

Goather watched the exchange and chuckled to himself. "Let the games begin."

4

THE LIFE TOKEN

I was half asleep when the nymphs came to my room the next morning. They styled me in a deep-green, knee-length dress with puffy off-the-shoulder sleeves and curled my hair into twists.

"Why aren't you happy?" Eudora cried. "You're officially among the elite."

"An elite class of assholes," I grumbled.

Jerks who sent cryptic notes and enchanted people against their will. I'd tried to speak to Goather last night; insisted I shouldn't be here.

The satyr had simply drawled, "We all know that isn't true."

Which meant that, for the time being, I was stuck.

When I was finally ready, Eudora ushered me towards the Resident Dining Hall. I studied the paintings as I passed. Based on the plaques beneath them; they were portraits of previous Game Winners—

Primaries, they were called. Each one looked as smug as the last.

"Get off!" someone shouted.

Ahead of me, three large guys surrounded a male centaur. He bucked as they tried to lasso him and climb onto his back.

What the fuck?

First the satyr, now this? Others simply walked by, or worse, pulled out their phones to film it.

Anger clawed its way up my throat.

"Oi!" I snapped and jogged over. "What do you think you're doing?"

The males arched their bushy brows—shifters in mid-transformation.

"Having a bit of fun," grunted a tall dark-skinned guy with hunched shoulders and tufts of fur growing on the backs of his hands. He dragged his tongue across enlarged canines. His stare dipped to my breasts. "You want to have some fun, too?"

I almost threw up in my mouth. "I'll pass, thanks."

He prowled towards me and I stepped back. "That's too bad. I hear your kind are a force in the sack."

My kind? He knew what I was? The cast, unknown?

Behind me, the centaur gripped the lasso that was around his neck and flung it to the tiles with a clatter.

That turned the shifters attention away from me and I subtly shuffled back.

"Try that again, and I'll trample you into the ground," snarled the centaur then he galloped off.

I went to follow but the shifter stepped in front of me.

"You ruined our fun," he growled. Black spread across the whites of his eyes. "Now, we'll have to play with you."

My mind went blank as the others moved closer. *Shit.*

"Now, now, Onzlo," a low voice rumbled. "Play nice."

I was stunned at how quickly the shifters straightened and stepped back. They seemed to shrink; not looking directly at the newcomer.

He was built, with cropped-blonde hair and pale blue eyes. The definition of boyband pretty.

He inclined his head and gestured with his hand. "After you."

I hesitated. Common sense said not to go with him, but the alternative was staying behind with the three assholes.

Sighing, I stalked ahead, and he fell in step beside me.

"I'm a wolf shifter," he said, as if guessing I needed an explanation. He shot the others a look over his shoulder. "Alpha."

I couldn't mask my surprise when the shifters bowed their heads.

"Impressive."

He chuckled and we entered the cafeteria. There were no plastic chairs, or cooks with hairnets like I'd expected. Instead, everything was carved from ancient wood. From the steepled ceiling to the towering pillars. Rectangular tables were covered with purple cloth and silver lace. The cooks wore uniforms and berets in the same color and worked with a wave of their hands.

Items moved on their command. Each cook had an ethereal beauty and long pointed ears—Elves.

As we maneuvered through the hall and dodged levitating plates, I felt the others watching me. Most wore guarded expressions, sizing up a potential threat. My dance last night had got the party started, but now people saw me as a game player, and I'd never let them know I'd been the victim.

The shifter sidled onto a bench, and I shuffled in beside him. Across from us was another male with unnatural green eyes and penny-brown skin.

He nodded in greeting. "Congratulations. You just survived your first walk of shade."

"Thanks," I snorted, then took out my Five Isles phone and tapped the symbol to pull up the holographic screen. The welcome pack had said to order meals via the Muncher app.

Four symbols were on the phone's homepage: camera, maps, Muncher and Enchant-a-gram, which, when I clicked on it, was the Five Isles version of social media, complete with a newsfeed and photographs.

I tapped on Muncher next, relieved that they had creamy Irish coffee. I quickly punched in my order.

"I'm Phoebus by the way; wolf shifter," the blonde said then gestured to green eyes. "This is Maximus; warlock."

I nodded. "Varialla; no one."

Maximus smirked. "No one is no one in the Eternal City."

He sounded like Eudora.

A plate of food and steaming cup of coffee spun towards me and I spared a second to marvel at the magic before I tucked in.

Someone behind me grunted, "Move over," and squished into the gap beside Phoebus. Lucinda Ironclaw.

The witch studied me then said, "You reek of power."

It wasn't an accusation or question. Merely an observation. One as bizarre as me being here in the first place.

I sniffed. "You smell like daffodils at springtime."

She snickered. "I just might like you."

We'd barely got the conversation going before a bell rang.

I flinched. "What's that?"

Lucinda grinned. "Initiation."

We headed out into the sprawling grounds of the Fortress. There, Goather waited. He wore a fitted green shirt; his orange hair slicked back between his horns and had a microphone hooked around his ear.

"Welcome, Initiates."

The light of one of the orbs zeroed in on him. Goather turned and spoke directly to it.

"Prepare yourselves for the next year. It will be one like none other and by the end of it, one of you will be crowned ruler of *De Cinque Istrovos.*"

Everyone around me cheered.

"However, your entrance into the Games isn't guaranteed. To qualify, you must successfully complete a series of challenges over the next four months. These trials will test your endurance, strength, and skill."

I straightened. So, there was a way out of this.

"The Trials will be carried out every ten days and those of you who pass, will advance to the next level.

However, those who rank the lowest, will be sent to compete in the Blood Battles to fight for their place."

"What?" I screeched without thinking.

Heads turned in my direction. Some snickered and others whispered to each other.

"The Royal Games are for the brave and the blessed dear, not the wimpy and the weak," hollered a pale girl with hair as red as her eyes.

Laughter filled the air.

Goather added, "Worry not. What you lack in strength and skill, you can make up in personality. It's important that the people stand behind the chosen Royal and so, if the viewers like you, they can vote to keep you safe. If you receive enough votes, your life may be spared."

I blinked at the satyr, yet no one else batted an eyelid.

"Another way to save yourself is to procure a life token."

The others nodded but I was sinking fast. The stakes rising with every word he said.

Why was death their answer to everything? If I try to leave, death. Rank low in the Games, death. Meanwhile, based on the note I got last night, if I stayed, someone may very well kill me.

Goather tapped on an orb and a giant projection of a silver coin embossed with the four-petalled symbol of the Five Isles, came into view. Engraved in its center were the words: *Life Token*.

"This token spares you from elimination—no Blood Battle required. Once a week, you'll have a chance to find one. And this week that opportunity, is now."

An excited hum rippled through the players.

"Since it's the first week, I'll make it easy," Goather went on. "The token you seek is on the branch of a Sycamore tree in Creature's Copse; marked by a red flag. You'll have twenty minutes to retrieve and return with the token. If someone, takes it from you along the way, the token is theirs."

The players shuffled around me. My heart pounded hard in my chest. I didn't know how I was supposed to survive four months of trials, but until I found a way out of this, I had to at least stay out of the bottom rank.

"On your honor, initiates." Goather bellowed.

Orbs sailed into position; readying to follow the hunt.

"May you go with the brave and the blessed." He pulled a shell-like horn from his satchel, pressed it to his lips, and blew.

The contestants took off. Shifters burst into beasts. Fae spread their wings and flew. Witches and warlocks summoned brooms with a whispered incantation and elves rushed off at inhuman speeds. All I could do was follow.

But the more we ran, the greater the gap between me and them became. Creatures Copse loomed ahead, a glorious medley of trees; the red flag clear in the distance, but it might as well have been an ocean away.

Spying a shortcut through a narrow gap of trees, I ducked through it and almost slammed into a cheetah who growled before he thundered on.

"Want to give me a ride?" I hollered.

The shifter skidded to a stop. As he spun to face me, he transformed into a glorious male with golden locks. His eyes were a shocking yellow.

He sneered. "You want a ride, sweet thing?"

I groaned.

Men! One thing on their mind even in the midst of a race that could literally save their lives.

I folded my arms. "That's right, Kitty. I want you to give me a ride all the way to the token."

A sweet tang coated my tongue. I frowned and licked my lips. The shifters eyes widened as his body transformed back into a cheetah. He seemed to struggle for a moment, then bowed his head.

"What are you doing?"

He didn't move; only waited.

Finally, with no hope-in-hell of getting the token otherwise, I climbed onto his back and clung to his fur. He took off at blinding speed.

Stunned, I shrieked; "Th-thanks."

However, by the time we reached the tree, a Fae had already taken off with the token. Everyone pivoted after him. Some tried to knock him from the sky. But he made it to Goather's side with the token in hand.

Defeated, I moved to dismount but the cheetah picked up speed then flung me from his back. I landed hard on my spine. Air ripped from my lungs.

Back in his human form, the shifter advanced; his yellow eyes wild with fury. "Bitch!" He roared. "What did you do to me?"

5

HOLY HOTNESS

I scrambled back from the snarling shifter as he pounced and gripped the laced front of my dress. He crouched over me; his nose almost crushed to mine and teeth bared. "You are her, aren't you?"

"What?"

He shook me so hard, my brain rattled in my skull. "You're her!"

Half his face shifted—part cheetah, part man. His nails turned to claws that cleaved through my dress and tore my skin. Blood whelped from the gashes. I gritted my teeth; ready to fight like I had so many times before, but a brutal force slammed into the shifter and threw him aside.

Stunned, I gaped up at Exekiel who stood over me, his expression marred with cold quiet rage.

"Rule Number Thirty-six," he bit out, "Players are not permitted to attack each other outside of the Games."

The shifter bounded to his feet. "She used that stinking gift on me," he bellowed.

"Careful, Lance," Goather warned. 'Remember the oath."

"Sod your oath!" Lance thrust a finger at me. "This little bitch shouldn't be here. She's a fucking—" He staggered; choking as blood bubbled from between his lips and dribbled down his chin. He clutched his throat, trying to speak; trying to breathe. His nose bled and red seeped from the corners of his eyes.

Someone shouted, "No!" and others jumped back just as Lance's head exploded.

Before I could even pretend to grasp what was going on, Exekiel scooped me up and soared into the sky. My stomach lurched. I'd barely recovered from the gut-wrenching sensation, when he descended. We landed in the gardens. Without a word, he tugged me into an alcove covered by a thin curtain of vines.

The space was narrow, our bodies practically forced together; wedged between lattice walls, climbing lianas and hanging plants.

"What's going on?" I whispered.

My thoughts crashed together. Words tangled in my throat. What the hell was going on?

Exekiel did a quick sweep of the alcove, I guessed, for cameras. When he found none, he growled, "Did he hurt you?"

"What?"

He went to the torn fabric of my dress and wrenched it down. My heart flipped when the swell of my breast was exposed but he didn't seem to notice. In that moment, his attention was on the slashes carved into my skin.

"You're bleeding."

My body ran hot from his touch; but the memory of the shifter left me cold.

"It looks worse than it is," I lied. It burnt like a bitch.

I held my breath as Exekiel reached up and pulled a leaf from a vine. It had jagged edges and a blue tip. I tracked the stroke of his tongue as he licked it.

"This will hurt." He pressed the leaf over the worst of the wounds, and I hissed. He wasn't lying.

His jaw clenched. "That bastard is lucky his head exploded."

My eyes shot to his and he returned my stare with an intensity that scorched through my soul. He brought another leaf to his lips and licked it then placed it on my smaller wounds. I shivered. The graze of his fingers was like strokes of fire in my skin.

I released a soft sound and his wings twitched. He could have concealed them; given us more room, but he didn't.

Finally, his gaze went to the curve of my breast. The shade of his eyes deepened to a merlot-red. My breaths turned shallow.

"I need to search you."

"What?"

"I believe your powers are manifesting." He gripped my arm and rolled up the sleeve. "If they are, they may have left a mark on your skin."

I tensed. I didn't know about any new marks appearing but there was one mark on my hip that I couldn't let him find. One that had been there since birth and was definitely connected to this world.

I yanked my arm out of his grip. "Like I said, I'm just an ordinary girl."

His teeth flashed when he grinned. "And I'm just the tooth fairy."

He dropped to his knees and his calloused fingers slid up the length of my leg; skirted beneath the hem of my dress. *Holy hotness.* My pulse spiked. He didn't go higher than mid-thigh but it was enough to make my head spin. An ache bloomed between my thighs.

"You'd make a pretty tooth fairy," I breathed; trying to focus on something other than his roaming hands. "Although her wings are more delicate."

My fingers trailed over the tips of Exekiel's arched wings with more force than I intended.

He shuddered. "Don't do that."

I didn't miss the tightening of his shoulders. My brows lifted. "No?" I did it again.

He gritted his teeth and the sight of him on his knees, snarling up at me, did something to my insides. "No."

I smirked, intrigued, and thoroughly enjoying a bit of payback.

"Or what?" I goaded and dragged my fingers lower. Savoring the soft, leathery texture of his powerful wings.

He vaulted to his feet so suddenly, my breath caught. In a flash, Exekiel's hands were on the backs of my thighs as he hoisted me up and forced my legs apart. Our centers met and I moaned when he pressed the swelling ridge of his length against me.

"Or…" he rocked his hips. My toes curled. My body pulled tight. "You'll find out what I feel like inside you."

Holy shit!

The plant pots clanked behind me as I trembled. My fingers hooked into the lattice wall whilst my other hand was braced on his wing. He was fascinating. Beautiful. And, in this moment, destructive.

Our eyes locked as we moved against each other. I couldn't speak, couldn't think. Too many thoughts blurred in my mind and all I felt; all I wanted, was him. As if all the fear, anger and confusion of the last few days, could be erased by the brush of his lips.

What the hell was going on? Why did he have this effect on me? I appreciated a good dry-hump as much as anyone but this had me straining for air, on the edge of oblivion. On the list of reasons, I had to leave this place, my response to him was high up there.

"A Fae's wings are strong but sensitive, little bud."

He jerked his hips harder, and my head struck the wall as I flung it back. A moan caught in my throat. What were we doing?

Exekiel was the bastard who'd brought me here, who treated me like some dastardly villain. I'd be a fool to give him any part of me. It felt like if I gave him just one sliver, he'd eventually take everything.

"I didn't know the Fae were such babies," I rasped; pleasure building between my thighs.

He chuckled and brought his mouth to my ear. "You have no idea."

His teeth grazed my earlobe and sparks shot through my skin.

"Varialla."

The sound of my name from his lips had my blood roaring.

"Yes?" I almost whimpered as he grinded into me.

"You're still touching me."

My fingers flexed on his wing; the thought of pulling back unbearable. How could I stop exploring every vein and indent? But if I didn't, we might never leave this alcove.

"Right."

Desperately, I ripped my hand away and gripped the lattice. My arms splayed; legs trapped around him as his fingers dug into my waist.

"Have I made myself clear?"

For a second, my senses were so overwhelmed, I registered nothing but the bright hue of his magenta eyes and the torturous feel of him between my legs.

"One more thing," I panted; wracked with need and self-loathing. "Do you think we'll ever have a conversation without you pinning me to the wall?"

His grin deepened. "Where's the fun in that?"

Exekiel thrust a final time and my breath hitched, our eyes intrinsically locked. He stayed against me a moment longer before he finally set me back on my feet and turned to leave.

"Who did he think I was?" I called; everything now flooding back without the shelter of his body. "The shifter. Why did he..." I trailed off; unable to voice the words aloud. Why did he explode?

"One thing I've learned over the centuries, is don't ask questions you don't want the answers to."

"Centuries?"

He smirked at me over his shoulder. "Be careful, little bud. The realm is watching and so am I."

Then he ducked out from beneath the alcove and left me panting against the wall.

6

SMILE, WITCHES

Too restless to return to my room, I wandered through the sprawling grounds of the Eternal City. The need to pace with my thoughts was overwhelming. I came across cafés and quaint shops. But everyone in them—camera crew, contestants and staff—eyed me with mistrust and contempt. What the hell had I done to them?

When my Five Isle's phone vibrated, I fished it out of the belt around my waist. Countless notifications that looked like bubbles bounced across the transparent screen. Inside each was the face of a contestant. I tapped on the winged-camera symbol for Enchant-a-gram, and the person's image appeared beside a speech bubble.

A Lillian Deamon wrote: **I can't believe the Gaming Council are letting her stay.**

Lillian's bubble popped and another floated onto the screen.

Wolfie Baron: **R.I.E.P** **Lance** #AddingYourLifeToTheTally

Lola Black: **It should have been her blood that stained my *Valyntina* sandals.**

Swallowing the chunks that rose in my throat, I clicked out of the app. I didn't know what I'd done to these people or why they blamed me for Lance's death, but one thing was clear: This world wasn't for me. Death penalty or not; I was going to find a way out.

The Five Isles brochure had said something about ley lines. Powerful points of magic that I might be able to use to escape. It would be difficult to get to them with cameras watching my every move, but I had to try.

I was almost back at Residence Manor when a low voice purred, "Where have you been?"

My heart fluttered as Exekiel landed in front of me. I'd been so lost in thought; I hadn't noticed him. Now, I couldn't notice anything else. His wings were splayed, black and shimmering violet. His dark hair was windblown, and he smelt like sea salt mixed with his own sensual musk.

I pursed my lips; fighting the urge to breathe him in.

"I went for a walk," I said dryly and stalked past.

He caught my hand, stopping me. A hot current crackled up my arm. "Where?"

My stomach tightened but I glowered at the overbearing bastard.

"Around," I huffed. "And stop touching me."

He smirked; clearly noticing how flustered I was. "What if I like the way you feel?"

I tore my hand away before I did something embarrassing and stormed inside the building.

Exekiel followed. "Whatever you're planning, little bud, stop."

"What?" I rounded a corner and marched down the corridor that led to my room.

"You think you can escape. You can't."

I clenched my fists. "I can do whatever I want, asshole. Not that I'm planning anything."

I threw him an up-yours smile and finally arrived at my door.

Exekiel grabbed me from behind; pulling me against his hard chest; his arms tight around my midriff. My eyes closed; pulse pounding. He ran his lips along my neck and I shivered.

"Don't do anything you'll regret, little bud."

"Like what?" I snarled. Invite him into my room? I was seriously considering it.

"If you run, I'll come after you."

I tried to pull away but he only yanked me closer— my back flushed to his chest. My rear crushed into his groin. The indent of his cock was unmistakable. My breath hitched. Lust clamoring in the pit of my stomach. What was he doing to me?

"If you hide," he growled and splayed his hand possessively over my stomach, "I'll find you."

Frantic, I fumbled in my dress pockets for the key; my movements sloppy. How did he always reduce me to some quivering idiot?

"Like I said," I rasped as his hands brushed beneath my breasts. "I'm not planning anything."

I shoved the key into the lock, relieved when it clicked open. I wrenched away and rushed inside but before I could slam the door, Exekiel wedged his foot between it and the doorframe.

"Don't make me hunt you, little bud." His magenta eyes deepened. "I'll never stop."

We glared at each other until he finally pulled his foot back. I slammed the door then sagged against it. My heart hammered in my chest. If I wasn't sure about leaving before, I was determined now. Somehow, I'd find a way back to Nottingham. My life hadn't been much there, but it had been mine. Here, I was defenseless and at the mercy of monsters and magical maniacs who wanted me dead for reasons I couldn't begin to understand.

I was sprawled on the bed, studying a map of the Five Isles, when someone knocked on the door.

"Who is it?"

"Friends."

I snorted. "I don't have friends."

But I recognized the voice as Lucinda, so got up and opened the door. The witch held up a plate of food and beside her, Maximus waved two wine bottles.

"At the very least, we're an alliance." Lucinda pushed past me and into the room. She gave the space a once over with her cool grey eyes then hopped up onto the bed. "Hungry?"

I snatched the plate and shoveled in mouthfuls of vegetables that looked like Skittles. I'd missed lunch and skipped dinner; not wanting to be in that hall with those people. Maximus joined us on the bed and popped open a wine bottle.

Frothing white bubbles spilled out of it and he caught them in metal chalices he'd brought. He handed one to each of us.

"Here's to surviving our first day." He raised his cup.

Lucinda whooped. I took a large gulp. I'd never had friends in my bed before. Heck, I'd never had friends. Even growing up, it hadn't been long before my so-called buddies—and family—abandoned me. Whispered conversations in the night before they packed their bags and left. Some were kind enough to drop me back with social services, but most simply fled.

Maximus pulled out his paper-thin Five Isle's phone and held it up in selfie mode. Our faces appeared on the hologram screen.

"Smile, witches."

Feeling better after some wine and food, I stuck out my tongue and winked at the camera, whilst Lucinda pouted, and Maximus blew a kiss. He took the snap, then underneath typed: #NoFucksGiven, and hit share.

Lucinda leaned back on her elbows. "So, about our alliance."

I drained my drink. Maximus was quick to refill it. "I don't do alliances. I look out for me. I'm the only one who ever has."

Lucinda arched a brow. "Would you like me to play a violin for your woes?"

Together, she and Maximus mimed playing a tiny violin and made a high-pitched sound.

I prodded them with my feet. "Point taken. Why me?"

"Because people don't like you." Lucinda grinned. "They don't like me either. I'm the High Priestess's favorite and they can't stand it." She finished off her drink. "Like it's my fault I'm better than them in every way."

I laughed. "Maybe it's because you say stuff like that."

"It's because people don't like people they can't fit inside a box. People who can't be molded because they aren't made out of clay but steel." Lucinda met my stare. "Something tells me, you're steel too."

"We know the Games. We can help you," Maximus added. "And you can help us with that exceptional power of yours."

"The power I have no access to?"

I didn't care what Lance had claimed.

Lucinda and Maximus exchanged a look.

"I wouldn't be so sure about that." Lucinda rummaged in her bag, pulled out a compact mirror and held it up.

The plate I held thudded to the floor as I gaped at my reflection. My eyes were no longer hazel. They were yellow and slitted like a snake.

"What is this?"

"No idea," Lucinda mused. "But it's definitely not your mother's gift."

My head snapped up. Twenty-four years ago, I'd been abandoned in Sherwood Forest, with nothing to say where I came from other than a golden symbol inked into my skin, and the name Varialla stitched onto a blanket. With everything that was going on, I hadn't stopped to consider that my parents could be in the Five Isles. That I might finally get the answers I'd always wanted.

"You know my mother?"

"Lucinda," Maximus warned.

The witch stretched out like a cat. "Unfortunately, we're sworn to secrecy, lest we want to end up like Lance.

My stomach dropped. "What?"

"Yep. All contestants had to swear the blood-oath. Break it and…" she curled then splayed her fingers in a gesture that represented exploding.

My heart seized. "An oath to keep me in the dark?"

"Sort of. This way, no one shows their hand. You don't know what we know and we don't know what you know."

"I don't know anything," I cried in frustration. "What is there to know?"

Lucinda mimed locking her lips.

I sighed. I shouldn't care. One way or another I was going to find a way off of these islands and back through the veil. It shouldn't matter who abandoned me or why. Or that the symbol I always thought was a strange birthmark, was clearly something more. But it did matter.

This place offered answers to questions I'd asked my entire life. But I'd have to survive a deadly tournament and claim a throne I didn't want, to get them.

I slumped back. My eyes drifted to the mirror.

"Have they done this all day?"

"No." Maximus considered. "It started when you laughed."

When I let my guard down—like I had with my foster families. Was that why they'd fled? Bolted in the night? Because their little girls' eyes had changed to that of a serpent?

"Even if it wasn't reflected in your eyes, we can feel your power," Lucinda stated. "When you do tap into it, we want to be on your side."

I snickered but she bumped me with her shoulder.

"I mean it. Power like yours could save the realm."

I eyed her; my brow raised. "I wasn't aware it needed saving."

Before Lucinda could reply, a female voice spoke into the room:

"All players are requested in the nearest common room. Attention: All players."

Together, we made our way to a gothic-chic common area with high-arched windows, blue velvet armchairs, and an ornate fireplace. A holographic version of Goather hovered before it and a crowd gathered around him.

"Welcome, initiates," he called. "It's time for the Trial of Ten to begin."

"Trial of Ten?"

"There are ten trials of initiation," Lucinda whispered. "He's going to tell us our first."

The hairs on the back of my neck stood on end and I couldn't shake the feeling that I was being watched. When I looked up, I locked eyes with Exekiel who leaned against a pilar. His jaw was taut and his eyes blazed that punishing shade of pink.

Crap. I quickly looked away and whispered, "Are my eyes still weird?"

"It's fine. Just keep your head down," Lucinda said. "No one's looking at you."

But Exekiel was looking at me. He always was.

7

LIE TO ME

The air in the common room thrummed with excitement. Camera-orbs panned over the audience's delighted expressions as Goather let the weight of his words land. The Trial of Ten had begun.

Finally, he said, "Your first Trial to advance to the next level of the Games, is to determine between what is real and what is fake. This week, you must use your mind and skill to conquer illusion." Goather's hologram ran its stare over us. "Everyone's illusion will be different and at different times. However, they must all be handled the same way."

The satyr revealed a golden dagger. Its hilt was peppered with rubies and its serrated blade was crusted in diamonds.

"Each of you will be given one of these. I suggest you carry it with you wherever you go because once inside your illusion, there are only two ways out. You must drive this blade through your own heart or through the heart of whoever you see before you."

The excitement in the room shifted to something sharper; colder. A few contestants shared guarded looks.

"Be warned that these blades are enchanted. If you hesitate or change your mind, it does not care. Once you position the weapon and your intention is set, the dagger will follow through." Goather twirled the weapon in his fingers. "If you're right, you will advance to the next level. If you're wrong…"

He didn't need to finish that sentence. If someone thought they were in an illusion and weren't, they would kill themselves or whoever they were with.

"Naturally, there's a catch. If you remain inside your illusion for longer than sixty minutes, you will never be able to leave."

My stomach dropped.

"You will be imprisoned by the false reality until you eventually waste away and die." He took a dramatic pause. "As with all things in the Games, this is a test of heart and skill, for you will need both to rule the Isles. Do you have what it takes to die for your Kingdom or to slay someone you love to protect the crown? Can your judgment truly be trusted? And can the people trust you?"

For the first time, I felt tendrils of fear from the other contestants.

"Each of you have a unique way to see through the deception based on your power level and aptitude. Spend every waking moment from now, trying to figure out what that is. Your illusion could strike at any minute. It could be happening right now."

His words struck like a blow to the gut.

"Goodnight, initiates. May you go with the brave and the blessed."

Goather's hologram flickered out. Conversation spilled through the room.

"Illusion?" Maximus cried. "Kill each other. Kill ourselves. Waste away and die. I didn't expect them to go easy on us but..." His dreadlocks swayed as he shook his head.

I couldn't concentrate. Exekiel's gaze bore into me and when I glanced up, he was headed my way.

"Shit." I didn't need his dominating alpha-hole energy right now. "See you tomorrow," I said to my potential allies. I was already backing out of the room.

Faster than I thought possible, I skidded down the corridor and hurtled back inside my room. I slammed the door and clicked the lock behind me. My heart rabbeted in my chest.

This was ridiculous. I was running away from a guy. Though, in my defense, he was a very disturbed and demanding guy. A Fae...with flipping wings, and some kind of vendetta against me. Like everyone else in the Five Isles. What was worse, was that I was drawn to him more than anyone else here. He was the epitome of a storm and, in me, he created lightning.

Desperate to put this day behind me, I shirked off my dress, wriggled out of my bra then collapsed onto the bed. Tomorrow was a new day. I'd revisit the idea of ley lines and how the hell I could get out of the Eternal City to find them. For now, I would savor my last few nights in an actual bed.

Something moved outside my window. I took in the sprawling night sky and my stomach pitched. Someone was out there. My hands flew over my bare breasts and

I gaped at the figure that descended on my balcony. Exekiel.

His wings were splayed as he prowled closer.

Shit! I bounded out of bed and rushed over to the terrace doors. They may have already been locked but I turned the key, just to be sure. A smirk claimed my lips. I didn't know what abilities the Fae had but didn't think walking through locked doors was one of them.

Exekiel's shadow fell over me.

I bristled; my arm protectively draped over my breasts.

"Look at me." His voice was coarse and commanding.

I knew what he wanted—to see if my eyes were still glowing yellow and slitted like a snake.

"Goodnight, Fae-boy."

I was tempted to close the curtain and return to bed but I needed to see him leave. There was no way I'd get any sleep thinking he was out here.

"Look. At. Me." Each word was uttered slowly; menacingly.

I clenched my jaw. The longer I refused, the longer he'd stay.

Finally, I looked up and met his stare. All air was sucked from the room. My throat closed as the pink of his eyes deepened and pulled me in. Even through the glass, I felt his heat.

His jaw ticked and something in his eyes said that mine had, at last, returned to normal. Probably because my guard wasn't down anymore. It was all the way up.

"If you're done staring into my eyes like some kind of creep, I'd really like to go back to bed.' I huffed;

needing this conversation to end or to at least put on a T-shirt.

I wore nothing but a pair of white lace panties; my arm uselessly cradled over my breasts where his gaze briefly lingered.

"You can tell a lot from someone's eyes," Exekiel murmured, dragging his stare back up to mine. "Earlier, I could have sworn yours were different."

I said nothing. I knew my rights. Although, in this world, did I have any?

"But now they've returned to the eyes of someone lost."

"Excuse me?"

"Someone who pretends to know who she is and what she wants but inside she's floundering. Screaming."

A scared little girl abandoned in the woods.

I bristled. His words cut deep.

"Let me guess, you occasionally moonlight as a therapist," I drawled.

His lips curved up in the corner as if he knew I was using humor in defense.

"Everything I see in your eyes I once saw in mine."

My brows lifted. "Are you telling me, that you, Exekiel V'alin; the Protector of the Realm, once felt lost?"

"Shocking, I know, but I wasn't always the suave, devilishly handsome Fae-male you see today."

"So, what were you?"

I shouldn't have asked. Shouldn't have wanted to know more about him...but I did. I wanted to know everything.

"A Bravinore Fae isn't born like other beings. They're put here to prove themselves worthy of their birthright among the Fates." His tone hardened. "No home. No family. Except the home we make and the family we forge for ourselves."

I swallowed thickly, shaking off the yoke of his sadness and how it replicated my own.

"So, you know what it's like to be left," I whispered.

I couldn't remember the last time I'd spoken about this with someone. Wasn't sure if I ever had. Counselors tried when I was growing up but I just wanted to forget. A Von Hastings didn't get abandoned after all.

Exekiel scratched the back of his neck. "I know more than you think." He looked at me like he really saw me; in a way no one else ever had. "I also had to find my way in a world I didn't know, little bud."

My breath stammered.

"And you became this." I gestured to the glorious expanse of him.

He smirked. "And you became…this."

His stare travelled down the glass, taking me in. Every unwaxed hair. Every faded scar. The swell of my breasts. The slope of my hips. Heat pulsed through me.

I was tempted to press myself to the window just to be closer to him. Almost forgot about my plans to leave this place.

Taking a step back, I folded my arms across my chest. "Remind me again, why you're here?"

Exekiel tilted his head to one side. "I wanted to check something."

"And?" My brow arched. He stepped closer. My breath faltered. "Did you get what you came for?"

His burning stare trailed over me. My heart pounded.

"Right now, there is only one thing I would come for."

His gaze travelled lower and landed on the spot between my thighs. I jerked and pressed my knees together.

"You're sick," I spat.

He chuckled. "I'm honest. Which is why," his stare snapped back to mine. It was no longer hot but bitter cold. "I don't like being lied to." His finger ran down the glass and stopped at my hip. "That's an interesting birthmark."

I reeled back. Ice in my veins. I'd forgotten. How had I been so stupid? I rushed to cover the symbol that had been imprinted on my skin since birth. One arm around my waist whilst the other clung to my breasts barely covering my nipples. It was too late. He'd already seen it; the mark of the Five Isles branded onto my skin in gold.

I fumbled over my words; didn't know what to say. I hadn't even known what the symbol meant until I saw it in the arena.

"You're the same as her," he snarled. "Go ahead; restart the war." His breath fogged up the window. "Once again, I'll end it."

I paled and tried to somehow explain but Exekiel spread his wings and surged into the sky.

"Shit!" I staggered back from the window, fisting my hair in my hand.

It was time to go. I didn't know what Exekiel planned to do with the knowledge of the Five Isles symbol on my skin but his entire demeanor promised pain. Promised a war. I had no clue what he'd meant by that but I wasn't sticking around to find out. I had to make a run for it and pray I made it across the veil and back to Nottingham, before anyone noticed I was gone.

8

RUN

Escape was the only thing on my mind. Not Trials, cameras, Games or symbols. Simply freedom. To not spend every second of the day puzzling out riddles and fearing for my life. I'd tried to leave last night but Exekiel had been circling the sky—as if he knew I planned to run. But he couldn't watch me forever, right?

Eudora whacked me in the head with her comb. "Well?" she snapped. "What do you think?"

I scowled at her from where I sat at the dressing table. The nymphs had been prodding me all morning, but I hadn't been paying attention. Now, I saw that Eudora had threaded my hair through gold beads and scooped it into a mass of curls on top of my head. She'd also added in red petals and let a few curls hang down the sides of my face.

"Believe it or not, hair isn't my top priority, right now."

She scoffed. "What could be more important than looking like a queen to gain the support of the people? They're your key between life and death, remember?"

"Exekiel may kill me, anyway," I grumbled. "He stopped by last night."

Eudora's eyes lit up. "The Shadow Saint, himself?"

I spluttered, "The what?"

"The Protector of the Realm. The fate's favorite of *Bravinore* descent," Eudora gushed. "He's practically up there with the gods."

"Apparently, he fucks like one as well," murmured a redheaded nymph with a large rose on either side of her head.

"He's Five Isles' most eligible bachelor and the most difficult," Eudora went on.

The others nodded with dreamy sighs.

"He barely says more than two words to anyone save for the Council, and he makes little time for romance."

"I don't need him for romance. I just need his coc—
"

"For Fate's sake, Cyrus," Eudora snapped. "We are in the company of a future queen. Possibly his mate considering his interest."

Laughter burst out of me. I'd forgotten all about the mate clause in this Game. The whole idea still seemed ridiculous.

"He was actually more interested in my mark."

I studied the nymph's reactions. They must have seen it when they bathed me but none of them had said anything. Now, they shared a glance.

"I see." Eudora said carefully. "And what exactly were the two of you doing for him to see it?"

"Seriously?" I cried. "That's all you have to say? Nothing about the symbol *inked* into my skin?"

She sniffed. "We aren't in the business of prying. The contestants' secrets are their own."

Unless they were about Exekiel, it seemed.

"It's not even my secret." I kicked my feet up on the dresser. "I don't know how it got there or how it's stayed intact all these years."

"Have you looked up enchanted ink in the library?"

"Library?"

"Best in the Five Isles…So, I'm told." Eudora grimaced. "Us nymphs aren't permitted to enter."

"What?"

"Rules of the Isles. Those who are lesser aren't given the same privileges."

"Lesser?" I shrieked.

Eudora shrugged but I shook my head. First the satyrs, the centaurs, and now the nymphs. There was clearly a divide between those of the Five Isles and those from beyond. A divide that, according to what Exekiel had said, maybe I was a part of.

Go ahead, restart the war.

"That's…awful."

"Maybe you'll be the royal who changes it," Cyrus suggested.

But I didn't plan on staying. Unease settled heavy on my chest. There was so much more to this world…to me.

Eudora tutted. "Rules are rules. Now, twirl."

I did and the sheer black dress I wore, swirled around me. It was floor-length with slits as high as my hip and crisscrossed around my neck. Light flowy sleeves fell off the shoulders and fitted to my wrists with

gold cuffs. It was stunning but impractical for Trials—
or great escapes.

When I pointed this out, Eudora countered, "It's
good practice. When Queens are called to fight, they're
usually in a dress."

The library was grander than I expected. Something that
Beauty and the Beast's Belle, would have envied. It was
at least six levels of spiraling shelves and rolling ladders.
A crystal chandelier draped from the glass-domed
ceiling where natural light spilled in. The floor was
polished red marble and the windows were gold-framed
arches.

"Can you be helped?" asked a gruff voice.

My gaze swept to a being who was no taller than my
hip. He had large bat-like ears and a drooping nose that
curled over thin lips.

I blinked. "Yes. I'm looking for information on ley
lines."

Enchanted ink be damned. As soon as the nymphs
mentioned a library, my thoughts went to my imminent
escape. A seed of uncertainty sprouted in my gut but I
ignored it. This world wasn't for me and, apparently, me
being here was only making things worse.

"Level three." The being, which I could only
describe as a goblin, ushered me onto an elevated
platform with gold metal rails and red velvet floor.
"Aisle six." He pulled a lever and I screeched as the
contraption descended to the lower ground. It stopped
in an archway that read: Level 3.

Stumbling out of the elevator contraption, I scanned
the aisles for number six. It didn't take long to find it,

and soon, I was sprawled on a large beanbag surrounded by a pile of books about shifters, ley lines and enchanted ink.

I'd barely put the pastry I'd swiped from the dining hall to my lips, when another goblin rushed towards me, waving a fist.

"No eating in the library," he barked. "What kind of monster are you?" He snatched the pastry away and stormed off muttering about crumbs and grease.

"What kind of monster, indeed?" A deep voice drawled.

I turned.

Phoebus, the shifter who'd rescued me, strode over and sat down.

"The hungry kind," I grumbled.

He grinned and handed me a thermos from his satchel. I opened it to find a thick potato stew. My stomach rumbled.

"No crumbs." He winked. "I'm convinced they sense them." He tossed me a spoon, next. "Enjoy."

My brows rose. 'Really?" I asked, already shoveling in a mouthful.

Phoebus chuckled and moved closer. I couldn't help breathing in his scent of earth and something wild. His arm brushed mine and small sparks skittered along my skin. Although it was nothing like when Exekiel touched me.

He gestured to one of the books. "Looking into what happened with your eyes?"

I wasn't surprised he knew. Maximus and Lucinda had made it clear he was part of their trio.

"Among other things." I licked stew from my chin.

"You really think your dad could've been a snake shifter?"

I shrugged. "It's a theory." One I was trying very hard not to care about. After decades of not knowing who I really was or where I'd come from, the prospect of answers was enticing. However, staying alive long enough to get those answers would be next to impossible in a world that wanted me dead.

Phoebus reached out and brushed his thumb down the side of my mouth. My heart stopped.

"You spilt some." He sucked the stew from his finger, his eyes on mine.

I gawked at him. Was everyone ridiculously attractive in this realm?

"Anyway, I'm supposed to find a book on witchcraft for Lucinda." Phoebus got to his feet. A part of me didn't want him to leave. "You're in charge of snacks next time."

"Done," I lied as I studied the book in my hands. There wouldn't be a next time. I'd just found the quickest route to one of the strongest ley lines and knew exactly what to do once I got there.

When night fell, I pulled on a pair of black pumps that Eudora had insisted were only for training and scribbled a hasty goodbye note. Grabbing the enchanted dagger—that I'd need to spill my blood where two of the ley lines converged—I tucked it into my belt, then crept out onto the terrace and swung myself over the rail. I'd gotten good at climbing on the many occasions I'd run away from social services. Now, I scaled down the castle trellis.

My feet touched the ground. I waited, watching the camera-orbs that drifted in the distance. There weren't as many as in the daytime. When they rotated, I ducked out of the shadows and darted across the grounds.

Gravel crunched beneath my feet when I reached the edge of the manicured lawns and stole towards Creature's Copse. It was apparently the quickest way out of the Eternal City—which, I'd learnt, in the library, was an entire city dedicated to those who were directly or indirectly involved in the Games.

I was almost at the tree line when five figures emerged from the shadows.

"We knew you'd try and free her, eventually," snarled a girl with pale skin and elven ears. I instantly recognized her as the girl from Enchant-a-Gram who'd said it should have been my blood on her shoes. Lola Black.

"Did you get what you came for?" growled a male with hulking biceps.

Mouth dry; I watched them closely. "Let me through."

"So, you can return with your army? No chance."

The man started to transform. Shifter. My stomach pitched.

"I suppose we should thank you," he sneered, through fangs. "Now everyone will think you escaped. Only we'll know that you're dead."

They began to close in around me; ready to punish me for something I didn't do, in a world I didn't belong. Instinctively, I reached for the dagger at my belt but I couldn't fight them all. My best chance was to run. So, I did.

"Get her!"

Heart racing, I pelted towards the trees. I flung all I had into the pound of my feet and thrust of my arms as I charged into the woods, towards hopeful freedom. The others bounded after me. A roar raged on my heels.

When I looked back, the shifter had transformed into a grotesque bear with drooping jowls and jagged teeth.

I steeled my nerves and ran faster, lunging over logs. Cold sweat on my brow.

"Where are you going, Devil Spawn?" Lola howled.

Pain shot through the back of my head. I staggered. A rock tumbled to the ground. Blood trickled from the wound it had made, and down my neck. Terror kept me moving. The dagger clutched firmly in hand.

A great white wolf with crimson eyes skidded into my path—cutting me off.

"It's over, shifter-slayer."

I swung around with the dagger raised. All I needed was a close enough target and murderous intent, and the weapon would follow through.

"Don't take another step," I shouted.

Their laughter bounced off the trees.

Chest heaving, I looked from the bear to the wolf— waiting for one or both to strike. Then blinding pain cleaved through my neck as a snake lunged from the grass and sank its fangs into my throat.

9

CHAOS AT THE CLIFFS

blaze of agony tore through my veins and the world ruptured. All I knew was pain and the pressure of the snake's bite as my knees buckled. I hit the ground.

Somewhere, Lola cackled. "Is she foaming at the mouth yet?"

Nauseous, I fought to break free. My movements sluggish and vision blurred.

"Use the femoral artery, Heskel. It's the main one in the thigh," commanded the bear shifter—now returned to his human form. "We want her to suffer."

The snake shifter—Heskel—ripped loose and I cried out then rolled over and retched. Cold sweat drenched my skin. Before I could try to piece myself together, Heskel bit into my thigh.

Sour chunks rose in my throat. Vicious laughter echoed off the trees.

"How poetic," a female with almond-colored skin and dark hair, spat. "She'll die just like her sister did."

My heart lurched. I'd had a sister. Did she have something to do with the mark of the Five Isles on my skin? Or with why I'd been left in the human realm as a child? As always, I was completely in the dark, and now, I would drown in its shadows. I'd convinced myself I didn't care. It had been the only way to get through each day when I was younger. But I cared. With every sliver of information into my past, I cared even more.

Pain spread—became a living thing in my bones. I gritted my teeth; refusing to give them the satisfaction of my screams even as my back bent and my head thrashed in the dirt. Tears pricked behind my eyes. I was going to die.

"That's enough." Lola snapped, "She won't suffer if she's unconscious."

Their haunting laughter filled the air.

Heskel finally drew back and transformed into a scrawny pale-skinned boy with auburn curls. His human form was laughable when compared to the monster he became. Fighting back a sob, I wanted to attack—to gouge out his beady orange eyes—but I couldn't move. His venom had left me paralyzed.

The bear shifter hefted me up under his arm and carried me like a sack of potatoes. Together, he and the others darted through the woods. Each with a single intent: To kill me.

I struggled to stay conscious as the edges of my vision faded. If I had any magic, now was a good time for it to show itself. But I felt nothing. No whisper of power or even the flutter of the breeze. The venom had numbed everything but my mind.

Soon, I detected the fresh scent of the sea as we ambled up a cliff. My heart spasmed with both longing and dread. I'd only been to the beach once before and it had ended in death.

As soon as I'd wriggled my toes in the seabed, there'd been a sudden and unusual surge of sharks. Many people had lost their lives and those who survived had looked at me like it was my fault. That was the first time I'd woken in an empty home. Five-years-old and my so-called family had fled during the night.

We reached the top of the cliff, and the bear shifter lifted me above his head. Violent waves crashed below. My eyes widened—the only things I could still move. I tried to twist free but my body wouldn't listen.

Lola sneered. "Drop her."

The shifter prowled closer to the cliff's edge; his grin sinister. "Goodbye shifter-slayer."

A blade cleaved through his skull. Blood and brain matter splattered my skin. His smile was still plastered across his face as his eyes grew wide and he toppled sideways off the cliff.

My stomach dipped as I was snatched from mid-air and flung to the ground.

Stunned, I blinked up at Exekiel who was now standing between me and my attackers. A strange white symbol of interconnected squares was illuminated on his forearm.

The wolf shifter pounced. Exekiel lunged—a blur of steel, wings and shadow. But as he battled the wolf, Heskel lashed out and kicked his curved blade off the edge of the cliff.

Exekiel didn't bat an eyelid. Hands raised, he whispered, "*Ulius.*"

Another mark lit up on the palm of his hand. This one like a green Trident.

The wolf rocked back but before he could run, Exekiel slammed his fist straight through the animal's side. Blood sprayed over him. The shifter screeched and fell; tongue flopping from its gaping mouth.

"Forgive us, Shadow Saint!" Heskel cried, as he thundered down the cliff.

All I saw was the sprawl of Exekiel's wings as he tore after the snake shifter. There was a high-pitched scream and a distant splash of something being thrown into the depths below.

"Why are you protecting her?" Lola shouted; her pale skin flushed. "She's the enemy." She thrust a finger at me. "She's their beacon of hope. She needs to die."

Exekiel rose like an angel of hell. Not from above, but from below. He surged up through the rock of the cliffs and grabbed Lola by the ankles. She screamed and fell backwards as she tried to pull free. Her head cracked against the stone.

Within seconds, Exekiel stood over her; his vermillion eyes so deep they appeared black in the moonlight. "Run!"

Lola scrambled to her feet with a hand pressed to the back of her head and took off. The dark-haired girl was close behind.

Exekiel barely spared them a glance before he swooped towards me. By now, the world was shaking. My head thumped the earth as I convulsed on the ground. Bitter white foam frothed from my lips; coated my tongue. Exekiel's mouth fell onto my neck.

His wings arced out at his shoulders and for a while, they were all I saw, backed by a swirling night sky. My vision blurred and sharpened.

Slowly, tingles peppered my skin. My fingers twitched in the earth.

I could move.

When he was done with my neck, Exekiel hiked up my blood-stained dress and fastened his mouth to my thigh. I gasped. I felt the pull of his lips as he sucked the poison from inside me and spat it on the ground. It burned almost as much as the toxin had going in. I bucked and, instinctively, tried to shove him away; my fingers twisting in his hair.

Exekiel gripped my wrists and pinned them to the ground. *Son of a bitch!* I writhed but he held fast. He sucked until the agony ebbed and I was able to breathe again. He sucked until I stopped fighting him and slumped back against the ground; exhausted. He sucked until every trace of poison had left my system.

Finally, he looked up at me from between my legs. My blood and the venom now coated his lips. My stomach pitched. The poison was in him.

"You're infected," I rasped.

Exekiel gritted his teeth. "*Thesona.*"

A symbol that looked like a backwards Z with a circle in its center glowed on his cheek. Almost instantly, the pallor of his skin brightened and the sheen of sweat that coated his brow faded.

"Are you alright?" he murmured.

"Yes." I couldn't believe it but I was—thanks to him.

Exekiel shuddered and rested his head on my thigh. "Are you?"

"Fantastic," he scoffed. The heat of his breath crossed between my legs.

I tensed. When he'd been sucking out the poison, all I'd been able to focus on was the pain. Now I was shockingly aware of how close his mouth was to my most intimate part.

Before I could say anything, Exekiel ran his tongue over the snake bite—one way and then the other. My heart thudded in my chest. Exekiel sighed deeply and the hands that pinned my wrists to the ground, moved to my hips.

My breathing slowed. My pulse pounded. Exekiel buried his nose between my legs and groaned. Gosh, the sound was primal. My insides spasmed.

"What are you doing?" I panted as he dragged his nose along my center. *Shit.* He was destroying me.

His hands slid lower and his fingers dug into the backs of my thighs as he pulled me closer. Sliding me through the cold, wet dirt and hitching my dress up even more.

My fingers curled into clumps of earth. "Exekiel?"

He pushed his mouth onto me. I gasped and quivered. My eyes closed. I could feel the imprint of his lips through the thin lace of my panties. The heat of his skin.

He growled. "You smell incredible."

Holy hotness!

What was I supposed to do now? I'd dreamt of Exekiel's mouth being there more times than I could count but now didn't seem like the time. I was still reeling after my brush with death and needed a second to breathe which was impossible to do with him touching me like this.

"Exekiel," I panted again but this time it was a plea. My fingers entwined in his hair. "I—"

His grip tightened and he breathed me in, savoring my scent. A low sound rumbled in the back of his throat.

Need pulsed through me. He was so warm, feral and he felt so fucking good. But this was a mistake. I couldn't trust him anymore than those bastards who'd tried to kill me. I didn't know much, but I knew there was a war brewing and we weren't allies in it.

His teeth grazed my clit and I bucked; my fingers tightening in his hair. God, what was I doing? Was I really going to let him lick me out on a mountaintop with my blood on his lips? He moaned and I almost pulled him closer but I couldn't. Exekiel was the enemy. A domineering Fae-bastard who considered me a threat.

"S-s-stop," I finally stammered.

He stilled—frozen like he was afraid to move—like he was holding himself back.

"Alright, little bud," he eventually purred against my sex and drew his face away.

I couldn't pretend I wasn't a little disappointed. However, his hands remained on my thighs, spreading me for him.

"You have five seconds to explain why you were out here before I kill you myself."

10

THE GAMING COUNCIL

Seriously?" I yanked my legs from Exekiel's grip and sat up. My head spun and I pressed a hand to it. "One minute, you save my life and the next, you threaten to kill me?"

Exekiel stared at my thighs—at the point where his mouth had just been.

I flushed and pressed my knees together. Was he part animal? Based on the sounds he made and the hunger in his eyes, I had to wonder. One thing was sure; sex with the Shadow Saint wouldn't be boring. Not that I would ever let it get that far.

"My eyes are up here, asshole," I forced myself to say.

He lifted his gaze; brows raised. "Were you saying something?"

I shook my head. "Just wondering if you're my hero or executioner."

Exekiel stood in one graceful motion and dusted off his hands. "Both." His wine-red eyes settled on me. "If anyone's going to kill you, little bud, it's going to be me."

I blinked. "You're insane." The world swayed as I clambered to my feet and ambled towards the cliffside. "Fucking mental."

"Where are you going?"

"Back to my cage."

Exekiel grabbed my arm and pulled me against him. My nipples tightened when they brushed his chest.

"Not until you tell me everything I want to know about that mark on your side." His stare sharpened; his arm locked around my waist.

I searched for a way to escape but I was still weak from the snake venom; my knees on the verge of giving out.

Before I could insist, I knew nothing, Exekiel shot into the sky—wings splayed and magenta eyes bright. I flung my arms around his neck with a shriek and buried my face in his shoulder. I was pretty sure he laughed as he angled our body's and soared through the Eternal City. *Smug bastard.* I still wasn't used to the sensation of flying without a plane especially when my head was spinning from snake venom and adrenaline.

Eventually, we landed outside an ancient looking fortress carved from black and green stone and surrounded by a moat.

"Where are we?"

He grabbed my hand and pulled me across the drawbridge. I tried not to focus on the warmth of his skin and the way his touch made my heart flutter.

"The Gaming Council."

I'd heard about the Council—about the blood-oath they'd made everyone swear—but I hadn't found any information on them in the welcome pack and, for some reason, this building wasn't on the map. These were the people I'd wanted to see in the beginning. To ask why they'd brought me here and demand that they let me leave.

However, now, my priorities had changed. There were too many unanswered questions—things I'd wonder about forever unless I stayed to figure out what they meant. Who had my attackers thought I was trying to save? Why had Lola called me a beacon of hope? Had I really been abandoned as a child or had my family hidden me to keep me safe? And what happened to my sister?

I eyed Exekiel as we passed beneath a gatehouse where guards patrolled. What were these people hiding?

We strode across a concrete courtyard inlaid with emeralds and arrived at a set of double doors forged from black iron. Pushing them open, Exekiel stalked inside and pulled me with him. The doors swung shut with an ominous clang.

We were in a grand circular chamber carved from red marble and ivory pillars; lit by a candle chandelier. Up ahead, on an elevated platform, six people were seated on green velvet-cushioned thrones. Two of the beings were clearly Fae with large, impressive wings. Another had skin like porcelain and prominent pointed ears—elf. The remaining three had no defining physical trait but the air hummed around them, thick with power.

"Varialla von Hastings," a redheaded woman with hazelnut skin and grey eyes leaned forwards. "She's smaller than I expected."

"And wearing less clothes," snickered the elf. "Not that I'm complaining."

His eyes did an appreciative sweep of my tattered dress. I was covered in filth and the flimsy fabric had torn in multiple places. It didn't help that Exekiel hadn't just lifted my dress to get to my thigh, he'd practically ripped it off. Now it barely covered my backside.

I frowned when his grip tightened on my hand and his jaw clenched. He looked like he was considering tearing out the elf's throat.

"Why is she here and in such a state?" snapped an elderly man with white-grey hair and deep wrinkles around his eyes and mouth.

"She was attacked," Exekiel announced.

"By?"

"Some of the other contestants. They sought revenge."

The elderly man gritted his teeth. "That kind of recklessness could bring a war on our heads," he spat. "We cannot risk her being killed outside of the Games."

So, inside the Games was fine? Maybe that's what they wanted.

Those around him nodded and I got the sense that he was in charge. Maybe because he was the eldest. The others didn't look a day over thirty, although their eyes held a wisdom that spoke of lifetimes.

"Even within the Games, we must tread carefully, Alexov." The redhead pursed her lips. "For all we know, they want her to be killed so they can make a martyr out of her."

I narrowed my eyes. Who were they talking about? I was clearly nothing more than a tool to these people— a means to an end. But what end? Why had Lola and the others wanted revenge? Who had Lance thought I was and what had he been about to reveal before his head exploded?

"The attack is not the only reason I've brought her here," Exekiel added.

Every eye pivoted to him.

"The mark of the Five-Isles has been branded onto her skin in enchanted ink."

The air snapped with tension. My skin prickled with a sick sense of foreboding.

"Has her mind shown you anything?"

My gaze snapped to Exekiel. It shouldn't have surprised me. He was Fae, and I'd learnt from Vivienne that it was all too easy for the Fae to get into my head. Now that I was staying, I'd have to find a way to block them.

"Not yet. She is either exceptionally trained or truly believes she knows nothing."

Alexov steepled his fingers. "It's possible a memory and magic suppressant has been used. Perhaps to help her blend in with the humans all this time."

The elf's pale green eyes danced. "Which means we need to do an extraction." He licked his lips. "I get to hold her down."

I yelped when Exekiel swept up onto the platform and landed before the elf. "Careful, Vladimir."

The elf's brows lifted. "Does my desire to pin Ms. Hastings beneath me, offend you?"

Exekiel clenched his fists.

Vladimir cocked his head. "It does." His eyes drifted from Exekiel to me and back. "Wait—Don't tell me, she's..." He threw his head back and laughed.

The other Council members tensed and stared from me to Exekiel. I frowned. What the hell was going on?

"Have you known this entire time?" Alexov growled.

"I had my suspicions but wasn't certain until tonight."

Vladimir crowed. "Did you smell something you liked?"

Exekiel rounded on the elf; teeth bared.

"Shit," Alexov cursed. "Vladimir can take over from now on."

"No," Exekiel snapped. "I'm the Protector of the Realm. She's my responsibility."

"She's also your—" he cut himself off.

His what? I looked between them. What had Exekiel discovered tonight?

"Perhaps he can use this to his advantage," the redhead mused.

The others looked at her.

She shrugged. "It is a powerful connection after all."

There was a strained silence I struggled to make sense of.

Finally, Alexov sighed. "Very well. For now, we will continue as planned."

He stood, taller than I expected. His stature broad— perhaps a shifter.

"Bring her."

Exekiel descended the platform and marched me through an archway and down a beige brick corridor with torches burning in wall sconces. He strode silently beside me; his jaw clenched and gaze fixed firmly ahead. Every now and then, Vladimir looked back at us and chuckled.

Exekiel drawled, "Fuck off, Vlad."

The elf grinned. I wished I was in on the joke but neither of them gave anything away.

We passed through a chamber where a cold blue light shimmered from the center of a plunge pool. Above it, hovered a shimmering beam of blue and green flecks. They drifted from the pool and straight up through the stone ceiling. Its power was potent—a sizzle across my skin.

I slowed. "What is that?"

"The Conduit," Vladimir boasted. "Our connection to the Fates and the gods beyond. It is what gave us your name and helped us find you, at last. Although," his eyes slid to Exekiel. "Not everyone needs the Conduit to commune with the gods."

A few of the symbols I'd seen on Exekiel's skin swirled within the ethereal channel. Maybe that was what it meant to be of the *Bravinore* race, a direct descendant of the Fates.

"Are you the only one?" I asked; curiosity getting the better of me,

Exekiel shook his head. "No."

Vladimir purred, "But he is the most powerful. The most destructive."

"Of course, he is," I drawled.

Exekiel shot me a dark look. I shrugged.

Eventually, we stepped into a low-lit chamber with strange tools hanging from the rocky walls and what looked like an iron throne in its center. The ground was a mixture of gravel and sand, and there was the metallic scent of blood.

The hairs on the back of my neck stood on end. "What exactly is an extraction?"

"You're about to find out." Vladimir snatched me away from Exekiel and shoved me onto the throne.

Before I could stand, the redhead whispered an incantation and steel manacles snapped around my arms and legs. I glared at the gathered Council; at Exekiel who stood in the shadows with his arms folded and cool disinterest in his pale pink eyes.

"A suppressant of this magnitude won't simply fade overnight." Alexov washed his hands in a nearby stone basin then moved towards me. "However, I'll be able to weaken it and overtime, it will disintegrate."

He pressed his foot down and the chair tilted, forcing me to lay back and stare up at his cold brown eyes. Shadows cast by the torchlight danced across his face.

"I expect you to keep a close eye on her, Exekiel." His eyes glinted as he lifted his hands and the air shimmered around us.

So, he wasn't a shifter, but a warlock with immeasurable power.

"You must make sure no other fools try to eliminate her until we know what her people have planned."

"I will." Exekiel stated. I looked at him—the hard lines of his face and the gleam of his eyes. "I'll watch her every second of every day."

Pain more violent than I'd ever felt speared through my skull. Like a drill was boring into my brain. My limbs locked up and my blood turned icy. The air became bitingly cold causing an ache in my lungs. I couldn't breathe.

A face flickered across my mind. Dark skin, pink hair; then she was gone. Replaced by a man with piercing blue eyes and golden-brown skin. He cradled me and kissed my forehead. My heart twisted. Was he my father? Before I could guess, the world tilted. A wave of nausea swept through me. And agony burned in my skull as if my brain was trying to break free.

Stop! I tried to scream but my mouth wouldn't work; my teeth clattered together. My tongue dangerously close to being bitten off.

Please stop.

11

WTF?

When I padded into the Resident Dining Hall for breakfast, I was basically a zombie. I communicated in grunts. My steps were sluggish and my eyes, heavy-lidded. The nymphs had styled my hair into a chignon and dressed me in a white peplum corset and black leather leggings, so I, at least, looked decent. But if it wasn't for them, I would've left my room with my heels on the wrong feet.

"What in the Isles did you do last night?" Lucinda tutted as she buttered a puffy bread roll.

"I survived a snake attack and was almost thrown off a cliff." I lifted my coffee cup in cheers.

I debated mentioning my meeting with the Council but now didn't seem like the place.

Lucinda, Maximus and Phoebus eyed me like I'd lost my mind. I didn't bother to elaborate. My head ached and my vision was still fuzzy from whatever the hell Alexov had done to me during the extraction.

Apparently, it had been successful. He'd managed to weaken the magical barrier that had been placed on me to make me forget the Five Isles and the power I possessed. Soon it would fade entirely.

But I couldn't afford to wait. The official Games began in four months and based on the snatches of conversation, I caught last night, the Council didn't want me in them. They planned to keep up the extractions until they learnt what my alleged people, had planned, and then…

This meant I had less than four months to uncover the truth on my own and to find a way to survive when I was no longer useful to them.

I noisily slurped on my creamy coffee; almost choking when Exekiel strode into the hall. Countless heads swiveled in his direction.

The Shadow Saint barely graced us with his presence, even during meals. He was usually off doing whatever it was the Protector of the Realm did. People leapt up to shake his hand and offer him their seat. Girls practically fell at his feet. Vivienne waved him over and I swallowed an irrational rush of envy when he nodded and went to join her.

"What brings him here?" Lucinda murmured.

As if to answer her question, Exekiel looked our way and his dark gaze settled on me. My skin warmed. Instantly, memories of the night before raced through my mind. Amidst flashes of Lola and the others almost killing me, and the Gaming Council's torture, one memory replayed itself more than any other. The moment I'd shared with Exekiel on the cliff. His mouth in places it shouldn't have been.

I quickly looked away and took another loud slurp of my drink. How did he always have this effect on me? The dry mouth. The racing heart.

"It's been ten seconds and he's still watching you." Lucinda arched a brow. "Tell me, Varialla, is the realm's most famous hottie the reason you're so tired this morning?"

I grumbled, "Yes and no."

"What?" Phoebus hissed.

"Long story."

"Shorten it." His tone was clipped; his blue eyes blazing.

Men.

Suddenly, I wished I had something stronger than coffee.

Before I could respond, heels clopped towards us. I looked up to find Vivienne standing with her hands on her hips. Her partially open wings were an impressive backdrop. Orbs followed after her.

"Clever girl," she spat. "I hear Exekiel's your new personal guard."

"What?"

"You tried to run. Now he has no choice but to babysit you every night—no longer able to warm my bed."

The words twisted inside my chest.

"Whatever you heard, is wrong. Exekiel is not my guard."

He couldn't be. For the first time in a long time, I'd woken up with a purpose—a determination I hadn't felt since childhood. Only now I wasn't determined to be the best daughter ever so that I'd be loved. I was determined to uncover the truth of my past—of where I came from and where I belonged.

According to what I'd learned, there was someone in the Isle of the Eternals that they thought I'd risk my life to save. There were people who impossibly saw me as a beacon of hope and there were contestants who wanted me dead. But I couldn't find out why with Exekiel breathing down my neck.

I'll watch her every second of every day. Those were the words he'd said right before the extraction. Had he actually meant them?

"Yes, he is," Vivienne snapped, slapping her hand down on the table hard enough to make the others jump. "I don't know what angle you're playing, but if you think you can come in here and get in my way, think again, bitch. Remember what I made you do at the opening ceremony?" She sneered, knowing that I hadn't told anyone that my dance that night had been a ruse. "I can make you do so much worse."

Exhausted with her ranting and this infuriating realm, I slammed down my cup. "Go fuck yourself, Vivienne."

She jerked back; her expression outraged. "What did you say to me?"

I planted my hands on the table and leaned forwards. "Go. Fuck. Yourself." A sweet tang trailed across the tip of my tongue.

Vivienne straightened, her eyes wide and cheeks rosy.

"Take it back," she whispered.

Her fingers flexed then slowly slid between her thighs.

My mouth dropped open. *What the fuck?*

85

Vivienne blanched and tore her hand away. Horror-struck, she gaped from me to the cameras, then raced from the Dining Hall. Everyone who was close enough to have witnessed the argument, burst out laughing.

I stared after her. "What just happened?"

Lucinda crowed, "Well, she was going to use her fingers to fu—

"I got that!"

What I didn't get was why. Then again, it wasn't the first time someone had blindly done what I'd said. When I was younger, people had often given in to my demands regardless of the consequences. It also wasn't the first time I'd tasted that honeyed flavor on my tongue. It'd happened the day I'd asked Lance to give me a ride. Was it part of my ability?

Lucinda threw her arm around my shoulders. "This is why I'm glad you're in our alliance."

I shook my head. "Did I just use compulsion?"

"Do you think you did?"

It wasn't a direct answer but I hadn't really expected one. They were sworn to tell me nothing, after all. However, if I had just used compulsion, it was a Fae ability, which could mean that my mother had been a Fae and my father, a Snake Shifter.

It was impossible to see through the illusions that Lucinda created using incantations. No matter how many times I tried, I failed to detect the difference between real and fake.

It didn't help that Exekiel was sprawled a few feet away on the grass. He was shirtless; hands propped behind his head which highlighted the swell of his

86

biceps, and on his bottom half, he wore a pair of black trousers that were just low enough to display the deep V-lines of his ripped torso. My toes curled. His wings were concealed and his eyes were closed, but I knew he was aware of my every move—an unwanted and unwelcome bodyguard.

"Concentrate," Lucinda snapped.

I cursed. Now that I actually wanted to be in the Games, I had three days—at most—to master illusion and somehow survive the First Trial. I didn't need to concentrate. I needed a miracle.

Phoebus jogged towards me with a bottle of water. "Breathe." He ran his hand across the back of my neck. "You're too tense."

I moaned around my mouthful of water as he massaged my shoulders.

"Just relax," he murmured, his lips brushing my temple.

He stepped unnecessarily close and I felt his body against my spine. I shivered. Phoebus was insanely attractive and was proving that he knew how to use his hands.

"I guess I just needed someone to help work out the tension," I purred.

Phoebus jerked back. His eyes were wide and he swiped at the air as if he saw something that wasn't there.

I frowned. "Phoebus?"

He snarled and twisted; half-shifted into his wolf form.

Someone chuckled then darkness swallowed me. A hand came up around my throat, the other rested on my hip. I blinked. I was in a cage of midnight-blue wings—

their owner right behind me. I didn't have to turn to know who it was. I weirdly recognized his scent. Exekiel.

He lowered his head and his hot breath fanned across the tip of my ear.

"If he touches you again, I'll break every bone in his hand."

"What?" I scoffed.

I couldn't help admiring the violet veins that ran through Exekiel's wings. He'd opened them slightly so a sliver of daylight could snake in overhead. Camera-orbs swooped closer. I groaned. I could only imagine how we must have looked.

"This is ridiculous." I tried to tug free.

Exekiel growled, "I mean it, little bud. I never considered myself a possessive man but I can't be held responsible for what I do when it comes to you." His grip tightened.

My heart raced. The pulse in my neck beat against his palm.

"Why do you even care?"

He drew me closer—the heat of his skin burned into me. "Because I'm very protective of what is mine." Cupping my chin, he guided my face; forcing me to look back at him. Our lips were so painfully close. "And you, Varialla, are mine."

I wanted to say no; that he was crazy, but the words stuck in my throat. Like an intrinsic part of me knew that he was right. That I was hopelessly and completely his.

12

BED HEAD

*Y*ou're mine. Exekiel's voice rattled through my skull. The memory of his fingers around my neck; his breath against my ear.

Flustered, I hefted up the lid of the illusion simulator. I'd been in the titanium tank for most of the morning but still couldn't tell the difference between illusion and reality.

I'm very protective of what is mine.

My stomach tightened. What the hell was wrong with me? Exekiel was an infuriating Fae-bastard who was working with the Gaming Council. He'd repeatedly threatened my life but still, like a fool, I couldn't stop thinking about him. Couldn't help wondering what he'd meant when he'd called me, his. Or why the slightest graze of his fingers left me breathless.

If he touches you again…

Cursing, I gave myself a mental shake. There was nothing attractive about a possessive alpha-hole, and I had more important things to focus on.

Four months to uncover the truth of who I was and how to survive, before the Council pulled secrets I didn't even know, from my mind and used them against me. Me and whoever they believed I was trying to protect...to save.

I glanced at the simulator's control screen where footage of my latest illusion experience replayed. Virtual Reality games paled in comparison to this machine. As soon as I'd settled into the leather seat and pressed my hands to the palm pads, it had lit up and transformed from an empty vessel into whatever creation it could conjure to manipulate my mind. I'd given myself one hour to see through each illusion. So far, I'd failed every time.

Frustrated, I did a quick scan for Exekiel who had taken to lurking nearby. When I saw no sign of him, I pulled out my textbook, *Illusion or Delusion*.

A voice blared over an intercom:

"Attention: All contestants are summoned for immediate etiquette training. Females to Training Tower, five. Males to tower three."

I groaned. Were they serious? Etiquette training in the middle of a Trial? Manners wouldn't help me if I was dead.

Using the map on my phone, it didn't take long to find the fifth tower that framed Residence Manor. Its roof was steepled and, like the others, a deep shade of purple. The walls were forged from black granite. Above an open archway, the Roman numeral for number five was painted in gold.

I stepped beneath it and up a spiraling stone staircase. At the top, was a red-carpeted room with floor-to-ceiling windows, and at least ten round tables covered in white linen.

"Welcome, initiates," called a nymph with ivory-pale skin, frosty blue lips and moose-like antlers. "Your First Trial is almost complete." Her voice was light and airy. "Three eves after the Blood Battles, there will be a banquet for those who survive. At these affairs, you will be critiqued on your etiquette. How well you do, will affect your rank."

Spying Lucinda near a stone pillar, I shuffled past the girls to join her.

The nymph gestured to the tables. "Today, you will learn the art of how to sit. Next, utensils, chewing and so on."

I snorted. "I'm pretty sure I know how to bite."

Playfully, I clamped my teeth around Lucinda's arm. The witch yelped and swatted me away, laughing. But my own laughter died when I spotted Lola Black across the room. Beside her, was the other girl that Exekiel had let escape.

"Ignore them," Lucinda snarled but looked like she wanted to tear them apart.

She'd been beyond disgusted when I told her what they'd done. I still couldn't believe they'd been allowed to stay even after Exekiel had identified them. Apparently, the Council felt that drawing attention to the situation would put my life in more danger, which was complete bullshit. The truth was they just didn't care and probably hoped Lola would try again when the time suited them.

Lucinda whispered, "Good old, rule number thirty-six."

The one Exekiel had recited the day Lance pounced on me: **Players are not permitted to attack each other outside of the Games.**

Still the sight of Lola had me reaching for the butter knife—not that it would do much damage. Combat training was definitely something I was going to take up. I'd always been good in a brawl but it couldn't hurt to keep my senses sharp.

"What happens if we break these rules?"

"The same thing that happens if we lose the Games," Lucinda whispered as the nymph prattled on about posture. "A Blood Battle. Any who survive are then bound to a life of service at the palace."

My blood ran cold. "Our only way out of the Games are to win, die or be forever enslaved?"

Lucinda shrugged. "Or rank in the top ten. They're given land, property and title." Her eyes filled with wonder.

However, all I could think was that out of one hundred contestants, I somehow had to rank amongst the highest—outlasting ninety other players who had probably been training for this their entire lives.

"Although, you don't have to worry about being enslaved."

"I don't?"

Lucinda snickered. "The Royal Court would never trust you in the palace. If you get forced into servitude, they'll kill you before you set foot through the door."

My stomach plummeted. "Thanks."

Lucinda grinned. "Think of it as motivation."

Etiquette training was where boredom went to die. I was starting to think it was the true Trial. On more than one occasion, I considered ramming a fork in my eye just to put an end to it, but finally the nymph excused us.

Wasting no time, I rushed back to the simulator. I was determined to detect something—*anything*—that would tell me it was an illusion. However, after more unsuccessful hours of trying, I returned to my room, dejected, and plodded towards my bed.

My eyes were barely open when I pulled back the covers and screamed. My heart punched in my chest and I tasted bile in the back of my throat. Hand crushed over my mouth; I reeled back from my bed.

Lifeless eyes stared back at me—the head of a Pegasus. Silver blood soaked into the sheets.

My stomach roiled and I shook my head, fighting down another scream that rose in my throat.

The door burst open. Exekiel charged in with his wings splayed and centaurs at his back. Their eyes fell on the Pegasus remains. I couldn't stop shaking.

A crowd started to gather in the corridor but three familiar faces pushed to the front.

"Step aside. Besties coming through," Lucinda huffed.

Her face paled when she noticed the head in my bed. Her eyes shot to me then back to the stained mattress.

Immediately, she fell to her knees and began to chant. A rush of magic filled the space. Phoebus shifted into a wolf and howled—the sound rang in my ears. Other wolf shifters did the same. Alpha.

Dimly, I was aware of Exekiel directing the centaurs to remove the head and ordering everyone to stay back. Power swirled around him. The ground rumbled at his feet.

"It is a dark day when someone slays a Pegasus," Maximus murmured; his head bowed as he came to stand beside me. "It is an unwelcome omen. A promise of innocence lost; of great suffering."

I swallowed thickly. Tears stinging my eyes.

"Who would do this?"

"Who wouldn't?" His sharp gaze studied those beyond the doorway. "This place isn't safe for you, Varialla. War is coming and you're its catalyst."

My gaze went to his. "What?"

His jaw clenched. "Be careful."

"What do you mean?"

He stayed silent. Clearly unable or unwilling to say more.

I wrapped my arms around myself, feeling violated and vulnerable. First the note, the attack in the woods, and now this. Max was right; I wasn't safe. If I ever hoped to be, I needed to learn the truth. Fast.

Magic thickened in the room as Lucinda led other witches through a purity spell to purge the tainted energy.

Water nymphs entered and sang around my bed; hands clasped. Tendrils of water swirled around them then soaked into my mattress. It glowed. I could practically taste the essence of their power.

"Cleansing spell," Maximus murmured.

I nodded. Although I doubted any amount of cleansing could make me feel clean in that bed again.

Phoebus shifted back into his human form and folded his arms around me. Savoring the comfort, I buried my face in his chest. He smelt half-wild, like peppermint in the woods.

"Don't worry." He stroked his hand down my back.

"Easier said than done," I grumbled.

However, the more these people tried to get me to leave, the more determined I was to stay. What were they hiding? Who was I?

Eventually the crowd thinned and everyone left except for Lucinda, Phoebus, Maximus and strangely...Exekiel. He leaned against the wall by the door with his arms folded. He was as good as a statue. A very built, distracting statue.

He wore a black tunic and deep red cape that matched the current shade of his eyes. His trousers were baggy and looped with buckles and chains. On his feet he wore nothing which weirdly felt...intimate. I gave myself a mental shake. I needed to get a grip.

"You're falling for him," Lucinda whispered.

I blanched. "What?"

I glanced at the others but thankfully Phoebus and Maximus were locked in a conversation about some concealment charm whoever hid the head in my bed must have used.

"Him," she jerked her head at Exekiel.

He was staring right at us and I wanted to screech at her to be less obvious. He clearly knew we were talking about him.

"Some believe the two of you are mates."

"What?" I let out a breathless laugh. "Why would they think that?"

"Because you can't keep your eyes off of each other."

It was only then that I realized I was staring at Exekiel…again. His own eyes raked over me; peeled me apart. *Holy shit*. I couldn't deny there was something between us. Something inexplicable and confusing, but mates? Not a chance. I was barely more than a human and he was an all-powerful Fae with connections to the gods.

I tore my stare away from him. "Those people are insane."

Lucinda arched a brow but thankfully let it drop.

"Maybe it's time we leave," she said, standing.

Phoebus and Maximus agreed and I followed them to the door. Phoebus shot Exekiel a questioning look.

The Shadow Saint simply said, "Sweet dreams."

Phoebus' gaze darkened but Lucinda took his hand and pulled him away.

Then it was just me and Exekiel. The room suddenly felt too small.

I looked from the open door to him.

"You're not planning on tucking me in, are you?"

His brow wrinkled. "Of course not. I was planning on reading you a bedtime story."

I bit back a laugh. His ability to deliver a punchline with barely a smile was a true talent. I ushered him towards the door.

"I think you're taking your warden duties a little too far."

Exekiel stopped in the doorway, a wall of hard stacked muscle. He was so close, I had to tip my head up to meet his piercing pink eyes. The air crackled between us. His gaze dropped to my mouth and I curled my upper lip between my teeth. He looked like he wanted to kiss me…to throw me down and…

His hand cupped my chin. My breath faltered.

"You're not my prisoner, little bud. But if you want me to chain you to that bed, all you have to do is ask."

My toes curled. I fumbled for a response but felt irritatingly tongue-tied.

'I—I…'

He grinned. "Don't hurt yourself."

Whilst I uselessly floundered for something witty to say, Exekiel purred, "Good night."

With that, he stepped out of the room and closed the door in my face.

13

ILLUSION OR DELUSION

Something stroked my breast, rousing me from sleep. My eyes sprang open and I gaped up at Exekiel.

He was sitting on the edge of the bed; one arm propped on the headboard as he teased my nipple with his other hand. I jerked. I'd kicked off my trousers before falling into bed but now Exekiel had unbuttoned my blouse; my breasts bared to him. My crotch barely covered by my red lace thong.

"Hello, little bud." His low voice shot through me.

I smacked his hand away and tried to pull my blouse closed. "What are you doing here?"

He lifted a brow; his eyes a pink so deep, they appeared red. "Don't you want me here? Or rather," his fingers brushed across my stomach and travelled South. "Don't you want me *here*?"

He pushed his hand between my thighs. My back arched and I moaned. What was happening?

Exekiel leaned closer. His breath shuddered across my parted lips. "Do you like that?"

He rubbed me slowly and watched every reaction play out on my face. I whimpered. I more than liked it. He was captivating. His touch made my cells burn.

I licked my lips and nodded. A heady rush swept through me. *Fuck*. His fingers were made for this.

"I like it," I panted.

He grinned in a way that made my nipples crown.

Shaking, I wrestled with my sanity. This was wild. He couldn't just break into my room and do what he wanted to me, whenever he wanted.

"Wait." I grabbed his wrist.

"I'm done waiting." Exekiel hooked his finger beneath the lace of my panties and tugged them aside.

My mind raced, settling on that night on the cliff. Exekiel's desire had been palpable and yet he'd stopped when I'd asked. Something was different about him tonight. Something was wrong.

"Is this an illusion?" I rasped as he peeled me open.

"Does it feel like one?" Exekiel sank a finger inside me.

I moaned, deeply; my nails digging into his wrist.

"S-s-stop," I stammered. But he didn't. He pumped his finger inside me and I bucked against his hand.

This isn't real. My mind screamed. Exekiel may have been an asshole but when I'd asked him to stop before, he'd stopped. It wasn't much to go on, but I weirdly felt like I knew him and this wasn't him.

I scrambled back on the bed. "This isn't real."

I jumped up, lunging towards the dresser where I kept the enchanted dagger. Why hadn't I slept with it under my pillow?

Exekiel bounded after me. His hands came up around my breasts and he yanked me back against him. His thumbs circled my nipples and a hot tight shiver pulled inside me.

"Let me fuck you, little bud."

This isn't real. And yet, I ached. The pressure of him behind me—the swell of his rigid length digging into my back. It would have been so easy to give myself over; to drink in every second of this whether it was real or not. But the clock was ticking and time was running out.

Frantic, I ripped away from him and ran. My fingers closed around the dagger. I swiveled; weapon raised but was careful not to position it. Uncertainty prickled up my spine.

"Is this an illusion?" I snapped.

A now familiar sweetness filled my mouth and I could almost see threads of red spool from my lips and fan across his face.

Exekiel blinked then snarled, "Why does it matter?"

He roughly grabbed my waist and pinned me against the dresser. The dagger shook in my hand but I refused to let it go.

"Answer the question."

'Real or fake, we're together." He ran his burning lips across my jaw. My eyes closed. My attraction to him was almost crippling.

"Answer me." I swallowed and raised the dagger higher. His eyes widened. It was so real, I hesitated. "Is this an illusion?"

The taste intensified in my mouth like sugared strawberries and pops of candy.

Exekiel strained, fighting the force of my ability. "It doesn't matter."

"It does," I cried, torn between desire and despair as he got on his knees and parted my thighs. "It matters because this isn't real, and I want all our firsts to be real."

Before I could change my mind, I angled the dagger and drove it through my heart.

The world went up in agony. I must have lost my mind. What kind of dumbass stabbed themselves in the heart?

Gasping for breath, I crumpled to my knees and felt the warmth of blood spill over my fingers. What had I done? Logic told me it was an illusion—Exekiel hadn't been able to deny it when I'd used my ability on him—but knowing didn't make it any less painful.

I slumped forwards; hands wrapped around the dagger's hilt; head pressed into the carpet. My ribs felt broken but I, somehow, sucked down great gulps of air until my mind started to clear and agony seeped away.

Eventually, I groaned and peeled my eyes open.

"Welcome back," a low voice drawled.

I flinched, surprised to find Exekiel crouched beside me, bathed in early morning sunlight. His forearms rested casually on his knees but his dark hair was tussled. A green trident glowed on the back of his hand and his wings were unfurled.

"What are you doing here?" I croaked.

The words eerily echoed the ones I'd said in the illusion.

A muscle ticked in his jaw. "You shouted my name."

"And you came running?" I half-smirked as I sat up and leaned against the dresser.

Though I knew he hadn't been far. Ever since the extraction, Exekiel barely let me out of his sight. He was just waiting for the secrets of my mind to be revealed to him. I really needed to work on a mental shield.

He dragged his thumb along his bottom lip. "I'll always come when you call, little bud. At least, until the secrets of your mind are revealed to me."

My eyes widened. "Get out of my head!"

His chuckle was deep and wicked. "But it's such a...*fascinating* place to be."

I narrowed my eyes. "You saw, didn't you? The illusion."

A full-blown smile stretched across his face. It was so at odds with his usual broody demeanor, and just as sexy.

He dusted off his hands as he got to his feet. "I might have."

I covered my face; mortified but couldn't help huffing out a laugh.

"To be honest, I'm impressed you were able to resist me."

I spluttered, "Get out."

He dodged as I swiped at him with my foot.

Hands tucked in his pockets; Exekiel strode towards the door. "By the way, nice tits."

"I grew them myself," I hollered as he left the room.

His laughter echoed down the hallway.

I was about to get up and slam the door when I realized the splintered wood was now strewn across the floor; the hinges busted. That explained how he'd gotten in.

There was something ominous in the air as I made my way to the Resident Dining Hall. One girl raced past in tears. A boy morphed his hand into a paw and punched the wall. Others were huddled around their Five Isles phones speaking in urgent tones.

Curious, I took out my own device and tapped the transparent face. The wires lit up and the holographic screen emerged.

Countless notification bubbles bounced across the surface but what caught my eye was a bubble with a red star next to it.

Inside were the words:

Fit for the Throne
(*Players Only*)

I tapped the notification and was met with a list of names. It was the players rankings.

Heart in my throat, I scrolled through the list. I did a little dance when I saw Lucinda ranked at number twelve. Apparently, she'd only been inside her illusion for fifteen minutes before she'd realized. Maximus was at number sixty-three.

Hands shaking, I continued to scroll. How long was I in that illusion? Those ranked in the seventies had taken up to fifty minutes to detect the magic. On I went; convinced I was about to find my name at the bottom— a definite contender in the Blood Battle. Then at number eighty-three at fifty-nine minutes was Varialla von Hastings.

Relief whistled through me. I was safe. And I'd surprisingly done better than Phoebus who ranked at eighty-seven.

By six other contestants' names was a skull. I guessed that meant they'd mistaken reality for illusion and killed themselves, or that they'd stayed passed the hour and become eternally trapped in their mind.

Although, Exekiel had killed three of them outside of the Trial. He'd killed them protecting me.

Shaking off the strange flutters that gave me, I strode into the dining hall and paced to where Lucinda sat with the boys.

"I need coffee." I collapsed on the bench and began punching in my order but something bleak in their expressions halted me. "What is it?"

Phoebus growled, "Did you check the rankings?"

"Yeah. We're safe."

"Not all of us." Lucinda looked to Phoebus.

I frowned. "You're eighty-seventh. Only those in the bottom ten go into the Battles."

"Yeah," he grunted, "and since six of us are dead there's only ninety-four contestants."

Which meant that anyone ranked at eighty-four or higher was going to be in the Blood Battle. My pulse skipped. I'd been so close.

"What about the public? Didn't Goather say they can vote to save you?"

Phoebus snickered. "I'm not that popular. Today I fight. And I either win or…"

"There's always the Truce Circle."

He hissed at Lucinda. His eyes shifted to that of a wolf.

"Truce Circle?" I asked.

"More like coward's circle," Phoebus spat. "The aim of the Blood Battle is to fight for your Kingdom or die trying. However, those who are afraid, are free to forfeit and enter the Truce Circle."

"That's bad?"

"You're stripped of your title, any worldly riches and forced into service at the palace."

"Better than dying, isn't it?"

I looked between the three of them for agreement, but none responded.

14

THE BLOOD BATTLES BEGIN

The air was thick with tension as the contestants, Council and crew headed to the open-air arena where the Blood Battles would take place.

For the occasion, I'd been outfitted in a dress made of chainmail. Silver spikes surged from my shoulders. Breastplates hung over my chest. Coils of chain tapered down my stomach and metal scales ruffled around my thighs. Apparently, it was official ceremonial attire.

Maximus and Lucinda flanked me; each one with their heads high and dressed in some form of armor. Hardly anyone spoke. Not even those who before had sung of war and honor.

We shuffled onto our stone seats and waited for the Battles to begin.

A ring of colored flames burst to life in the heart of the arena—the Truce Circle. Moments after, Goather trotted out. Behind him, the Council carried the Conduit on a bronze pedestal with four handles and a pool of water in its center.

Gasps rippled through the crowd. My heart leapt. There was something fascinating about the glittering green and blue flecks that shimmered towards the sky.

Once the Conduit was in position, Goather lifted his arms. "It is time for the Mating March; our player's last hope of saving themselves."

Goblins played a haunting melody on flutes and violins as the contestants trekked out onto the sand.

"If they correctly identify their mate, they prove that they can rule with their head *and* their heart. As a result, five seconds will be taken off their time, which would raise their rank and potentially free them from the Battles."

I straightened. So, this was why mates mattered. One by one, the contestants marched around the Conduit and named the one they thought was their match but it was obvious they were guessing. We'd only been here a few weeks.

Phoebus marched next. His hair was smoothed back and his chin tipped high; chest bare.

"Varialla von Hastings."

What? That was the worst guess he could have made.

"You realize it's rare for those of a different cast to be mated."

"Rare but not impossible."

Goather inclined his head and scribbled my name down on a piece of parchment that he passed into the Conduit. Like with the other players, the Conduit turned red and the paper was burned to dust.

In the end, none were saved from taking part and the Battle began with a gong.

They fought against each other with every weapon they had. Their powers, potions and spells. Others wielded actual spears and swords that had been placed in the arena.

Phoebus spent most of his time in wolf form. He tore off the head of an elf and clawed out the guts of a lion shifter. Blood sprayed across the sand. The audience began to chant and stamp their feet.

"Who will be victorious?" Goather roared.

It was all a show; a game.

My knuckles paled from how tightly I gripped the stone seat beneath me.

A Fae drove a spear through Phoebus's hind legs. He swiveled around with a fierce growl and lunged. The Fae splayed his wings, flipped over Phoebus and struck again. This time carving through his side. I screamed. The crowd bellowed.

Not Phoebus. So many dead already littered the ground.

The pair continued to brawl but the Fae had more than weapons. He was fast, strong and his wings made it easy for him to dodge every one of Phoebus's attacks.

One brutal kick sent Phoebus sprawling. Before he could rise, the Fae impaled him on spears end. Phoebus let out a howl of pain and his wolf form quickly shifted back to human. He shuddered; bloodied hands trying to pry the steel from his chest.

"The Truce Circle," I shouted over the roars of the crowd. "Go to the Truce Circle."

He was close enough to crawl.

His blue eyes met mine and, in that moment, I knew he would never surrender. He would win or die.

Phoebus roared and kicked the Fae back. Muscles trembling, he tore the spear from his body and threw it to the sand. He didn't try to shift—he was too battered.

He charged the Fae. The two went down in a fit of fists and for a time, it was anyone's game. Then a flash of silver glinted in the setting sun. A sword.

"Phoebus!" I screamed.

Bloodlust rose in the stands.

"For the Isle of the Eternals!" The Fae raised his weapon and carved off Phoebus' head.

I woke with what felt like the world's worst hangover though I hadn't had a drink. My head throbbed. My throat ached and my mouth was bone-dry. Did the Blood Battles really happen? Was Phoebus truly gone? The swish of the blade slicing through his neck echoed in my mind. The thump of his head as it rolled.

I exhaled heavily. I was used to being abandoned but never like this. The crowd had barely shed a tear. After a moment of silence, they'd hailed the victor and praised the bravery of the fallen. It had all been natural to them—the only outcome. As if the Truce Circle hadn't been right there; a rainbow of flickering flames.

My stomach turned. This wasn't a Game. This was a death sentence.

However, one good thing did come from yesterday. During the Mating March, Goather had told Phoebus that it was rare for those of different casts to be mated. This meant they didn't think I was a Shifter. That whatever power I possessed that they all despised, came from one of the other Isles—Wiccan's Wharf, Fae Reef or Elf Bay.

I rolled out of bed, got dressed in the plain black dress Eudora had laid out for me and made my way to the library. The corridors were deserted—even the camera-orbs had been turned off.

Sadness struck me the second I entered the book-scented aisles. I was instantly reminded of Phoebus...I still had his flask.

Sighing, I searched for books related to the realm's various abilities. I needed to find something connected to what I was. Some clue on how to unlock this incredible power everyone insisted I had. Sleuth and sass wouldn't be enough to help me survive. To learn the truth.

For years, I'd convinced myself that I didn't care who'd abandoned me or why. I was a lone wolf and proud of it. But the child in me had never stopped hoping—dreaming—that one day I'd find answers. Now, for the first time, it seemed possible. And nothing was going to stop me.

After hours spent looking into the possibility of being a Fae, elf or witch, I discovered that I wasn't either. The Fae were the only ones who could compel someone to do something without needing an incantation but none of them tasted something sweet when they used their ability. So, what the hell was I? Where did I belong?

When I returned to my room, the nymphs were waiting for me, with arms folded.

Eudora snapped, "Where have you been?"

She didn't wait for an answer as she ushered me into the bath chamber and the others tugged at my clothes.

"What's going on?"

"The fallen have received their overnight blessing," Eudora stated as she swirled soap in the bathing pool. "It's time for the burial."

Of course. Goather had mentioned the burial ceremony after the Battle but I hadn't been paying much attention.

The girls made quick work of scrubbing me clean. I didn't even argue about doing my own privates. My mind was elsewhere, on battles, blood and secrets. On rolling heads and heckled threats.

"If someone had an ability that no one else in the Five Isles had, what would that mean?" I asked as I climbed out of the water and was patted dry.

The nymphs exchanged a look.

"It would mean that the ability didn't come from the Five Isles."

They led me into the bedroom.

"I thought only people from the Isles could participate in the Games."

Eudora nodded. "That's right. Only the Fate's Chosen."

I'd read about them in the welcome pack. The four Chosen races that were each blessed with their own island that drifted around the Isle of the Eternals—where I currently was. The island where only the greatest among them dwelled, guardians of the Conduit. The four Chosen races were elves, shifters, Fae, and witches.

Any outside of that, including centaurs and nymphs lived in the Outer Isles. It didn't go into much detail about them but based on what I'd witnessed so far, they weren't seen as equals. Were there more beings out there? Was *I* one of them?

Was that why everyone hated me? Because I was half creed—half worthy in their eyes?

After lathering on lotions and scents, Cyrus started on my makeup. Peoni cornrowed the right side of my hair up to the center of my head then let the curly ends tumble down to the left. Eudora revealed another chainmail dress. This one was light and forged from delicate chains and mesh. Only the shoulder plates were solid metal.

It took the three of them to wrestle me into it, but soon, I stood before the mirror.

My brows lifted. "Am I going to a burial or a brothel? I look like a gladiator's wet dream."

Since the dress was made out of thin chains; an indecent amount of skin showed through the interlacing links. It was floor-length with long sleeves but also tight-fitted and had a front slit that came up to my inner thigh.

Eudora huffed, "You look like a queen."

I snickered. "No queen I've ever seen."

Eventually, the nymphs added their final touches and sent me on my way.

Centaur-drawn chariots carried us to the mourning site. It was a beautiful beach strung with fairy lights. My heart fluttered. Despite the situation, there was something about the ocean that soothed me.

Everyone was gathered by the water where the fallen lay wrapped in leaves and twine. Floating lanterns were attached to them by golden thread and each lantern had been lit.

I found Maximus and Lucinda near the front. We nodded to each other and joined hands. I'd never needed or even wanted friends before, but now I was glad they were here.

The Council arrived and marched towards the dead.

Alexov stood before us. His robes black as pitch and his expression grim.

"We are here today, to honor those who gave their lives out of love for their Kingdom." His voice lilted with the ebb and flow of the waves.

Despite how much I hated him, I let his words wash over me.

He spoke of glory and hope, then finally said, "Now we send these souls to rest. May they go with the brave and the blessed."

Witches stepped forward and enchanted the lanterns to rise, carrying the bodies with them. It was haunting and beautiful.

"Let them drift towards the Fates and burn among the stars." As if Alexov's words ignited the flames, the lanterns' fires grew and encased the dead.

I sucked in a breath whilst the others sang a song of farewell. I wished I knew the words.

15

DON'T *SEA* ME

The burial was a celebration of life. Earlier had been about mourning—meals sent to our rooms; camera-orbs turned off—but now a great feast was spread out on a clear sheet of glass that floated in midair. Camera-orbs soared overhead. Goblins swayed on a sandbank and played lively music. People danced, shared stories of the fallen and drank way too much.

I downed my third shot of something called *crudel* then linked arms with Maximus and skipped around in circles.

"Whilst you two frolic, our enemies are identifying their mates," Lucinda drawled.

Although she showed no signs of leaving the eerily perfect rendition of a skull that she was building in the sand.

"I wouldn't even know where to start." I scoffed. "Do I just rub up against every...whatever I am?"

"Not quite. You must recognize each other's souls." Lucinda sliced a dagger across her palm and sprinkled droplets of blood onto the skull.

"Also, it doesn't matter what you are. It's rare for those of a different cast to be mated but sometimes, if the bond is strong enough, it overrides the natural order. Usually to the disgust of everyone involved." She chuckled.

The skull mimicked her. I swallowed a scream. So that was blood magic.

"As with all things, people are free to reject or accept the bond. That being said, when it happens between two different casts, it's usually because the bond is impossible to deny which is why the Fates ordained it."

I didn't know why my eyes chose that moment to find Exekiel. He was darkly handsome in a chainmail trench coat and fitted black trousers, locked in conversation with the Council.

As if he felt me staring, his eyes lifted and settled on mine. I quickly looked away. Exekiel was dangerous. Not only for the ways he could kill a man but for the way he made me feel.

"Just think, if you'd taken half a second longer, we could have been burning you tonight," Vivienne purred behind me. I turned. "What a pity."

She didn't wait for me to respond as she bumped me with her shoulder and strode passed. Her three lackeys giggled and followed after.

"Always a pleasure," I drawled.

She was disturbingly correct. Just half a second had put me at number eighty-three instead of eighty-four.

And, apparently, if any of them had guessed their mate, it would have been me facing the Blood Battle.

After another round of dancing with Maximus, I needed to clear the drunken haze from my mind. Ordinary alcohol had never affected me as much as this.

I strolled towards the ocean and kicked off my shoes. My toes scrunched in the sand as the water lapped around my feet. Every ripple echoed in my skin. Every touch seemed to draw me in.

I gazed at the sea the way one would gaze at the stars and whispered, "Now what?"

The ground trembled.

Tense, I glanced around to see if anyone else noticed. The celebration carried on, oblivious. They didn't feel the earth tremor or see the strange shimmers that appeared on the water's surface.

The mark on my side throbbed and I pressed my hand to it. It shifted beneath my fingers—rotating, reshaping.

What the heck?

Heart racing, I peered through the chains of my dress. It was hard to see in the torchlight but I was almost certain that the symbol had changed. No longer that of the Five Isles but instead of a centaur.

My mind reeled. Every beat of my heart felt like thunder. Glowing tendrils continued to ripple through the water. I took a final look behind me. Everyone from the Council was huddled together including Exekiel. For once, no one was watching me.

I snatched up my shoes and raced along the shore, tracking the shimmers. It was like they were there solely for me. Leading me to the answers I longed for. If I knew how to swim, I would've dived into the depths of the water to follow them.

When the light faded, I'd almost reached the tree line at the edge of the beach where the rocky cliffs rose. I was far from the burial site now. Its music pulsed faintly in the distance.

I shook my head. Had the water really glowed? Or was it the result of too much *crude*?

"I knew you'd make a run for it."

I wheeled around and came face-to-face with two burly shifters and one slender Fae. Atlas, Nikolai and Cora.

Cora stepped towards me, her blonde ponytail bouncing.

I took a step back, slipping on the slick pebbles behind me.

"Lucky for you," she hissed. "We enjoy the chase."

Claws shot from the ends of Nikolai and Atlas' fingers and Cora spread her mammoth blue wings.

Shit. My stomach pitched. *Extra shit with shit shavings on the side.*

I turned heel and fled. Darting through the trees, I tried not to lose my footing. How was I here again? Being hunted for just existing?

Something swiped dangerously close to my back. I shrieked and pivoted direction; gripping onto a tree trunk to carry my momentum.

It was useless. The boys easily followed, tracking my scent. And when they lost sight, Cora soared overhead, bellowing when she saw me.

Nikolai was now a lion larger than I'd ever seen. And Atlas had become a kind of yeti. He was half the size of the tallest tree with thick white fur, giant yellow teeth and terrifying red eyes.

He made an unsettling sound that rumbled through me and shook the trees. Now would have been a good time for my magic to surface but nothing stirred. It was like searching for a thread of nylon, hidden in hay.

A stitch started in my side. I couldn't outrun them much longer. Desperate, I dove behind the nearest tree and clamped my hand over my mouth to stifle my heavy breaths.

The beasts prowled closer. Their animalistic growls sent shivers up my spine.

Don't see me. Don't see me. I silently chanted to myself. Eyes closed and body pressed against the tree, I tried to blend in with it. Tried not to move; not to blink too loudly. *Don't see me.*

The yeti stepped out in front of me and my nostrils stung when I detected his bitter scent of rotted meat. I clamped my lips together, swallowing a whimper. *Don't see me.* I pleaded.

Again, my tongue turned sugar-sweet. I drank in the flavor like a fine wine.

The yeti's eyes drooped downwards landing on me. I stayed perfectly still. I could run but the lion wasn't far and Cora still circled overhead.

The yeti blinked, shook his head and narrowed his eyes at me. I gulped. His large head tilted then he huffed and stalked away.

"Where is she?" Cora shouted.

My heart hammered in my chest. Couldn't they see me? They couldn't see me!

"She can't have gone far."

Heart racing, I slid down the tree trunk and tried to catch my breath. Knees hugged to my chest, I continued to chant, *don't see me*, over and over again.

I woke to sunrays beating down on me through a canopy of trees. Everything was quiet except for the slap of the ocean and the screech of some unholy bird. I groaned; my body creaking.

I'd fallen asleep. Leaves and twigs clung to my hair. Flecks of tree bark pocked my skin. I pushed to my feet, lifted the flap of my breastplate and revealed the hidden pocket that held my Five Isles phone and lipstick. A necessity according to Eudora.

Pulling up the holographic screen, I went to Maps and began my long walk back to Residence Manor.

A pale figure with pointed ears and spring-green eyes, stormed towards me when I eventually rounded the corner to my room. Vladimir—the Council's elf.

"Where the hell have you been?" His sharp jaw clenched. "We've been up half the night searching for you."

"Sorry to ruin your beauty sleep."

His hand closed around my neck as he slammed me against the wall.

Panic speared through me. My head spun.

Couldn't I get at least five minutes between death threats?

"Don't get smart with me, you treacherous little bitch."

I was too exhausted to point out that I'd never actually done anything to these people. They didn't care either way.

Vladimir leaned closer. His porcelain skin shimmered in the sunlight that snaked through the arched-glassless windows.

"Everyone thinks you're better to us alive rather than dead." He scoffed. "I do not share their sentiment. I think we should exterminate the lot of you before you come for us all."

There was so much hatred in his eyes that I couldn't understand. I wanted to look away but also needed this reminder that I wasn't welcome. That if I didn't find a way to unlock my power soon, I would die here. And just when I'd found something worth living for. A life I never thought I'd have. Family. A home. The truth of who I was. It was all within my grasp.

"I don't know what you're talking about," I croaked. My throat dry.

"Save it," he barked, pressing harder on my neck. "I know you're working with them and I'm going to prove it."

I frowned. *Working with who?*

Finally, he released me with a sickened grunt.

"I'll let the others know I found you." With that, Vladimir smoothed back his hair and strode away.

Eudora hastily threaded pearls through my high-bun whilst Cyrus applied blush to my cheeks and Peoni tugged on my sandals. The disaster of the day was forgotten as everything hinged on tonight.

Tonight, more than ever, I needed to look—and act—the part of a Queen. It was the first banquet of the season. A chance to schmooze with the noblemen and women of the realm; to climb higher in the ranks.

"Do not give the Primary's a reason to fault you," Eudora insisted. "They're the winners of previous Games, and though their 100-year reign has ended, they're still in a position of influence. They'll be rooting for you, of all people, to fail."

Of course, they would. I'd only been allowed into the Games because they couldn't defy the Conduit. And, apparently, killing me could incite a war with my kind—whoever they were.

"Primary's bad. Got it." I blew the nymphs a kiss to disguise the rapid beating of my heart, then rushed from the room. I was late; already failing the first rule of our etiquette training: Always be on time.

My gradient blue gown swished around my ankles as I raced into the courtyard towards the last Pegasus-pulled-chariot. I hiked up the ruffled tulle layers of my dress and climbed in; careful not to tread on the off-the-shoulder sleeves that fell below my knees. Then I was off.

Voices sailed from chariots up ahead; people singing and gossiping about the noblemen we'd meet. But I was barely listening. My thoughts were on the mark on my hip that last night had changed to a centaur and had only reverted back to normal earlier this evening. It definitely meant something. The question was, what?

16

The First Banquet

The chariot slowed outside Infinity Hall—a grand black marble fortress that blended with the night, except for gold towers that were shaped like the sharp edge of a pencil.

I followed the crowd as we were led through a set of frosted glass doors and into an opulent banquet hall. Grapevines decorated the beamed ceiling and framed a grand candle chandelier. Long tables covered in white linen stretched down the hall with centerpieces of small leafless trees.

I scanned the place settings for my name.

"You aren't down here, Ms. Hastings."

Goather came up beside me wearing a tight-fitted jacket. He gestured to a table on a raised platform at the head of the room. There sat a group of people in extravagant robes. Probably from the Royal Court.

"Fan favorites have special seating."

My brows lifted. "As in me?"

"Indeed." Goather hooked my arm around his and led me through the hall. "The public are quite taken with you and your antics."

By antics did he mean getting attacked by Lance, the Pegasus head in my bed, or coercing Vivienne to inappropriately touch herself? The list was endless.

"I believe you're sitting next to me," he announced.

I forced a smile as we settled into high-backed seats with purple padded cushions.

It was no surprise that Exekiel and Vivienne had also been invited to the table but I lit up when I saw Lucinda. She was on the other side of Goather in a beautiful peach gown. Our eyes locked. Lucinda's glittered with pride but carried a hint of warning. The same warning, I felt in my bones. Tonight, was more than a feast. It was a test; a day of judgement, and the entire realm was watching.

On my right, must have been a Primary. His tall-hat was plum-purple, the same shade as his hooded cape. A gold Five Isles medal was pinned to his breast and a sash hung across his chest. His brown wings on display.

He picked up his silver goblet and swirled the drink in his hand. "Varialla von Hastings."

Remembering my training, I bowed my head. "It's an honor."

"The honor is mine; I assure you." The man scooped up my hand and pressed his full lips to my knuckles.

Countless cameras turned in our direction.

"And you are?"

"Adir Degalos; First Primary." He grinned—all teeth. His face was well-cut—even handsome. "I daresay this evening just got a lot more interesting."

I couldn't tell if that was a compliment but I smiled and dipped my head, all the same.

Thankfully, Goather dominated most of the conversation throughout the starters and main course. The satyr was only silent when the Primary's spoke of their experiences in the Games—what it felt like to witness their first Blood Battle, how they rose in the ranks, the challenge of finding their mate.

"Which reminds me, when we last spoke, Vivienne, you believed that Exekiel was your mate." Goather looked between the pair who'd been seated together. "Is this still the case?"

Exekiel's deep pink eyes flickered to mine. My heart flipped and I looked away but not before the others caught the exchange.

Goather grinned. "Or perhaps the public is right in their suspicions?"

Now every eye swung from me to Exekiel. I smothered a groan.

"I suppose that would explain this footage from the other week." As if summoned, an orb drifted closer and Goather tapped a button on its side.

A holographic scene emerged from the lens. My stomach dropped. It was footage of me and Exekiel the day he'd taken me away from Lance. There was thankfully no sound but the cameras had caught Exekiel dragging me into the alcove and shielding us behind the vines. After, all that could be seen were our legs but that was enough.

Our legs showed how closely we were standing together. Showed when Exekiel dropped to his knees. Worse, it showed my legs disappearing as they were wrapped around his waist.

Heat rippled through me as I remembered the way he'd moved between my legs. The way he'd felt. The smooth texture of his wings and warmth of his breath. My hand tightened around my goblet.

Goather purred, "What exactly were you two doing in there?"

"Talking," I blurted and took a swig from my cup.

"Yes. Fluent body language." He snickered.

Those around the table chuckled. Exekiel's expression remained infuriatingly unreadable.

"Don't be coy," said a resplendent elf in a lavender gown as she sucked sorbet from her spoon. "Mated or not, the audience are loving it. Perhaps you'll both indulge us with a dance."

"No," I snapped then rushed to add, "I'm not familiar with the dances here."

Or any dance that wasn't Beyoncé's Single Ladies routine.

"No matter. The male leads and with our dear Exekiel, you'll be in excellent hands."

I cursed. I didn't want to think about his hands; about the things they'd done to me in the illusion or how they made me feel.

Exekiel grinned as if he'd read my mind even though I'd been practicing Mind-Shield.

He stood and extended his hand. "Little bud?"

I bristled; my eyes narrowing. Had he seriously just used that ridiculous pet name in front of everyone?

I snarled. "My sorbet will melt."

The table swelled with laugher.

Goather prodded me in the side. "We'll get you another one."

Reluctantly, I stood and accepted Exekiel's hand. A current rippled between us and I did my best to ignore it.

I reminded myself that I had to appear to play the game; to want to be a part of this world. I had to convince the Primary's that they were still the puppet masters and that I hadn't seen the strings.

Exekiel led me out onto the dance floor between the contestants and the Court. His dark tailcoat whipped behind him as he turned to face me. All eyes were on us.

He interlaced our fingers and drew me close. "Let's give the people what they want."

His hands slid over my waist and grasped my hips. Sparks danced along my skin. I didn't know what to do with my hands so I rested them on his biceps as he rocked us to the music—a slow sultry pace. I tried not to focus on his dizzying scent of woodsmoke and warm apples, or the hard press of his body against mine.

He lowered his head and ran his nose up my cheek. *Dear God.* My entire body trembled.

"Varialla, have you been working on your Mind-Shield?"

I swallowed thickly. "Didn't I tell you to stay out of my head?"

Orbs drifted closer.

"Why?" he murmured. "What are you hiding?"

His hips moved against mine and my mind briefly went blank.

"Isn't that how this works?" I finally uttered. "You have your secrets. I have mine."

The music shifted. Exekiel spun me away then pulled me back. Stepped one way then another. I followed him easily as if I could sense what he would do next. We were completely in sync.

Finally, he brought my body flush to his and pulled me onto my tiptoes so our hips were almost aligned. Lost in the moment, we grinded to the seductive beat.

"The secrets we keep are for the good of the Kingdom," he murmured.

I scoffed. "According to you."

With a low growl, Exekiel cupped my ass. I barely suppressed a moan.

Shit. What was happening? It was like an inferno blazed between us, fusing our bodies together. Etiquette out the damn window.

The orbs light flashed intensely. I jerked back but Exekiel held me in place, his grip almost painful.

"What will Vivienne think?" I said, breathlessly. The way his fingers trailed up and down my spine was wreaking havoc on my insides.

He chuckled. "There has never been anything but physical satisfaction between Vivienne and I."

That didn't make me feel any better.

"And I haven't touched her in decades."

"That's not what I heard."

He cocked his head; his magenta eyes probing. "Careful. You sound jealous."

I snickered. "I assure you, I'm not. Last time I checked, you didn't like me and I didn't like you."

He dipped me. His strong hand travelling to the back of my thigh as he hooked my leg around him. Our centers met. I bit down on my bottom lip; fought the rise of pleasure that coursed through me.

"I don't have to like you, little bud, to want to fuck you." He emphasized this by thrusting his hips.

My body tightened. My pulse pounded like a jackhammer. Our eyes locked—a blaze of desire and disdain. He wanted me as much as I wanted him. I could taste it. Our hips met in a rhythmic grind over and over. His length thickened against me and I hissed through my teeth.

He was destroying me, tearing down my defenses. My leg locked in his grip. I needed to get away. To break the trance, he threatened to trap me in.

As if my prayers were answered, a slender finger trailed down my arm, but it made my skin crawl.

I looked up to see Adir smirking down at me. "Mind if I cut in?"

17

YOU'RE MINE

I wanted to refuse when Adir offered me his hand but I couldn't. If the First Primary of the Five Isles had a thing for me, I had to exploit it. Had to do whatever I needed to, to survive. To get answers.

Besides there were rules to be followed—roles to be played. Me, the clueless foreigner from the human realm and he, the mighty Primary; ruler of the Five Isles, who'd been kind enough to honor me with a dance.

He winked. "I can take her from here, Protector."

Exekiel's grip tightened around me. His bright eyes held mine and a muscle ticked in his jaw. Only for a heartbeat, he let something other than cool indifference slip through—a fleeting look of rage and desire. The intensity of it, made it hard to breathe.

I barely noticed when the Primary dragged me away. I was only aware of Exekiel and the growing distance between us. What was wrong with me? Why was I so hyperaware of this male? Why did everything he do leave me craving more?

"I've been waiting all night to get you in my arms," Adir purred.

His fingers fisted in the ruffles of my dress and grazed the swell of my backside.

My gaze shot to his. As handsome as the Primary was, there was something about him that made my heckles rise. Maybe it was Eudora's warning but I didn't trust the smarmy bastard.

"I must admit, I'm surprised the Conduit deemed you worthy," Adir went on. "After the war, I was sure your kind would never grace these shores again."

I froze; torn between pushing the asshole and his roaming hands, off of me, or staying to learn more. Had he just confirmed that I was part outlier? That I belonged beyond the borders of the Five Isles?

"What do you mean?"

He spun me away then greedily pulled me back. My body pressed to his. It had the direct opposite effect to being in Exekiel's arms.

"Surely, you've noticed the other contestant's hostility towards you." His breath beat over my shoulder. "Your kind cost this realm a lot. Took so many innocent lives."

Adir stroked his fingers down the back of my neck. I shuddered in revulsion but masked it as desire. The orbs drifted closer.

In the background, I heard Goather say, "None of us ever thought we'd see this day. The First Primary and our guest from beyond the veil in what looks like the start of a budding romance." His tone was in full presenter mode, and I knew he must have been speaking to one of the cameras.

"What kind am I, Primary?"

He grinned and brought his lips close to my ear. "Naughty girl. You know I can't tell you that."

I almost threw up in my mouth.

"Doesn't it seem unfair that everyone knows what I am, except me? How can I atone for the sins of my kind when I don't know what they are?" My tongue turned sweet. I latched onto it. "Maybe you could tell me exactly what my kind did and I can try to make it up to you."

Pink filaments, that only I could see, slithered from between my lips. The Primary blinked.

Smiling coyly, I curled my arms around his neck and drew him close. I was getting good at this.

"Tell me everything."

Adir held me closer; his eyes hooded. One hand curved around the back of my leg as he pressed me against him.

I swallowed bile that rose in my throat. For the truth, I could endure this—his bitter breath and greedy hands.

"Tell me," I coaxed. "What did my kind do to the Isles?"

"That's enough." The uninvited voice was low and thick with warning.

I didn't have to turn to know that Exekiel stood behind me.

Adir blinked again. His bleary gaze drifted to the Shadow Saint.

"What's that?" His tone turned brusque. The pink essence receded and he was back to being a royal bastard.

"Walk away, Primary. Ms. Hastings is done dancing for the night."

Adir laughed. "I never took you as the jealous type, Protector. Besides, there's no guarantee she's your mate."

I couldn't believe how casually he said it—that Exekiel and I might be *destined* for each other. It was laughable, impossible…

The Shadow Saint prowled closer; voice quiet—probably to avoid a scene, but it came out more menacing. "Walk away."

Adir scoffed. "How can I walk away from such a fine creature?" His hand slid beneath the slit in my dress and grazed my bare thigh.

I fought every instinct to punch him in the face and somehow managed to giggle instead. I needed this man on my side. I'd come so close to learning…something.

The guttural sound Exekiel made was barely human. "I was defending this realm when you were still sucking on your mother's tits, Primary. I would thank you not to question my command."

Fury flashed across Adir's face and he finally rounded on the Protector.

My jaw clenched. All I'd wanted was some answers. Not a dick measuring contest. And who the hell did Exekiel think he was? He couldn't go around threatening every guy that touched me like some possessive tyrant. I didn't belong to him. I wasn't anything to him.

132

Liar. My mind whispered but I shook off the thought.

"Believe it or not, I don't need you to rescue me," I snapped.

Exekiel chuckled darkly. "You're not the one I'm saving." His gaze slid over me and I felt as if he'd stripped me bare. "It's the Primary who needs rescuing from you. If that means that he gets his hands off of you in the process, I consider that a bonus."

I swallowed. Of course. His warning for Adir to get away from me was because somehow Exekiel had known what I was doing. Had he sensed my power?

He returned his attention to Adir who's brow furrowed. "Sorry to ruin your fun, Primary, but my little bud has thorns."

I glared at him.

Exekiel's deep pink eyes gleamed. "I suspect she's pure Poison Ivy."

"She's just a girl." Adir scoffed. "Her kind are well and truly beaten and she's not foolish enough to follow in their footsteps."

My nostrils flared.

Exekiel smirked at my furious expression, as if he knew and was delighted that I wanted to tear the Primary apart. "Think what you will, Primary. Either way, get your hands off of her."

I flushed. There was an edge in his tone—a violence in his stare. It wasn't something that should turn me on but everything about him seemed to.

Adir shook his head but ultimately the Protector of the Realm won. With a heavy sigh, the Primary took my hand in his and brushed his lips over my knuckles.

"Perhaps you can visit me in my private chambers one day."

I couldn't think of anything worse. However, the Primary clearly didn't see me as a threat. He underestimated me and my abilities and I could use that to my advantage.

I smiled. "I'd like that."

Adir bowed his head and, at last, strode away.

"Excellent performance."

I bristled as I turned to Exekiel. "I could say the same to you."

He arched a brow. "Oh?"

"You didn't stop us from dancing just to protect the Primary," I spat. "You did it because you have this ridiculous idea that somehow, I'm yours and nobody else can touch me."

His silence said it all.

I stepped closer and prodded him in the chest. "Well, you're wrong. No part of me belongs to you in any way. You have no say in who I talk to or dance with or even if I decide to let the Primary rail me all night long."

Exekiel blinked. "We both know the only one who'll be fucking you, is me."

My heart skipped and I stumbled back. Before I could recover, Exekiel gripped my chin and tipped my head up, forcing me to look at him. Heat coursed through my veins.

"But you're welcome to try and live out some fantasy with Adir Degalos if you think he can make you feel the way I do."

He trailed his fingers down my neck and they came to rest on my pulse. "If you think he can make your heart race like I do."

I shook. This was crazy—the effect he had on me; the rush I felt from his touch. It was powerful and pathetic.

"You're delusional," I snarled.

Exekiel dragged his thumb along my bottom lip. "No matter what happens or how badly you try to deny it, little bud, at the end of the day, you're mine and I am infuriatingly yours."

I wanted to retort but was left utterly tongue-tied—my mouth dry. What did he mean by that? I licked my lips and his eyes tracked the movement; his body a hairsbreadth from mine. His head bowed so his lips were close.

"Tell me, I'm wrong."

"You're wrong," I whispered then jerked free and stormed away.

I didn't have time for his arrogant Fae-bastard bullshit. All he was doing was messing with my head and getting in the way.

With no desire to return to everyone's intrigued gazes at the table, I veered towards the veranda. The doors were flung wide to welcome the evening air. Fairy lights twinkled on leafless trees.

I paced the marble platform and tried to focus on what mattered. Not Exekiel but what Adir had said about a war; the countless deaths and his invitation for me to get him alone. To use my magic—as weak as it was—to get answers.

"Sorry to interrupt."

I spun around at the sound of a man's voice and was met with a centaur. He was tall with hazel skin; his lower half, the body of a black stallion. His hooves clopped as he trotted towards me with a tray in his hand. A beautiful cocktail the color of the ocean in a winding glass was perched on the platter. The outer rim of the glass was decorated with glittering sand and there was a pattern of shells around the base.

"Signature cocktail for a fan favorite," he said and held out the tray.

I was only half paying attention as I took the glass. "Thanks."

"And the shell." The Centaur nodded to the largest shell on the tray—a conch shell. "They say if you listen closely, you can hear the ocean."

Something in his voice snagged my attention. I finally lifted my eyes to his, and there was something unsaid within them. Immediately I thought of the mark on my hip. It couldn't be a coincidence that last night it had turned into a centaur and now he stood before me.

Slowly, I picked up the shell and held it to my ear. Instead of hearing the ocean, I heard a voice.

18

A ROUND OF TOKEN TRIVIA

My bedroom door flew open. I shoved the shell beneath my pillow and bolted upright. I'd listened to its message at least a hundred times already.

"Tomorrow, your dinner will be served in your rooms. Be there."

The voice that spoke had been low and commanding—a man who wasn't used to being denied.

"Alright lady, spill." Maximus flipped his dreadlocks as he and Lucinda hopped up onto my bed. "What happened last night?"

I groaned. On the chariot rides home, all anyone had been able to talk about was a potential romance brewing between me and the Primary. Apparently, Adir hadn't danced with anyone else. Not that I noticed.

I'd been too distracted by the shell burning a hole in my garter where I'd hidden it and by Exekiel who'd danced with Vivienne and the Primary's mate for most of the evening. I hadn't been able to keep my eyes off of him. I couldn't help feeling smug that he'd held none of them as possessively as he'd held me.

You're mine.

Lucinda sprawled across the foot of the bed. "By the way, if your intention was to seduce the Primary, you should have told us."

I snorted. "That was not my intention." At least, not at first. "What's the point of having a mate anyway, if you're going to behave like that?" I shuddered at the memory of Adir's groping hands.

Lucinda shrugged. "Like I said, the mate bond can be rejected. Our First Primary's love each other but they each have a consort from their own cast to appease their kind."

Considering how prejudiced these people were, I wasn't surprised. Adir was Fae and his mate; an elf. I could only imagine the shitshow that went down when that was discovered.

Maximus grinned. "And, by the looks of it, our Primary wanted to add you to his harem."

I snickered. "To be honest, right now, I'd do about anything to get some answers."

"Does that include doing the Primary? Because you might have to."

We all laughed even as I whacked him with a cushion.

"Although, the library holds as many answers as the cyber-grid if you know where to look."

The cyber-grid, I'd learned, was the Five Isles version of the internet. However, contestants were barred from it and the outside world during the Games.

"Speaking of the library, we need to check out its books on potions," Lucinda interjected. "Apparently, the Second Trial will involve a tonic."

"How do you know that?"

"You're not the only one who's mastered the art of seduction." Lucinda winked.

After a quick breakfast, we headed to the library. As always, I thought of Phoebus.

"Did your source say what kind of tonic?" I whispered as we traipsed down the aisles. There were countless books on potions—some to alter one's appearance, others for medical advancements, history of herbs, skin serums etcetera.

"No. They risked enough just giving me a heads-up." Lucinda took down a book on advanced brewology. "It's safe to say, it won't be something simple. However, I have a vast understanding of potions. All I need is a guide on herbs, roots, and such, and I'll be able to put the recipe together."

"Maybe whilst we look, you can tell us whether you're leaning more towards Team Exekiel or Team Primary." Maximus grinned.

I laughed. He was worse than the viewers.

My stomach twisted as I followed the other contestants out onto the stage. It had been a couple of weeks since I was last here. So much had changed since then.

Like the first time, there were two rows of red-cushioned chairs centerstage for the first twenty-five chosen by the Conduit. I sat on chair number five. The remaining contestants settled in the seats arranged along the outer edge of the stage. Goather waited on a platform in a frilly azure shirt.

Unlike the first time, two podiums stood on either end of the stage. The audience howled with wild applause and Goather raised his microphone to his lips.

"Welcome, initiates. Congratulations on finishing your first Trial of the Trial of Ten. And thank you for being so entertaining whilst doing it."

Again, the people cheered.

"The hot topics on everyone's lips are Camal Silverhound and his ability to sniff out his illusion in less than two minutes—second only to the Shadow Saint."

I recognized the bronze-skinned contestant who'd sat on the table with us at the banquet. He waved as the crowd applauded.

"The viewers also can't get enough of the love triangle blossoming between Exekiel V'alin, the Primary and our foreign temptress—Varialla von Hastings."

My ears rang with the force of applause. I covered my face in my hands and shook my head—the perfect image of a blushing schoolgirl. It was like Exekiel said—give the people what they want.

They held the strings to my survival in the second Trial if I ranked in the bottom ten. It also might convince the Council and anyone else who was watching that I was wholly dedicated to the Games and had no interest in discovering the truth of who I was or what they'd done to my kind—my family. I was innocent. They could leave their Primary with me.

"Tell us, Ms. Hastings, when will you put these boys out of their misery?"

I forced a laugh. "It's funny; everyone sees a romance but all I see are two very different males who are kind to me..." I slid my gaze to Exekiel and frowned. "Sometimes."

The audience fell into fits of laughter. Exekiel's lips quirked.

"Our Shadow Saint isn't exactly known for his charm." Goather hooted.

"You can say that again."

The audience erupted and I giggled. Just like the naïve little girl they wanted me to be.

"Ms. Hastings doesn't want to be charmed," Exekiel's voice cut through the laughter. His heated gaze fixed on mine. "She wants to be taken; held captive—a prisoner of passion and unending love. She wants to be desired, treasured and never abandoned again."

My throat constricted. Silence followed; so complete, I could have heard a feather hit the floor. His words ricocheted through my body and resonated through the entire room. I could practically hear the women's panties melting and some of the males. Was this what he was offering me? When he wasn't threatening my life?

I am infuriatingly yours.

Did he seriously think he was my mate? Could I keep pretending that he wasn't? It was easier to deny how I felt about him. Safer that way. Attachments only gave people the power to hurt you. Considering Exekiel was of the Five Isles and I clearly wasn't, whatever we were, could only end in pain.

Goather blinked. "I daresay that was pretty charming."

The auditorium burst with shouts of agreement. Exekiel held my gaze.

Look away. I willed him, because I didn't have the strength to.

Finally, Goather bellowed, "On that glorious note, let Token Trivia begin. Whoever wins the final round, will be given the elusive Life Token and spared from elimination should they find themselves in the bottom rank in the upcoming Trial."

Contestants were called up to the podiums and pitted against each other. Goather asked a series of questions and whoever answered the most, the fastest, went on to the next round. Once again, Exekiel didn't take part. I couldn't tell if it was arrogance or justified confidence that made him so sure he wouldn't need the token.

Then it was my turn. I sighed. I was up against Vivienne who'd answered almost every question correctly so far. Considering I knew nothing of this world, the life token was as good as gone.

Resigned, I stepped up to the podium. The energy in the auditorium changed. Everyone knew of the animosity between us—our supposed fight over Exekiel; me hexing Vivienne.

"Question one," Goather began. "Powerful ley lines run throughout the Five Isles. Where is the most powerful line?"

Stunned that I knew the answer, I punched the globe-like buzzer on my podium and shouted, "On the outskirts of the Isle of the Eternals between Creature's Copse and Gargoyle's Lagoon."

Goather's brows lifted. "I can't help wondering how you know that."

I shrugged. "I'd planned to use the lines to escape."

The audience laughed. I grinned to myself. The more honest I was now, the less likely they were to notice when I lied.

Vivienne answered the next five questions without taking a breath.

"Finally, for a chance to win the Life Token, how do we deal with traitors?"

I didn't bother reaching for my buzzer.

"We bind their power, give them thirty months of thirty lashings and imprison them in Blacktomb Bay." Vivienne turned her cold gaze on me and smirked. "We make sure they feel the pain of every wrongdoing they ever inflicted. And we make sure they never escape."

My feet wore a groove into the carpet as I paced my chambers with the shell pressed to my ear. The message replayed:

"Tomorrow, your dinner will be served in your rooms. Be there."

The dinner bell rang a while ago but I was still waiting; chewing on my bottom lip. Trying to figure out what the message meant, and who had sent it.

A knock sounded on the door. I took a second to brace myself before I pulled it open. A centaur stood in the doorway—the same one from the banquet.

He bowed his head. "Ms. Hastings."

In his hand, he carried a covered silver platter. On his cloaked back, a basket of bread.

After a moment's pause, he said, "Shall I set this up in your room?"

"Yes." Giving myself a mental shake, I stepped aside to let him pass.

He unceremoniously dumped the tray and basket onto my dresser. When the door clicked shut, he removed the cloak draped over his hindquarters to reveal someone harnessed beneath his stomach. The figure dropped to the floor, rolled out from under the centaur and bounded to his feet.

I stumbled back.

Shaking his head, the male breathed, "Congratulations, Danimous. It's true what they say about a horse's—"

The centaur, Danimous, smacked him across the head.

The man chuckled. He appeared to be in his mid to late-thirties. He had warm golden-brown skin, full lips and piercing blue eyes, like chips of ice bobbing on the ocean. Though there was no water around, droplets clung to his long black corkscrew curls and rolled down his cheeks. His fingers were webbed and there were the faint lines of gills on his neck. He seemed, somehow, familiar.

When he finally turned to face me, he grinned. "There she is."

19

WEREWOLVES & WOES

It was official. The Five Isles was a realm of impossible power, and panty-soaking men. I studied the shirtless newcomer as he circled me like a vulture assessing his prey. He couldn't have been more perfect than if he was carved by Michelangelo; his jaw square and shirtless abs, stacked. Cut-off black shorts hung low at his hips. He seemed to carry a permanent scent of the sea and I couldn't stop staring at his webbed fingers and the gills on his neck. What the heck was he? The Five Isles version of Aquaman?

"Fuck, you're as gorgeous as your mother."

He moved with lightning speed and was suddenly in front of me, my face cradled in his hands. His voice was familiar—the voice from the shell. His face, I now realized was the same I'd seen during the extraction. A man I thought could have been my father.

"Fucking beautiful."

His mouth descended on mine. I stiffened. Definitely not my dad then. Though by the way he was kissing me, I could see myself calling him "daddy".

My skin flushed and my fingers curled in his shirt. A part of me relished the feel of his mouth on mine but my mind screamed. This was mental. I didn't know this man. He'd just snuck into my room and shoved his tongue in my mouth. He groaned, pressing closer. I lurched back and slammed my knee into his groin.

Aqua-freak's eyes crossed and he stumbled back; his hands cupped around himself.

"You're just as violent as her, as well," he panted.

"Who are you?"

"Loch Orqanz—Guardian of the Siren Sea. Leader of the revolution." He adjusted himself and moved towards me, looking like he wanted to pick up where we left off. "Mate-sworn to the heir of the Coral Court."

"Get to the point."

He tsked and scooped my hands up in his. "So impatient."

I tried to twist free, but he used my momentum against me, and spun me around until my back was crushed to his chest; my arms strapped across my stomach.

"I was looking forward to taking my time with you."

I blanched when he licked the lobe of my ear. *What the hell?*

I was about to throw my head back and shatter every bone in his perfect nose when screams rang from the corridor.

"Right on time."

"What?" I hissed; still struggling in his grip.

"Someone would've noticed you weren't at dinner. We had to create a diversion."

With no other way to escape, I flung my head back. Loch skipped aside to avoid the crushing blow and I rushed towards the door. He blocked my path.

"Leave them to their fate. Only those who are too stupid to run are in any real danger."

"That's all of them!"

He snickered. I glared. I'd meant that the players would never run. They were warriors; their people's champion and they wouldn't go down without a fight. Not Exekiel. Not Lucinda. None.

I tried to duck around him but he grabbed my arm and pulled me back.

"Get off me."

I didn't know what I'd do if I ran out there, but the sounds coming from beyond the door were horrifying. Nothing could be worse than what I was imagining and anything was better than hiding from an attack that had started because of me.

I didn't trust the Five Isler's but I didn't trust Loch either. He was shrouded in an air of murder and madness. For all I knew, he was butchering my allies.

"You owe these people nothing," he snarled. "They are the enemy. They seek to mount your head on a stick and make ornaments of your scales."

I frowned. Nothing he said was making sense.

The screams grew louder and the thud of racing feet pounded passed the door.

"Sounds like some are running."

Again, I tugged against him but his hold was firm.

"Who will you trust?" he snapped. "Those who tell you nothing? Who want you blinded by the dark? Those who hold your mother captive? Or will you trust me—the voice of your people?"

I froze. Was that who Lola and the others had thought I was trying to save the night I'd tried to escape—my *mother*?

Loch pressed, "Our Kingdom is in danger. Our people are impoverished and set to starve. The only way we can save them, is with you."

He released me, as if he knew I wouldn't run. That my curiosity would keep me in place despite the cries that raged from the hall.

"In order to protect our people and, one day, rescue your mother, you must win the Games and claim the Eternal Throne." His words were rushed now. Apparently, we were running out of time.

"Then you will rule outright and none can defy you. You can order the execution of the Royal Court and let your people dismember any fools who try to stop you." He sneered, coldly. "You can save yourself and change the world."

There was a wild fervor in his eyes. A thirst for revenge, I recognized. Hurt that had twisted into something cruel. Alarm bells rang in my mind but Loch claimed to know where I came from. Had known my mother. He had the answers I desperately wanted. And perhaps a way for me to survive in a world where everyone wanted me dead.

Beyond the walls, glass shattered and something roared. Goosebumps rippled my flesh. I was a skilled fighter. I'd spent most of my life fending off assholes—thieves, crooks, people who desired revenge, others who desired my body. But fighting magic or beasts was foreign to me. I glanced again at Loch's webbed fingers; the unnatural hue of his crystal blue eyes.

Something slammed into the door. Our heads whipped in its direction.

Gripping my waist, Loch pulled me close and whispered, "My sexy siren savage, it's time for you to take back control of your life."

Another bang. Someone was trying to get in.

"Look for my messages." He brushed the symbol on my hip. I shivered, hating the delicious tingle of his touch. "I'll communicate as often as I can."

"Through my mark."

He dipped his head.

"You're the one who changed it into a centaur."

Another fierce bang. The door rattled on its hinges.

"Ms. Hastings, are you in there?"

Loch winked. "I should leave."

He stepped back, dug into the leather pouch on his weapons belt and drew out an obsidian glass dagger—its blade curved. The hilt was gold and embossed with scales. The end forked like a mermaid's tail. "You'll need this." He held it out to me. "It's the only weapon powerful enough to pierce a Bravinore Fae's heart."

"What?"

Another bang. The entire room shook.

"In order for our plan to work, we must rid ourselves of the one bastard powerful enough to stop us—Exekiel V'alin."

My blood ran cold.

Outside the door, someone shouted, "Varialla!"

Loch bared his teeth; each one sharp as a piranha's. "Speak of the devil."

A green trident glowed on the door. The wood cracked then flew off its hinges, splintering into the room. In the same instant, Loch dove behind Danimous. The centaur turned to gather the trays, cloaking Loch from sight, and I concealed the obsidian blade beneath the sleeve of my gown.

Exekiel charged in—two elves at his back; his wings splayed and dark eyes burning red.

He scanned the room and when he found me standing there, relief flickered in his eyes, before it turned to rage.

"Have you lost your hearing, Ms. Hastings? Why didn't you answer the door?"

"I advised her to remain hidden until it was safe," Danimous replied easily, as if he'd rehearsed it, which he probably had. "What's going on out there?"

"Werewolves."

"*Werewolves?*"

Exekiel's cold stare slid to me. Knowing that looking away would only make me appear guilty, I held his gaze. My body flushed beneath its intensity. *Sheesh*— whatever attraction I'd felt for Loch, had nothing on this. This burning thing inside me that longed to be wrapped in the Shadow Saints arms. That ached for his touch and pulled me towards him.

It was hard to stay still. I was so tempted to rush forwards. To feel his lips on mine and erase the stroke of Loch's.

"You were at the gala." Exekiel was speaking to Danimous but his stare never left mine.

The centaur seemed surprised but I wasn't. If anyone was going to remember the face of a seemingly insignificant server in a crowded room, it was Exekiel.

"Danimous Evalon." He bowed his head. "Third of his name and servant to the Eternal Court."

"And yet, you're here."

A muscle ticked in Exekiel's jaw as his stare raked over me; ignited an ache inside me.

"Primary Adir is fond of Ms. Hastings and asked me to deliver this meal, along with his invitation for her to join him in his chambers at week's end."

I masked my surprise. Was that true?

"Ms. Hastings regrettably declines."

"That isn't up to you," I scoffed.

Exekiel's brow arched and he prowled towards me. "Haven't we been over this?"

My skin heated as I recalled what he'd said the night of the banquet.

The only one who'll be fucking you, is me.

"Decline."

I gritted my teeth. I wasn't a dog to be ordered, and I sure as shit wasn't taking orders from him. Besides, I needed this meeting with Adir. Needed to wear down his defenses and get answers to the medley of questions that plagued my every step. Who was I? Why was there a divide between the Isles? Why was my mother their prisoner?

The Primary could offer an alternate perspective to the strange aquarian-male who was currently strapped to a centaur's underbelly.

I turned to Danimous. "I accept."

"Then so do I."

My attention snapped to Exekiel. "What?"

"It is my job to protect this realm, Varialla and you are its greatest threat. I cannot stop whatever flirtation you think you've formed with the Primary." His teeth flashed. "But if you go to this dinner, then so will I."

I glared at him. He glared right back, a glint of triumph in his vermillion eyes.

Finally, I snarled, "I decline."

Danimous didn't waste any time. He dipped his head and trotted from the room.

"Was that so hard?" Exekiel's voice was low and irritatingly seductive. His scent intoxicating the closer he came.

My stomach tightened. What was wrong with me? Exekiel was the enemy. He knew they had my mother imprisoned. As Protector of the Realm, he'd probably chained her himself. He wanted to keep me ignorant; caged. Wanted me to fail.

Still, when he grasped my arm and pulled me close, I didn't want to pull away.

"Why was the centaur here?"

I swallowed. The urge to say and do anything to please him, crashed into me. Exekiel's grip tightened and I tensed. Any higher and his fingers would brush the weapon Loch had given me.

I backed away but he followed.

"Well?"

"What?"

"Why was he here?"

I jerked free, yelping when I fell backwards onto the bed.

"He just told you why," I snapped.

Exekiel stood over me, hunger and hatred in his eyes. "Wrong answer."

20

BETTER THAN I IMAGINED

Before I could move, Exekiel knelt over me. One knee pressed between my legs. Hot sparks shot through my system. I blinked, momentarily blinded by lust. If he realized, he didn't show it.

His hand wrapped around my neck and he drew me to him. "Why was Danimous here?"

I clenched my teeth; tormented by his touch—caught between desire and disgust.

"To invite me to dinner," I snarled, wishing he'd move back.

His closeness disarmed me and created a visceral need to please him; to utter all my secrets and share my darkest desires.

"Don't lie to me."

His knee stroked between my legs. My fingers curled into the soft sheets.

"Why was he here?"

I opened my mouth to confess, then promptly closed it. What was going on? Why did I feel so compelled by him? Not like when Vivienne had used compulsion on me, but deeper; more demanding. Was this the mate bond? This desire to give him everything? It was a want that went soul deep—the same want I felt for his body; his kiss.

I scrambled back to get away from him. Exekiel followed and leaned over me, his eyes bright.

"Varialla."

I trembled. I loved when he said my name. It was rare and beautiful—like an eclipse at midday.

"If the Primary wanted to send you an invitation, why wouldn't he go through the proper channels?"

"You'd have to ask him."

I pushed up; trying to throw him off balance, but Exekiel bore down on me. I slipped from my elbows onto my back. *Shit.*

"You're either with us or against us, little bud. Which one is it?"

"I'm with me." Just like I always was.

Exekiel's grip tightened around my neck. Not enough to cut off my air, but enough to make my heart race and my body thrum. *Gah!* I was enjoying this way too much. By the glint in his eyes, he was enjoying it too.

"The only reason I'm alive right now is because the Council are afraid that if I'm killed, it'll somehow start a war, and because you intend to use me to find out what my people have planned." I spat, clinging to my anger and mistrust. "But I won't let you use me."

He sneered and brought his lips close to mine. "The only way I plan on using you, is when you're naked. Bent on all fours or splayed out on your back."

He leaned closer, slipping both his legs between mine. My stomach knotted and I pressed my lips together to stifle a moan.

"And you wouldn't just let me. You'd beg me."

Arousal shot through my system. My laugh, breathless. "You'd like that, wouldn't you, asshole?"

He groaned and moved his hips. *Oh shit.* "You have no idea."

We came together, moving slow at first then more forceful; desperate. Exekiel hooked his arm beneath my waist and dragged me further onto the bed. The obsidian dagger in my sleeve slipped but I didn't care. He moved into me and my hips bowed beneath his. He felt incredible.

I didn't know how we'd gone from threatening each other to this, but there was no going back.

"Shit," I panted. This wasn't supposed to happen. Exekiel was a bastard; my enemy...my *mate*?

"Something wrong?" His hand tracked the slopes of my breast.

I hissed, my mind and body at war. "Aside from the fact that I hate you?"

Exekiel wrenched down the top of my dress and my breast toppled free. He grasped it fully in his large hand. His grin predatory.

"No, you don't."

My eyes slammed shut as Exekiel sucked my nipple into his mouth. His tongue hot and teasing.

I panted and drew him closer; my fingers tangled in his hair.

Distantly, I heard footsteps thudding from the room. I'd forgotten all about the elves Exekiel had come with and apparently, he had as well. I could only imagine the rumors that would follow. The foreign temptress with the Protector of the Realm in her bed.

My knees were bent and my off-the-shoulder lilac dress was bunched around my thighs with Exekiel moving between them. One hand coiled around my neck. The other on my waist.

"What about the werewolves?"

Again, I felt desperate to tell him everything. The pressure of his body unraveled me, *weakened* me…and he knew it.

Clarity shot through me. He was using our bond against me. That's what the redhead of the Council had said—that he could use our connection to his advantage. This must have been what she'd meant. Clever little asshole.

I grunted. "What about them?"

Exekiel kissed my breast. "How did they break through the barrier?"

His tongue curled around my nipple. Desire pulsed deep in my core.

"How should I know?" I breathed.

Shit. He was only doing this to wear me down and it was working.

"Don't you?"

His mouth traveled upwards; over my collarbone, along my neck and up to my jaw. I shuddered.

"Why don't you use your little gift and compel me to tell you?"

"That would violate our bond," he murmured against my lips.

Gosh, I wanted to kiss him.

"What bond?" I whispered, my eyelids fluttering.

"The bond you so desperately want to deny."

Exekiel's lips crashed into mine. The contact was electric. Like riding the waves of lightning. His tongue, his touch raged a storm inside me. All I could do was try not to get swept away.

"Open your legs."

Despite myself, I eagerly obeyed. Exekiel's fingers found their home. Within seconds, he slid his hand inside my silk panties and stroked my warm, wet center.

I knew I should stop this but I couldn't. Not when I wanted it just as badly.

"You feel better than I imagined," he growled, then pushed a finger inside me. My back arched and I moved with him as he soaked his finger on my sex and inserted another.

I hissed through clenched teeth. My body alight with desire.

"When one uses their magic to coerce their mate on things that truly matter, it drains them; blackens the bond and tarnishes the soul," he explained as his fingers flicked and pumped inside me.

His thumb pressed down on my clit and I cried out. It took me a while to remember what we'd been talking about.

"Secrets must be shared willingly, body's given freely. Nothing between mates is forced. It never has to be." He grinned. "You are going to tell me everything."

I shook; overwhelmed by the beat of his fingers.

It was ridiculous and dangerous. There was so much I didn't know about Exekiel, about this whole twisted situation. I'd just been given a dagger to kill him for flips sake—not that I was going to. But then…maybe I should stop to think why they thought I would—*should*.

Exekiel grinded into me, forcing his fingers deeper. My head tipped back as pleasure speared through my core.

Shaking, I grasped his shoulders and tried to stay focused as he brought me so close to the brink.

"In that case," I rasped. "Tell me about my mother."

His gaze darkened as he realized his mistake. By pointing out my weakness to him, he'd inadvertently confessed his own weakness to me. Whatever I wanted, he would eventually give.

Exekiel chuckled darkly. "Nice try."

I half-laughed then moaned when he worked me harder.

My hand pushed between our bodies and I palmed his cock. I'd never wanted anything more. For a second, I forgot that this was a battle for information. All I felt was him, hard and thick in my hand.

Exekiel groaned as I stroked him through the fabric of his trousers. Up, down. Up, down.

"Fuck," he breathed.

My head spun. The way his hips moved was a heart-stopping preview of how he'd move inside me—if we ever went that far, which of course, we wouldn't.

His fingers took on an intoxicating rhythm as I tugged on his rigid length; barely able to catch my breath.

"Why is it like this with you?" I panted.

Exekiel ran his burning lips along my jaw. "It will only ever be like this with me."

He fingered me faster; harder. My hips rolled; my lips parted. Chest heaving.

"That's it, little bud," he praised. "Fuck my hand."

I did. Tight on the thrust of his fingers, I rocked into his motions; my hand fisted around his shaft, rubbing him.

Our eyes locked. Without words, our lips met—a demand of the soul. Undeniable and profound. I had never been kissed like this before.

It was all-consuming and irresistible. My body sang. My legs shook. Then I erupted. My soul shattered across the stars.

Exekiel continued to move into the pump of my hand. I stroked him with relish; wanting him to chase my high.

A voice purred, "Well, well."

We broke apart and I glared at Vladimir who stood in the doorway. Orbs were at the elf's back, recording everything. His hand was pressed inside his robes as he openly touched himself.

Sicko.

How long had he and the cameras been there? Exekiel slid off the bed and Vladimir waggled his brows as he caught a glimpse of the wet between my thighs.

"Talk about putting on a show."

21

SECRETS AND STITCHES

After adjusting his trousers, Exekiel left to deal with the aftermath of the werewolf attack, leaving me to deal with the aftermath of him. Of his hands on me in places I never thought they'd be.

Reeling from the violent orgasm he inspired just from his fingers, I pressed my legs together and exhaled. Of all the things that had happened tonight—aquarian males, obsidian-glass daggers, and werewolves—Exekiel's burning touch was the one that made my head spin.

Desperate to get away from the cameras that bobbed in my busted doorway, I strode into my bath chamber. What I really needed was an ice-cold shower, but I gladly settled for the bathing pool that bubbled like a hot spring. I stripped down—tucking the glass-dagger beneath my discarded dress—and dove in.

The second the water hit my arm, it burned. I bolted to the surface. Blood spilled from a gash on my bicep. I must have cut myself on the blade whilst Exekiel and I were…

I drew in a breath and redirected my thoughts. What mattered was the wound. How hadn't I felt it at the time? Then again, I'd felt nothing but Exekiel. Been aware of nothing but Exekiel.

"Word of advice; if you're going to get freaky with the most desirable male in *De Cinque Istrovos*, do it behind closed doors."

I swiveled at the sound of Lucinda's voice.

"Almost every female out there wants your head."

I snickered. "What else is new?"

Lucinda chuckled but her laughter halted when she noticed the seeping gash.

"What happened?"

"Nothing."

"Nothing?"

"Nothing I can't handle." I shrugged then winced as pain shot down my arm.

Lucinda arched a brow. "Is this you handling it?"

"It looks worse than it—"

"Spare me the lone-wolf, bullshit," she drawled. "Everyone needs someone sometimes and you need me to take care of that before it gets infected."

My mouth twisted. Lucinda was right. The wound hadn't stopped bleeding which wasn't a good sign. Plus, the blood made it difficult for me to see just how bad it was, and the gash had been carved by an enchanted blade. Still, I wasn't used to asking for or accepting help.

Lucinda shook her head. "Come on." She left the room then returned with a toweled bathrobe. "You can sleep in my room tonight. Handy-Hooves will have your door fixed by tomorrow."

Inwardly grateful, I wriggled into the robe and followed the witch into the corridor. Windows had been shattered, statues toppled and blood smeared across the tiles. My stomach turned.

"Werewolves did this?"

"Can you blame them?"

I frowned. "What does that mean?"

As a full-blooded witch of the Five Isles, I expected her to be furious at the outlanders that did this.

Lucinda searched the corridor before whispering, "You must've noticed how outliers are treated here—or rather *mis*treated."

She pushed open the door to her rooms. They were identical to mine, only her color scheme was purple and silver.

"It's barbaric," she added once the door clicked shut. "All of them are being punished for what one outlander race did."

She gestured for me to sit at the dresser and retrieved a small wooden chest of salves.

"What did they do?"

"Started a war." Lucinda took out some cotton wool and began to clean the gash. "There was a time when the Isle of the Eternals stood alone. A place where everyone went to worship at the Conduit and collect fragments of the magic it offered to sustain their land. But, one night, four of the Isles miraculously converged around the Eternal Isle and became known as the Blessed."

I nodded. The Fate's Chosen.

"Naturally, jealousy reared its head and led to countless battles but nothing too severe. Not until a certain race insisted, they had a claim in the Five-Isles and refused to yield their blessing."

I flinched when Lucinda applied a salve. "Did they have a claim?"

She shrugged. "They had particular traits that could be argued to belong to one of the Chosen."

The shifters. I guessed. Loch had called me a siren. Those who lived in water with tails but could shift into human form and therefore could argue to belong to the shifters.

"That was the end of everything. A war like no other raged. It only ended when the leader was eventually captured and the outlands were cut off. Now they're only welcome in the Isles upon invitation—their right to worship at the Conduit stripped." Her lips pinched. "They're no longer seen as worthy. No longer receive parcels of magic to sustain their lands and have to pay extortionate tolls to benefit from basic resources. Although…" she smirked. "Some of us manage to smuggle small magic specs out."

My brows lifted. "You?"

"When I can." Lucinda squinted as she stitched the wound. "One race shouldn't ruin it for the rest."

"How come the outliers don't revolt?"

"Can't. A powerful barrier keeps them out. Crafted by the Protector, himself."

Exekiel. The male whose mouth I'd had branded on mine not long ago. I clenched my fists. A fresh wave of blood spilled from the gash.

Lucinda tutted. "What the hell did this?"

I hesitated. I didn't know if I could trust the witch but Lucinda had revealed a secret to me and I needed to trust someone. I couldn't get through this alone.

"An obsidian-glass dagger."

The witch's eyes widened. "Where did you get a weapon like that?"

The day began with nymphs. After tracking me down in Lucinda's room, Eudora and the others outfitted me in a pair of baggy khaki-green trousers with a wrap-around sash that made them look like a skirt, and a green crop top that tied around my midriff and neck. My golden bangles were heavy and my earrings long. Hair pulled up in an afro puff.

Cyrus and I shared a look when the redhead purred, "I polished your shell."

But before I could unpack that sentence, a bell rang and Second Trial began.

Now at the border of Creature's Copse with the other contestants—most who shot me murderous glares—I waited.

Orbs circled overhead as Goather paraded out before us, microphone in hand.

"Today, you'll brew a potion."

Lucinda grinned—it was just as her informant had said.

"One to change your eye color."

"Wickleberry root, Mirror wheat, powdered slug," Lucinda hissed, reminding me of the ingredients.

She'd spent the last few days grilling Max and I on various serums. Now I just had to remember which one did what.

"A longworm and a crushed gilstone," I finished.

"You catch on fast."

"I had a good teacher."

She smiled at me. It was the most genuine one since we'd met and I couldn't help returning it. Something had shifted in our friendship last night.

I'd showed Lucinda the glass dagger and told her how I'd gotten it. She told me about how being the most powerful in her coven had led to her being bullied or challenged when she was younger, when all she'd wanted was friendship. It was why she'd eventually found comfort with the outlanders.

One day, she'd discovered a crack in the barrier and used her power to widen it. Not much but enough to talk to a stranger—a female giant who'd been out for a stroll.

My mind boggled at this. Werewolves, giants, centaurs and sirens—what else lived beyond the barrier? What else had been forced into exile and poverty?

"In these woods," Goather continued, drawing back my attention, "are the ingredients you seek. However, there isn't enough for you all."

The air thrummed with tension.

"This is, of course, a race. By the end, three of you will not have the ingredients you need to pass the Second Trial and will automatically be entered into the Blood Battles."

The orbs panned closer, taking measure of everyone's reaction.

"You have one hour. Go with the brave." Goather raised a hand and contestants began to shove one another to get to the front. "Go with the blessed."

A white haze fell over the crowd. Everyone leapt back and I yelped as I was shrouded in the mist. The world spun; my feet swept from under me, until I finally landed hard in a dirt pile in the middle of the woods.

Disoriented, I studied the endless trees for some idea of where I was. I could hear other contestants landing nearby but none were close enough to see.

My stomach twisted. I'd hoped to do this Trial with Max and Lucinda. Or, at least, have a bit longer to pick their brains. But I was completely alone.

Somewhere Goather boomed, "Let the Trial begin."

I bounded to my feet and began to search for the ingredients. Some were found in nature but others, like gilstone, would have had to be planted by the crew and there was only a limited amount. I searched for it first.

From the books in the library, I knew it was a pearlescent cylinder of rock that sometimes rang like a bell.

I hurried through the woods, making out the sounds of other contestants as they did the same. Some whooped when they found what they were looking for. I cursed. Every path looked the same. Every tree a stretch of bark and low-hanging leaves.

Camera-orbs followed at my back and somewhere the hands of a clock ticked. The sound deafening. Ticking with the pound of my heart.

"Fifty minutes," Goather's voice echoed through the forest.

I wiped sweat from my brow and continued on. There was the faint tinkle of wind chimes in the breeze. My heart leapt and I pivoted, following the sound.

It was coming from overhead. My gaze shot upwards, searching the tree branches. At last, I spied a chunk of a cylindrical stone hanging from a chain.

But how the heck did I reach it?

Wiping my hands on my khaki trousers, I pounced on the tree. My feet swung, searching for purchase. My toes, at last, hooking in a small nook of the trunk.

Stretching up, I reached for the branch above my head. My fingers caught and I heaved myself up. Going as fast as I could without slipping to my death.

"There!" someone shouted.

My head snapped in the direction of the voice.

Vector, a lean elf with long dark hair and wide blue eyes hurtled towards me. No, not me—the gilstone.

Shit.

I sped up. My teeth gritted. I'd climbed out of windows and scaled down trees many times during my escapes from social services, but none as large as this. And climbing up a tree was proving harder than down. But I didn't stop.

"Give up!" Vector shouted. He was almost at the base of the tree now.

"Forty Minutes!" Goather boomed.

Crap!

Higher and higher I climbed. The bark bit into my palms as I clung to the branches. Scents of pine and earth filled my nose.

Vector reached the base of the tree and wasted no time coming after me.

Fear spiked in my chest. I was skilled but he was better. His body moved with the agility of a dancer. There was no way he could reach the gilstone with me ahead of him but I wouldn't put it passed the bastard to push me out of the tree.

I climbed faster. My lungs burned and fingers groaned. The height was dizzying. Smaller trees shrinking below. My legs began to shake but I pushed on. Failure wasn't an option.

Failure meant death—not just for me but for the entire Outer Isles. Though Loch and Lucinda were on opposite sides, they both claimed that those in exile were wasting away. My family among them. And Loch seemed to think, I could save them. I just had to survive long enough to find out how.

My foot slipped and I screamed as I almost vaulted from the tree.

Vector's laugh was cruel and rasping as he leapt gracefully from branch to branch. He was gaining on me, fast.

The gilstone was close now but I'd need to let go of the tree trunk and leap for a branch no thicker than my arm. The stone swung from the end of it.

Looking down was a mistake. My stomach pitched. I yanked my gaze back up and drew in a ragged breath.

Vector was almost upon me. There was no time to hesitate.

Closing my eyes, I gathered my courage and jumped. For a moment, I was suspended in the air, soaring above the ground, then my hands latched onto the branch and the branch snapped.

22

THIRD TRIAL TWIST

D own I went. The gilstone toppled beside me. Frantic, I reached out and caught its chain between two fingers.

Vector swiped after me as I tumbled through the leaves. I slammed into a branch and pain exploded through my side. The air rushed from my lungs.

Arms pinwheeling, I tried to grab onto something to slow my descent. Snatching at branches before my fingers slipped and I was, once again, falling.

I landed with an oomph in a mound of leaves. A sharp pain shot through my ankle and I yelped. Gingerly, I rolled it; hissing through my teeth. It was already starting to swell.

Groaning, I used a tree stump to hobble to my feet. Dragging the gilstone chain with me, I tucked it into my satchel. One ingredient down. Four to go.

"Thirty minutes," Goather called.

Damn. If the other ingredients were as hard to get as this, I wouldn't make it. I'd be forced into a Blood Battle I wasn't prepared for. Heck, I was unprepared for this entire realm.

Bracing myself, I pushed off the tree and limped off in search of another ingredient.

A glimmer of silver caught my eye. I swiveled and pounced on a longworm as the silvery-slimed creature attempted to burrow underground.

Dirt sprayed around me. I clawed after the insect but it slipped through my fingers only to be plucked up by another.

'Hey!' I snapped.

"Hi."

My breath caught and I gaped up at Exekiel. Of course, he looked effortlessly gorgeous in black cargo pants and a fitted blue T-shirt that outlined his abs. Where I was sprawled out and caked in mud.

He grinned from where he squatted over me. His deep pink eyes gleaming. Memories of last night took hold.

Swallowing, I pushed up to my knees. "That worm is mine."

His brow lifted. "Is it?"

I swiped for the insect but Exekiel dodged and dropped it into his satchel.

I snarled in frustration, "You're such a pain in the ass!"

"Care to test that theory?" His voice dipped low, curling in the pit of my stomach. "I suspect I'd only hurt going in. After that, I think you'd enjoy it."

Holy shit!

Faster than I could blink, Exekiel was on his knees behind me; his hands on my hips.

"Don't you?"

I forgot how to speak. His wings cloaked me as he pushed on my back, forcing me to bend forwards. I braced my hands on the soft earth. My heart ratcheted in my chest. But I didn't argue.

"If only Vlad hadn't interrupted us last night. We might have found out."

Exekiel subtly moved his hips. My entire body tingled. I should have been shoving him off. I had less than thirty minutes to get the ingredients for this potion, and this thing between me and him had already gone too far. But I couldn't pull away. I was addicted to the feel of him.

He leaned in, bringing his lips close to my ear. "Maybe later, we can find out how much of a pain in your ass, I can be."

My toes curled. "You're sick."

Exekiel chuckled. "You have no idea."

His lips brushed the back of my neck, then he spread his wings and was gone.

I almost collapsed. My mind so clouded by lust, I couldn't see straight.

Focus.

Another longworm skittered passed. I lunged on it and wrestled the insect into my sack.

Leaning on my undamaged ankle, I stood and continued on through the forest.

"Twenty minutes," Goather called.

Desperate, I searched for any clue of where to go next.

Someone whooped and I followed their whispers of excitement. Finally, I spotted the patch of Mirror wheat they must have found. I scooped up a handful of the red wheat that briefly reflected my face and shoved it into my bag. Now all I needed was powdered slug and wickleberry root.

"Ten minutes."

I trekked on, my hope fading. The woods seemed endless and I had no idea where to go. The sweet taste of magic filled my mouth but I didn't see how compulsion could help me with this.

"Vee!"

Turning, I spotted Maximus jogging by; his dreadlocks bouncing.

"Catch," he called.

I held up my hand and caught a rough knotted root. *Wickleberry!*

"Have you found longworms?"

"Over there," I pointed and he blew me a kiss as he raced past.

The clock overhead chimed and Goather's voice called, "Five minutes."

My stomach pitched.

The woods were emptying as more of the contestants gathered what they needed and left. They each had an ability to track—whether through spells or smells. But what did sirens do?

They sang…

What's your favorite song? Suddenly, the question Goather asked me all those weeks ago didn't seem so random. Finally, I was in on the joke.

Panicked, I drew on my magic. A sweet taste hit the back of my throat and a haunting melody spilled from my lips. It struck something in the distance then tugged me towards it.

Camera-orbs soared overhead and I hummed quieter. No one knew I'd figured out what I was, and I wanted to keep it that way.

I arrived at a clearing where a vial of golden slug-dust hung from a low branch. I raced towards it. A mammoth wing knocked me back.

Blinking, I saw Vivienne. She didn't reach for the vial which suggested she didn't need it. She was only there to stop me.

"Tell your werewolves, we say hi," she snarled then flung out her wings and sent the last vial spinning into the tree trunk. The glass shattered. Powdered slug puffed into the air then scattered across the ground.

"Five seconds."

I lunged. Slug be damned. I would gladly enter the Blood Battles as long as I could rip Vivienne to pieces first.

We went down. My fist inches from the bitch's face when we were spirited away. Time was up.

We materialized centerstage in the Gamers Dome. The audience howled around us.

"Captivating entrance, ladies," Goather boomed over his microphone.

I blinked in the garish light. I was still straddled across Vivienne—the scruff of her blouse in my hand.

"Nevertheless, your fight will have to wait." Goather gestured for us to take our place at one of the many podiums that had been set up onstage.

Vivienne sneered. Reluctantly, I released her and stalked to an empty stand, but not before I pocketed the vial of slug powder that she'd dropped during our skirmish.

"I'm sure you've all noticed the *Guagulon* paste, by now." Goather called.

I studied the small pot of glittery, blue gel that rested on the podium beside various apparatus.

"And I'm sure you all know what it does."

The audience and contestants cheered. I frowned.

"You see, this Trial is not about simply altering your eye color. It's about altering what your eyes see. By combining the ingredients, you have collected and adding just a smear of *Guagulon*, you will be transported to another place." Goather paced before us, his hooves clopping. "However, unlike the illusion, everything that happens in this place, will be entirely real."

He paused as the camera-orbs panned the auditorium and the audience roared with bloodlust.

"That's right. It's time for the—"

The audience bellowed, "Third Trial Twist!"

Third? What the heck was going on? I tried to catch Lucinda's eye but the witch was caught in the high. Her eyes bright and her grin sharp.

"Welcome to the next level." Goather's voice echoed across the auditorium. "It is time to truly get to know yourselves and exactly what kind of ruler you would be."

The audience howled.

"The potion you're about to make will reveal your inner desires. It will rip out your heart and show it to you. It will erase all logic and pull out pure primal instinct." His grin was feral. "This Trial could narrow down the identity of your mate and will awaken the inner warrior you will need to survive the Games."

I swallowed. My thoughts racing. His explanation only left me with more questions.

"Prepare your potions, Initiates. Your time starts…now."

I got to work; adding what I remembered of the potion to a twisted vial. The ingredients popped and burbled—the color shifting.

Vivienne shrieked, "That bitch stole my slug."

I snickered as I added that very ingredient to my brew.

Some of the audience laughed. Others applauded.

Goather turned to the seething brunette. "What happens to you, is what you allow, Ms. Foraglade. If you're the sort of leader who can be so easily deceived then perhaps, you're not the leader we need."

Vivienne's pale cheeks colored. If looks could kill, hers would have flayed the flesh from Goather's bones.

"I'm afraid you must forfeit," he gestured to those who hadn't been able to gather all the ingredients. They sat to one side, knowing they were destined for the Blood Battle. "Unless you have allies, willing to help you. A true leader commands true allegiance after all." He shrugged and trotted away.

I didn't watch what Vivienne did next. The clock was ticking and I had to see this through to the end. I couldn't keep pretending that I didn't care about where I came from. Or claim that my mother was a bitch who'd abandoned me for dead. The truth was impossible but painfully clear. She'd done it to protect me from the very people I was now surrounded by and I had to find out why. What happened to her? To my family. It was only a matter of time before they did the same to me.

All around me, contestants shrieked as their potions exploded—their measurements off. Others yelped as it melted through the vial and cleaved through the podium. One by one, their rank fell.

Finally, Goather yelled, "Vials up!"

I lifted my potion along with the other players, hoping I got it right.

"A word of advice, going forward, initiates: Kill or be killed!" Goather kissed his fist. "May you go with the brave and the blessed."

I swallowed my nerves and brought the vial to my lips.

"To the brave and the blessed," I whispered.

Then I drank.

23

A QUEEN DOESN'T YIELD

Spirited from the auditorium, I emerged in the Eternal City arena. The stands were packed. The noise deafening. Midday sun; bright and punishing.

"Well done, Initiates," Goather bellowed from where he strutted across the sand. "You have survived phase one of the Third Trial Twist."

Around him, other contestants were gathered in small groups—most female.

I searched those beside me. Three girls I barely recognized, Maura, a bear shifter, and Vivienne. Apparently, the Fae-bitch had had allies to help with her potion after all.

Every player was dressed in some type of battle armor. I wore a brass crop top, chainmail skirt and leather sandals that tied around my calf. The straps thankfully added extra support for my aching ankle.

Spiked cuffs were fitted on my wrists and my hair was braided into a crown with a few tendrils left free.

"It's time to awaken your inner beast," Goather bellowed.

The audience cheered. A line of grey stone columns materialized on the other side of the arena. Chained to each one was a shirtless male contestant, and a couple of females. My blood ran cold. Countless camera-orbs zoomed closer.

"Over the last few weeks, you've each been trying to identify your mate. Now, you've been grouped based on who you think it is." Goather turned to a girl and guy dressed in silver armor. "You both believe Michael is your mate." He gestured to another group. "You think yours is André." On he went, until, finally, he turned to my group. "You think Exekiel is yours."

I stiffened, wanting to argue. Exekiel couldn't be my mate. He was the bastard who'd kidnapped me, built a barrier to block out the innocent and who was most likely responsible for my mother's captivity. But the Game didn't care about any of that. The potion had pulled out my truest desire and that was Exekiel, whether I liked it or not.

"Today, you will prove how far you're willing to go for those you love—for your people; your Kingdom."

Hulking men stalked across the arena. Each stopped beside a stone column. The fine hairs on the back of my neck stood on end. Something was wrong.

A band of goblins on the edge of the grounds, beat on their drums.

Goather bellowed,

> *Be the first to reach your mate.*
> *Save them from this cruel fate.*

Seal it with a kiss that's true.
Show the realm, they belong to you."

The hulking men revealed whips in their beefy hands. My gut tightened. Was this the cruel fate? Torture, unless they were saved by true-love's kiss? I swallowed bile that rose in my throat. It was like a fairytale for the Dark Ages. This couldn't be real. But Goather had warned us that it was. Only the stage had changed.

"In this Trial, you have two options, Initiates: Fight to the death or yield."

The brawny men raised their whips. Gasps rang through the arena—the air taut. I gaped from Exekiel who stood tall with his brow rested on the column, to the enrapt audience.

Goather's grin twisted. "However, a true Queen never yields."

The audience roared. My gaze shot back to Exekiel and I mentally mapped out a path to him through the other chained players. A shell-horn sounded and the Trial began.

Whips cracked across spines and I hurtled forwards. The distant sound of Exekiel's grunt was like thunder in my bones. I shouldn't have been able to hear it but I did—connected to him in a way I couldn't explain. My ankle barked but I blocked out the pain. All that mattered was reaching Exekiel.

A force slammed into my legs and I went down. My chin smacked the ground. My skull rattled and vision swayed.

Maura, a shifter, clung to my legs and screeched, "Exekiel's mine."

Another lash struck his back. Another grunt. I choked on a gasp. Twisting, I kicked Maura in the face with my good leg. I had to get to him—I *had* to. It felt like his torture was mine.

Maura's head whipped back but she clung on. "All he sees is you."

Pain burst through the side of my head. My ears rang. Then heavy bear paws fell over my nose and mouth, smothering me.

My eyes shot wide. Maura's face was twisted. Her nose changed to a bear's snout. *Shit.* She was shifting.

I thrashed—the sand grating my skin. Sweat stinging my eyes. My lungs tight and seizing.

Blindly, my fingers searched for something I could use to fend Maura off before her shift was complete. There was no way I'd survive being mauled by a bear.

At last, my hand curled around a large stone. Vision spotting, I smashed the rock into the side of Maura's head. She didn't release me and I hit her again. Harder.

The half-bear cackled. A deep, growling sound that sent splinters of ice through my veins. Before my eyes, tufts of fur sprouted along her arms and her teeth protruded.

A man screamed. It wasn't Exekiel but my heart thumped inside my chest as if it was trying to beat out of it. Exekiel was being tortured, beaten bloody and instead of trying to save him, this bitch was slowing me down.

My anger became an extra limb weighing on my soul. With a warrior's cry, I clutched the rock tighter and swung. I struck her again and again. Eventually, Maura fell backwards and I went with her.

Blood pounded in my ears and pulsed in my veins. I tried to tame my breathing but it was impossible. Just as Goather said, the potion unleashed pure primal instinct and my instinct was to protect my mate.

I struck again until Maura's haunting laughter silenced and her head caved in. Until she slumped unseeing, unmoving on the ground. Only then, did the ringing in my ears stop and the rock rolled from my hand. It was stained with blood that splattered across the sand.

I scrambled back. My breathing heavy.

For a fleeting second, my mind went blank. Then the shouts of the crowd, the cries of men and the snap of whips flooded back in.

I half crawled, half ran as I stumbled to my feet and charged towards the column.

The metallic scent of blood was thick in the air. Exekiel's muscled back flayed and raw. My stomach turned. I ran faster than I ever had despite how my ankle screamed and my vision swam. I darted around others being beaten and ducked under fists.

Vivienne and a blonde battled ahead of me. The other girls already unconscious or worse.

The whips cracked more furiously. In spite of himself, Exekiel barked in pain; his fists clenched. His back shredded to bloody pulp.

Why isn't he healing? I ran faster, my lungs burning. How big was this arena?

Translucent spikes fixed along the edge of the whip glinted in the sunlight—obsidian glass. My gut lurched. Apparently, Exekiel could heal from it but it would take time—time he didn't have between lashes. He gritted his teeth; his dark hair damp with sweat and muscles strained against the binds.

I'm coming.

Vivienne let out a battle shriek and the elf she'd been fighting hurtled through the air and fell in an awkward heap. I hobbled forwards, my foot dragging behind me.

Vivienne took off, getting closer to Exekiel—to saving him—but the elf lunged to her feet and charged after her.

I changed course, veering away from Exekiel. Vivienne wheeled around to defend herself just as I flung myself at the elf and trapped her in a headlock.

"Go!" I screamed at Vivienne.

Though she had a black eye, busted nose, and her white wings were stained red, she was in better shape than I was.

She frowned then smirked. "If I save him, he is seen as my mate."

Camera-orbs swooped closer—hovering as if they paused for my reply.

"Just go," I shouted.

I knew what it meant but she had a better chance of reaching Exekiel; of ending his torture.

"I don't care who saves him! Just save him!" My grip tightened around the elf's neck as she thrashed. "Go!"

Vivienne sneered then darted off. Her wings flapped as she surged towards the column where Exekiel was bound.

Her lips crashed into his and the audience cheered wildly.

Pain lanced through my chest as my heart cracked.

24

THE KISS THAT SHATTERED THE EARTH

I rested my throbbing head on the sand, harrowed by the riotous applause of the people. Vivienne had won. She'd rescued Exekiel with a kiss and now he sagged against the rock; battered but free.

It should have been me. It was a useless, immature thought, but I seethed as Vivienne brushed the hair from his brow. As the people saw her as his mate. Why did I care?

"Get up!" Lucinda crouched in front of me. My vision swam. "It's not over."

The witch's dark skin seemed to melt—drip from her jaw. I blinked. The potion was playing tricks on my mind; just as it had pulled out my primal instincts and drove me to do things I wouldn't normally do. My gaze drifted to Maura's lifeless body.

"Get up!" Lucinda shouted again. "It's the boys turn."

Before she could elaborate, the world transformed once more.

Something cold bit into my wrists. My stomach pitched. The audience continued to holler, but now it was the mostly female contestants who were topless and chained to the stone columns. The males and some females, who stood in groups around Goather. Each one was beaten and bloody. Some barely able to stand.

Goather shouted, "Time for Round Two!"

The audience stamped their feet. Their shouts rang through the arena. The hulking men returned, whips in hand.

My mouth went dry. My heart hammered in my chest. I knew from the earlier battle, that even if I could control my magic, I didn't have access to it. The only way to be freed, was by my mate.

"I can't say I'm surprised that our foreign temptress has a whopping eight males in her corner," Goather boomed.

Confused, I craned my neck to see the group of men who sought to claim me as their mate. There was at least one from each cast. Some, I hadn't said more than two words to. Again, I thought of what sirens did best. Lure men in…perhaps without a song.

However, only one male caught and held my attention—his pink eyes so deep, I could lose myself in them. Exekiel. His skin was clammy and pale. His jaw clenched. It was obvious he was in pain. All the players were. But the strength in his stare promised violence; said that he would destroy heaven and hell to reach me. My chest squeezed.

Goather blew the horn. Exekiel charged like a storm of chaos. Though he moved slower than usual, he was fast. He easily sidestepped the warlock that rushed him and rolled beneath the leopard shifter who pounced—his fur matted with blood.

I didn't see what happened next as the whip tore across my spine. Air shot from my lungs. A scream torn from my throat.

Somewhere the shifter roared. He couldn't hold his transformation for long and I caught a glimpse of him as he collapsed in a bloody heap.

The whip struck again. I gasped. I prided myself on being unbreakable, but this would break me. Again and again, the punisher struck.

I lost count at eight lashings. My vision blurred and bile burned in my throat. All I registered was a constant rush of searing agony and Exekiel's distant fury. The rumble of his power through the earth.

In the brief second between blows, I searched the sands for him.

"Exekiel." It was a whisper but his eyes shot to mine as if he'd heard it.

A massive gorilla lumbered up behind him and knocked him aside.

Exekiel staggered. His damp hair fell across his forehead, shuddered above those violent pink eyes. Shadows seemed to surround him as he gritted his teeth and his wings ripped through his shredded back; flesh and sinew torn. His knees buckled and he hit the ground. Sand plumed around him.

The whip cracked across my spine. I could barely discern between blows anymore.

My punisher grinned, clearly enjoying himself. His gaze lustful as my body jerked, and blood whelped up from the wounds he carved. His hungry stare lingered on where my bare breasts juddered against the cold stone.

"Beautiful creature," he hissed then brought the whip down again.

Spit sprayed from the corners of my mouth. Nausea churned in my gut. I was going to black out. I was going to die.

"Don't you dare," a voice whispered against my lips.

Then I was consumed—claimed by a kiss that shattered the earth. It was as if my savior was breathing life back into me. The chains vanished and I fell against him.

I could hardly open my eyes but I knew from his scent, his touch, that Exekiel had saved me. Craving him, I opened my mouth and accepted the sweep of his tongue.

The audience erupted. My body shook. Tears rimmed my eyes. Nothing had ever felt more right.

Exekiel pressed his hands to my back. I whimpered but he whispered, "*Thesona.*"

Power pulsed from his fingertips and seeped into my skin, cooling the worst of my lacerations. Power he couldn't use on himself when the wounds were caused by Obsidian glass.

I cupped his face in my trembling hands. Our eyes searched each other, then his mouth claimed mine again. My mate, my hero…my enemy.

The Blood Battles were postponed since the infirmary was full of the wounded. The less brutalized were ordered to rest in their rooms. Thanks to Exekiel and some herbs and paste that Lucinda's mysterious source had sent, after two days, all I had was a dull pain in my spine and faint lines where the whip had struck.

My exhaustion, however, was all-consuming. I groaned as I was woken by my pillow vibrating. Reaching for the shell I kept hidden beneath it, I brought it to my ear.

Loch spoke: *"The day they mourn, go to Creature's Copse to the place where the Pegasus play."*

I frowned. The Copse was home to the Pegasus and other creatures but I didn't know exactly where they stayed.

The day of Mourning would follow after tomorrow's Blood Battle—where those who'd failed the Third Trial would meet a bitter end or forever be enslaved. Which meant the rankings would be posted in the morning.

My stomach knotted. I had no idea how I scored in the Trial. I'd managed to stay alive but hadn't been the one to save Exekiel.

My skin flushed at the thought of him; at the memory of his kiss. Groaning, I flung my arm over my face. I couldn't seriously be falling for him. Mate or not, he was working against me. Trying to condemn the outlanders and me.

A knock sounded on my balcony door. Frowning, I slid out of bed and padded towards the window. I peeked through a gap in the curtain and my stomach flipped. Exekiel waited beyond the glass bathed in sunset. His magenta eyes moved to where I stood as if he sensed me through the fabric.

He didn't have to ask. Before I could think about what I was doing, I unlatched the door and held it open. He stepped inside; his height dwarfed mine.

Some color had returned to his skin; his bare torso wrapped in ointment-soaked bandages.

Finding my voice, I whispered, "What are you doing here?"

"I couldn't spend another night in the infirmary."

That didn't explain why he'd come here but my argument died when he trailed his finger down my cheek and along my neck.

"All I kept thinking about was you. Wondering if you taste as good as you felt."

I swallowed thickly. "W-what do you mean?"

Exekiel stepped forwards and used his hips to press me into the door. I remained frozen as his hands trailed over the slope of my breasts that were framed by my lilac negligee. My body shuddered. Eyelids fluttering. He caressed me lower.

"Let me show you."

He gave me a second to refuse before he pushed his hand between my legs.

My head kicked back; striking the cool glass as he slid aside my underwear and peeled me open.

I gasped, shaking under his touch.

He groaned. "You feel so good."

"Yeah?" I panted.

"Yeah."

My nipples crowned. My fists clenched as warmth pulsed between my thighs. "Yeah?"

"Yeah."

With one arm around my waist, Exekiel scooped me up and I wrapped my legs around him. He carried me towards the bed; his fingers still pumping inside me.

"I'm willing to bet you taste even better."

My breath hitched as he laid me down and settled beside me. His fingers undid me so easily. His mouth would shatter my world.

God, what was I doing? I couldn't get involved with the monster who supported the exile of my people; the family I'd never known but missed every day. The male who was possibly responsible for my sister's *death*.

"M-maybe y-you should leave," I stammered as he fingered me to the edge of my sanity.

"Or" he purred, as he trailed kisses across my shoulder, over my breast and down my abdomen. I whimpered. "Maybe you should part your pretty thighs and let me have a taste."

Fuck! Need and logic warred inside me.

Exekiel grinned as he slid off my underwear and his shoulders forced my legs apart. I didn't try to stop him.

"Well?" he breathed; his fingers still working me hard.

I rocked into his touch; unable to deny him but knowing I should.

However, one look in my eyes and he knew I was his. Exekiel lowered his head and dragged his tongue up my center. I moaned. Hot shivers catapulted through my core.

Shit.

We weren't lovers. Not even friends. But something that overrode all logic and consumed us both.

One lick and he was gone. Exekiel feasted on me; a wet banquet spread before him. My legs splayed and thighs pinned in his grasp.

I quaked. My body coiled tight.

This is wrong.

His tongue plunged deeper, jabbing and stroking. My back arched as I tugged on his hair and struggled to breathe. He was trained for this. Forget flying, illusion and strength; this was his superpower—making me come.

"Fuck, Princess," he growled. "I want you dripping down my throat."

I bucked.

Exekiel ate me like his favorite ice cream. His tongue swirled around my sensitive nub as his fingers dipped inside me.

Fuck. This was messed up. I had a weapon tucked away for the sole purpose of killing this man, yet here I was, grinding on his tongue.

Blood pumped between my thighs.

"Shit," I rasped.

My legs locked up as my release strained against the seam.

"Mmmm," Exekiel murmured.

The vibration rolled through me and my release tore free with an eternal scream. Weightless and wild, I convulsed all over my enemy's ruthless tongue.

25

WHERE THE PEGASUS PLAY

Mild amusement glinted in Exekiel's eyes when I ushered him out of my room, and via the balcony since there was less chance of him being seen.

He leaned in the doorway, his hair disheveled. His lips quirked to one side. It took all I had inside me to not drag him back to bed and ride him 'til sun-up.

"Are you ashamed of me, little bud?"

I inwardly scoffed. Exekiel was smart, cunning, powerful and unbearably gorgeous. Over six-feet of chorded muscle bound within tanned skin. He had a face that was chiseled by the gods and a mouth that knew exactly how to push me over the edge as if he'd tasted me a thousand times.

No, I wasn't ashamed of him. I was confused and *terrified*. Confused by the way he looked at me, with such endless hunger in his eyes. And terrified of the way I felt about him.

I couldn't shake the sense that this could all be a ruse. A way to use our connection against me and gain information. And I couldn't let that happen. My life and potentially the lives of countless others, depended on it.

"I'm tired," I lied. "Besides, your wounds have opened and I don't want blood all over my sheets."

Exekiel studied me. "I'll try to bleed less, next time."

"There won't be a next time." I pushed back my shoulders and hoped I sounded more confident than I felt.

"You still don't get it."

Moving closer, Exekiel maneuvered me back against the door and planted his hands at either side of my head. "I could do so many things to you, right now." He leaned in. Our breath entwined. "I could have you wet and shaking." His lips brushed mine lighting a fire in my belly. "And you wouldn't do a thing to stop me."

His hand trailed down my neck and cradled my breast. His hot breath fanned over my skin. "Because you're mine."

I whimpered, my body tight with need.

"Mine." He kissed me, passionately; endlessly. "And I," his fingers curled around my hand and brought it to his rigid erection. My heart kicked. "Am yours."

His mouth descended on me. I shook as I stroked his stiff cock. He moaned; deepening the kiss, threatening to have us toppling back onto the bed.

But finally—*finally*—he pulled back. "Until next time, little bud."

With his wings concealed and healing, he darted across the terrace and leapt over the rail. My heart leapt with him as if he carried it in the palm of his hand.

The ratings were in. Apparently, being willing to kill for my mate—my kingdom, increased my rank by twenty points. This meant that by taking Maura's life, I'd saved my own. The thought made me sick. Lucinda insisted that I'd had no choice. Kill or be killed. But that didn't make me feel any better about it.

The only good thing was that since Trials Two and Three had been combined—first, making the potion, then rescuing our mate—there'd only been one Blood Battle. Now the players were left to convalesce and mourn for three whole days. Cameras cut down to a minimum.

I dressed and slipped out of my room at the first whisper of dawn. In case someone saw me, I strolled casually, like I simply fancied a walk. Loch hadn't specified a time to meet but it was easier to sneak out under the cover of darkness. Quietly, I skulked across the landscaped grounds and finally ducked into the Copse.

Where the Pegasus play…Where the hell was that?

I stumbled more times than I could count, lumbering through churned earth and over raised roots with only the milky light of the early morning to guide me.

Eventually, I felt the familiar prickle of a Pegasus' power. Caught a whiff of their wings—like pinecones and cinnamon. Aromas I wouldn't have noticed before but since coming to the Five Isles, my senses had sharpened. As if my body was flourishing in the world where it belonged.

Balancing on smooth rocks, I hobbled across a narrow stream where glowing fish leapt and followed the scent.

My jaw dropped when I came to a field of golden grass swaying in the morning breeze. Countless Pegasus grazed and pranced through willow trees. They were majestic beasts; larger than any horse, with wings that spanned meters. They were various shades of silver, gold, black and white and each had delicate markings on their feathers. No matter how many times I'd seen them, the awe never went away.

I jumped when a familiar voice drawled, "Temptress."

My heart beat in my throat and I swiveled around. Goather stood behind me; his lips curved in a smirk. *Crap!*

Perhaps reading my panic, he added, "Loch sent me."

My brow furrowed. He knew Loch.

"Come on, I need to get back before someone notices I'm gone." Goather trotted ahead. "I didn't spend decades undercover for it to fall apart now."

I hesitated. This could be a trap. Then again, he did know Loch's name and seemed to know when and where to meet me.

Tentatively, I followed. "You're a spy?"

"I am."

I wanted to believe him. However, this world was riddled with deception and duplicity. And everyone knew more than I did.

"Why?"

"Because satyrs are as exiled as the rest. I was simply fortunate enough to be on this side of the Isles when they split." He ducked under a branch. "Elf Bay and Creatures Copse were once joined. But when the land-shift happened and the four chosen casts became bound with the Isle of the Eternals, Creature's Copse was split. Half connected to the Five-Isles and the other on the outlands—no longer worthy."

There was a sharp edge to his tone. "Since I'm on this side, I've been given certain privileges and position but I'm still not worthy enough to warrant a claim to the Throne." He gestured to his goat-legs.

"Aren't you as worthy as the Shifters?"

Goather scanned the skies where the sun rose and quickened his pace.

"That was what the sirens argued. For the satyrs, nymphs and themselves. Who decides what is worthy and what isn't, when we were all technically Chosen?"

Before I could reply, he pressed a finger to his lips. Seconds later, a camera-orb drifted overhead. He tugged my hand and we crouched low in the shrubs. When it passed, we continued on in silence.

We came to the edge of a vibrant lagoon. The topaz-blue surface steady and shimmering.

"This is where I leave you." Goather pointed to boulders nearest the tree line. "He'll meet you there."

I nodded and made my way to the rocks. The lagoon was bright, but deep and veiled in mist—impossible to see the bottom. I settled on the bank and studied the point where the inlet met the sea.

My thoughts drifted to what Goather had said. Just like Lucinda and Eudora, he didn't support the Five Isles. There were two sides to every story but I was becoming increasingly convinced, that trusting Loch was the right move.

The water rippled and Loch emerged from beneath its surface. Droplets dripped down his dark skin. His eyes almost identical to the blue of the lagoon.

He grinned his sharpened teeth and purred, "There she is."

As he swam towards me, I caught a flash of his tail. His scales a deep red with iridescent flecks of green. My chest tightened. Knowing Loch was a siren and seeing it, were two very different things.

He cut through the water like a shark—the sight unnerving.

My fingers were wedged into the graveled ground by the time he reached me.

"Is this where you explain what the hell is going on?"

He chuckled. "This is where I show you. Get in."

I eyed the murky water then looked back at him; brows raised.

"We can't stay here. Someone will see us." He looked up as if expecting an orb to fly over.

My mouth twisted. "Then where are we going?"

"The Coral Court, of course."

My heart skipped. My stomach a medley of anticipation and dread. We were returning to the place I'd apparently been born. The place where it all began…and ended.

"I…can't swim."

Loch snickered. "Get in."

Curiosity overriding my fear, I sunk down into the surprisingly warm water. It was as deep as I'd suspected and my feet kicked as I tried to stay afloat. I couldn't swim.

'Relax."

196

That was easier said than done but I looked into Loch's piercing eyes and took a calming breath. The water swirled around my legs and suddenly, I instinctively knew what to do. It was like stepping into myself—a part of me that had been buried long ago.

"Follow me."

Loch's tail flicked as he swam towards the lip of the lagoon that led to the open ocean. I followed; stunned when my legs and arms effortlessly mimicked the moves, I'd seen on television. I was *swimming*.

We slowed when we neared the magical pulse of the barrier. My stomach rolled. Countless bodies with tails were nailed to wooden poles set in the rocky reef. Most skeletal but some relatively fresh.

"What is this?" I whispered, spying guards on patrol.

"A warning to our people."

I blanched. Some of the skeletons were small—*children*. One of the newer women bore an obvious swollen stomach.

"The Protector did most of these himself."

Chunks rose in my throat. The more I learnt about Exekiel, the more I questioned the connection between us. If he was as powerful as people said, then wasn't it possible that he'd magically manipulated me, somehow? Convinced me to think I could be mated to such a monster?

"That one there." Loch indicated a skeleton with a silver crown upon its head. "That was your sister— Corina Merlantis."

26

THE CORAL COURT

Riding on Loch's muscled back, I plunged into the depths of the ocean. My nerves on edge. I was bombarded by memories of sharks on shore from the one and only time I'd ventured into the sea as a child. But I was equally enthralled by the gills Loch's magic had given me, and the filament in my nostrils to stop the water from flying up my nose.

A vast translucent dome glistened near the seabed and Loch veered towards it. We swam through a gate of seaweed and were met with a shimmering pearl path that cut through mounds of rock and veered off in various directions. Along its edge were houses made of coral and seashells. Within, countless faces peered out through glassless windows. Others eagerly rushed into the street.

Loch greeted them all with a wave. I could barely smile. My mind was racing. The sirens bowed; their tails curled around them.

"Their princess has come," Loch murmured. His words shot through me like a bolt of ice.

I'd started to put the pieces together but this confirmed it. I was heir to the Coral Court, my mother the captured queen.

We came to a grand castle made of peach coral and worn stone. It was tall with domed-spires and arched windows; its double-doors forged from polished shells that opened at Loch's touch.

I whistled—surprised for the hundredth time when water didn't choke me. The palace was beautiful. Its furniture made from shells and sand-filled cushions. Light flooded in from glow fish that swam in a floor-to-ceiling glass cylinder and refracted across the pearl tiles.

Loch paced ahead. "We'll begin your training after the celebration."

"Celebration?"

"In honor of your return."

'Oh.' I swallowed. "And…the training?"

He shrugged. "You're our weapon, Princess. It's time we sharpen the blade. Born of both sides, only you among us can claim the throne and free our people." His stare was resolute. "Only you can slay the Bravinore Fae and welcome in our army."

Unease crept up my spine. He spoke about murder like it was natural. I suppose for him, it was. This war had been going on for centuries and it wasn't about killing, but about surviving. About fighting for those who couldn't fight for themselves.

"Everything must be timed perfectly. Kill the Bravinore before you win the Games and you will be tried as an enemy. But slaughter him as the new Primary and no one can argue." He grinned at me. "Then you will deliver our message of change. Of the Outer Isles freed from exile and your first order as Primary will be to execute all those in the current Royal Court."

I let out a breath. I'd spent my life as a nobody and now I was being called to become a queen. It was the stuff of an abandoned girl's dreams…and nightmares.

"In the meantime, get close to Primary Adir and learn what you can of the Royal Court. Uncover its weaknesses and its strengths whilst at the same time, convincing them of your innocence."

I nodded. I wasn't entirely sure I could kill anyone—least of all Exekiel—but it felt good to have a plan, some semblance of hope; of control. Some direction as I struggled to navigate through the dark.

Loch turned down another pearlescent corridor. "By the way, you'll need to bathe before you meet the others." He threw me a dark look. "You reek of the Protector."

It was an effort to mask my shock. "You know what they say." I forced a shrug. "Keep your friends close…"

"And your enemies closer." Loch pushed open a sand-crafted door and swam into an oval chamber with giant oysters lining its walls. Like the rest of the castle, the space was lit by glow fish that swam within glass walls.

"You remember he's your enemy, then?"

"Yes."

I did now and I wouldn't let myself forget again. Exekiel was a killer. His barrier and its butchered bodies were proof of that.

"Good. I can't say I'm not jealous you let the bastard taste you."

My mouth dropped open. Loch couldn't only smell Exekiel, he could smell what I'd let him do to me.

"I was hoping to have that honor myself." He waggled his brows.

"Get in line." I cringed. "That came out wrong. I just mean I seem to be attracting random guys."

Loch laughed. "Ah yes, the curse of the Siren— being irresistible." He gestured to the nearest oyster. "Come. You'll want to see this."

He waved his hand and the shell creaked open. Within was a pearl the size of a small toddler. On it was an image of me the first time I ran away from social services.

"What is this?"

"A record of your life. It's how we watched over you."

I blinked. Shell after shell opened. Each one linked to a moment in my life.

"How?"

Loch stroked the mark on my hip. It tingled beneath his touch.

The further we went, the younger my depictions became, until I was looking at myself as a baby. Someone I almost recognized stood over me with a bright smile.

I stepped closer. "I know her."

"That's Corina."

My sister. I couldn't look away from her smiling face, pink hair and ochre skin. I even heard her voice— a familiar lullaby.

"We stored memories in your mark." Loch explained. "To make your return easier."

I let out a breath. Easier wasn't the word I'd use but I definitely remembered—the love, the laughter and song that rang around me. My heart ached. This was what had been taken from me, all because the Five Isles had wanted to keep the power of the Conduit to themselves. Their greed led to war and yet they blamed us for it because we refused to kneel.

I didn't know how long I stared at the pearls; at memories I'd forgotten and others that were imprinted on my skin.

Eventually, Loch murmured, "We should strengthen your mind shield after training. I imagine the Protector's been trying to worm his way in."

"Him and the Council."

"What?"

The sharpness in his tone tore my stare away from the pearls.

"They performed an extraction a few weeks ago."

"Shit!" Loch snarled, "They won't believe you've been able to keep them out this long on your own. We'll have to give them something; control what they see and keep the rest guarded."

By the rest, he meant his plan for me to win the Games so I could publicly execute the current leaders and make way for my reign. Become a queen of land and sea.

Once I'd bathed—which seemed redundant since we were underwater—I dressed in a cream strapless gown, Loch had left for me. The bottom half was shredded—resembling seaweed, and the upper half was encrusted with shells.

His stare lingered when I met him in the hallway. "Beautiful. Almost as stunning as me."

I snickered. "Almost."

He was shirtless but wore a crown of weeds and steel breastplates patterned with shells.

"Maybe we should skip this party and I take you into that room and fu—"

"Move," I half-laughed, cutting him off.

Loch grinned; all teeth, then led me down a dark seagrass-covered passageway. I gnawed on my bottom lip wondering what I'd find at the end.

The sound of pipe music fluttered through reeds, carrying the murmur of distant voices. My nerves spiked. We were almost there.

Suddenly, Loch turned and pressed me into the wall.

I gasped. "What are you doing?"

His slender fingers curled into my hips. "Savoring this moment before I have to share you." He buried his nose in my neck and inhaled. Tendrils of desire rippled down my spine. I didn't know why my body responded to him like it did. Not powerful and overwhelming like Exekiel, but sharp and undeniable.

"My delicious Mate-Sworn."

I shivered. "What exactly is that?" He'd mentioned it before.

"An intention sworn the day our eggs were laid; a vow between our bodies and souls."

Was that what I was feeling?

My thoughts trailed back to Exekiel—the connection with him was so much deeper; sweeter.

Stop thinking about him!

Loch groaned and something long and hard slid from beneath his scales as he moved into me.

My breath caught. This was weird.

"At the end of this, it will be you and I on the throne."

"Loch," I panted. I couldn't deny the aquarian-male was ridiculously attractive. And lust seemed to be a baseline of this bond.

"Princess."

"My people are waiting." It was strange that it didn't feel strange to say those words.

Loch's eyes gleamed as he pulled back. "Your Ladyship."

Taking my hand, he pulled me into a glass-domed ballroom where sirens swam above a glass floor. Glow fish darted within.

I was instantly surrounded. Sirens shook my hands and welcomed me home. *Home.* One beaming girl with russet-brown skin and wide grey eyes pulled me into an embrace.

"Finally!" she yanked me through the crowd. "Let's drink."

The girls purple tail whipped through the water. I struggled to keep up. We came to a shell-encrusted bar and the girl pressed a fruity pink drink into my hand.

"Come on, we have a lot of time to make up for." She drank deeply. "I'm Colette, by the way."

"Varialla Merlantis," rasped an elderly man beside us.

I stiffened when he pulled me into a hug. It was warm and familiar. He'd held me before. My throat closed; eyes stung with unshed tears.

The evening wore on and more sirens came to share their stories and support. I tried to remain wary—trust was earned after all—but it was impossible not to get swept up in the wave of affection. More love than I'd ever felt. These were my people. Where I belonged. They knew my secret but didn't fear or despise me for it.

I danced and laughed and vowed to free them. To rid the world of the barrier and change the way things were run.

Eventually breathless, I slumped against the bar and gulped down another drink.

A sandy-brown skinned girl with wide brown eyes, swam up to me. She didn't look older than six.

"Are you going to save my mummy?" Her small voice was almost lost beneath the music. "She needs the blessing of the Conduit but we can't get to it." Her bottom lip trembled. "There are so many sick here, since the blessing was taken."

My chest tightened. Loch had told me all about it. How the Conduits magic helped cure the sick, fertilized the lands for food. The sirens were living on rations of sea grapes and seaweed and even they had started to wither.

I clasped the girl's hands. "Yes. I will save us all."

Being back at the Coral Court had enhanced my memories and emotion towards it—made them as sharp as the day they were created. And I would use them to fuel my determination. To help me go through with Loch's plan.

If Exekiel died, the barrier would die with him, and there'd be no one powerful enough to stop the Outer Isles from attacking. From taking what was taken from them.

I recoiled from the thought of killing Exekiel but balled my hands into fists. Sure, the Shadow Saint was gorgeous, but I wasn't going to sacrifice myself and the lives of these people for the sake of a pretty face.

Whatever existed between me and him would only ever be used as a weapon against me. There was no real connection between us. But this was real. This was what I'd craved my entire life. A safe place to call home with people who loved me. I'd finally found, and I wasn't going to let them go.

27

DON'T DRINK THE FAERIE WINE

I returned to my rooms in Residence Manor brimming with new determination. I pushed aside thoughts of Exekiel; the Fae-male who made my blood pound and heart race. And focused on the goal: Taking down his barrier, no matter what. Getting close to Adir and sussing out the Royal Court.

My muscles groaned and I stretched. Training had been intense. My knuckles raw from punching; toes bruised and legs throbbing. All I wanted was to collapse into bed but Loch had given me a mission. One that had to be carried out tonight. Danimous was waiting.

I eased out of my sweat-and-sea-soaked clothes, bathed and changed into a backless black minidress that shimmered with sequins. There were plenty of parties happening tonight to honor those who fell during the Battles, which gave me the perfect excuse for being out after dark.

Once ready, I crept through the vast gardens of the Eternal City. Music droned in the distance. A heavy bass backed by wolves' howls. Something else soft and lilting, akin to the elven taste.

With the map of the Five Isles on my phone, I followed the path that led to where Loch had indicated. After a while, I realized it'd brought me near the Gaming Council. I was about to rush past when someone said my name. A familiar voice that drifted up from the other side of the wall. Vladimir.

"We agreed she'd die in the Games," the elf growled.

"Yes, but only when it looks like an accident," a female replied. "Being whipped to death isn't an accident. And if he hadn't saved her, one of the others would have."

"Not if he prolonged the fight with them like we suggested. Made it too late for anyone to save her."

I froze. They were talking about the Trial. Exekiel was supposed to let me die.

"You know I'm right, Gwendoline. You saw that kiss."

"It was for the cameras—to strengthen their bond. This is the plan, Vlad. She has to believe it, to succumb."

My heart twisted. I'd had my suspicions but there it was. Whatever this sick connection between Exekiel and I was, it couldn't be trusted.

Vladimir scoffed. "And what if he succumbs to her? You remember what happened the last time one of us was foolish enough to do that."

The silence that followed was somber.

"At this rate, she'll be in the winner's ring with a Fanclub—an *army* we gave her—at her back."

Gwendoline sighed. "So dramatic." Her footsteps moved closer to the wall—to him. "If Ms. Hastings doesn't truly die in the Games, Exekiel will kill her and make it look like she did." Her breathing turned heavy. A low groan came from Vladimir. "But first, we must extract every secret we can from her head."

He moaned. There was the distinct rustle of fabric; the thunk of a weapons belt hitting the ground.

I ran. Fear and fury churned in my gut. I knew it. Exekiel was a trained assassin and I was next on his list. Loch was right. There was no reasoning with these people. There was only one way for this to end.

I hurtled through the trees beyond the Council. Firelight flickered ahead. Laughter and music rang through the branches.

Before I realized where I was, I stumbled into a raging Fae party. The winged beings danced with abandon. Feathers and flowers were woven into their hair. The males' bare chests were painted with random markings. The females' breasts barely covered with leaves.

Someone shoved a drink into my hand. I gulped it down; needing to stifle my anger and steady my racing heart. The path ahead of me was bathed in blood but it was the only way to survive; to save the exiled and to finally put an end to the divide. One final war for eternal peace. And I would be its catalyst.

The drink hit almost instantly. My mood shifted; heart soaring. A familiar scent drifted towards me on the breeze and my body thrummed. I was consumed by a need for the one who carried that scent—my mate, my enemy. Like a bloodhound, I sought Exekiel through the crowd. He was there. I could smell him and I *needed* him.

A male grabbed my hand. Together, we laughed and twirled through the Fae. Then finally, I saw him, seated on a log with a girl on either side. They draped themselves over him but Exekiel didn't seem to notice as he spoke with another male. Still, I bristled at the sight.

His eyes shot to mine as if he'd sensed me. They changed from their lethal pink to a burning red. My pulse pounded.

In one fluid motion, Exekiel prowled towards me; his wings half splayed behind him. A pair of black shorts hung off his hips to reveal the indents of his V-muscles. I couldn't help noticing how they pointed like an arrow to his cock. I drew in a ragged breath.

Holy hotness.

"What are you doing here?" he snarled.

Anger and sanity forgotten; I closed the gap between us. My breasts grazed his sculpted chest and I swallowed a moan. My legs pressed together. Exekiel's nostrils flared as if he scented that need.

"Hi," I breathed.

His gaze slid to the chalice I held. "Who the fuck gave you faerie-wine?"

"Who cares?" I smirked and curled my fingers around his cock.

Exekiel went hard in my hand. The veins in his neck jumped. My whole body reacted to him—lit up.

"Fuck me, Protector." I couldn't believe I said the words but the wine had loosened my tongue.

Exekiel growled, "Go home. The faerie-wine has gotten to your head."

But the only thing that had gotten to me was him. His intoxicating scent; his overwhelming presence. A *need* for him.

Slowly, torturously, I stroked his length. Up and down.

Exekiel gritted his teeth. "I can only be a gentleman for so long, little bud."

I grinned; relishing the way his body responded to me against his will. "You haven't been a gentleman a day in your life."

Exekiel's muscles tightened when I rubbed him again, making sure my thumb brushed the tip. He groaned. His shorts were thin and it was easy to find his hulking cock within.

"Fuck me," I pleaded.

The wine hadn't messed with my head; it had cleared it. I knew with certainty that this was what I wanted—him. It was always him. No one else would ever be enough. There was no way I could kill him without experiencing him, just once.

Exekiel bit out a curse and grabbed my arm. He hauled me towards the edge of the clearing and through the trees.

"Go home," he barked but when he turned to leave, I cut him off.

My eyes flashed. "Make me."

With force that surprised us both, I slammed him against a tree. Exekiel's eyes widened and the scent of his arousal struck the back of my throat.

I moaned and got on my knees. I needed him in a way I had never needed anyone. My fingers slid over his length and raked down his chorded thighs.

"Fuck." Exekiel's head tipped back against the trunk; his breathing labored. "You don't know what you're doing."

I licked my lips. "I'm begging to suck your cock."

His face creased with conflicted desire but he didn't stop me as I shimmied down his shorts. His length sprang free. My breath hitched. Heat throbbed between my thighs. He was magnificent. As long and thick as my forearm.

"Varialla," he groaned; the word strained.

I looked up at him as I wrapped my hand around his root. His hips bucked. I smirked and stroked him from base to tip. He was velvet wrapped around steel. My mouth watered.

"Yes?" I purred.

"You're not accustomed to faerie-wine," Exekiel grunted as I continued to rub him; savoring the way he pulsed in my hand.

"I had one glass," I countered. My lips were so agonizingly close to the bead of arousal on the head of his cock. Every fiber in my being wanted to lick it clean. "Just enough to know that I need you inside me, one way or another."

Exekiel groaned and couldn't help moving into the pump of my hand.

"Let me do this," I begged.

I hadn't drunk enough to cloud my mind. But the drink had made me braver—truer to myself.

His jaw clenched but when my tongue slid from between my lips and circled the tip of his rigid cock, Exekiel gripped the back of my head and held me there.

He seemed to collect himself; to steady his breathing.

I waited a heartbeat, then widened my mouth to take in more of him. I sucked hard; cheeks clamped around his perfect shaft. Exekiel jerked and let out a deep moan.

My mouth filled with saliva as I greedily worked my hand and tongue over his cock. His muscles tensed; eyes heavy-lidded as he stared down at me and watched me suck him. My hand pumping at the root; squeezing, stroking.

His stare was a brand that scorched my entire being. Wet slicked between my thighs. Needing more of him, I swallowed another inch.

"Fates," he rasped. "Yes. Just like that."

His fingers flexed, tangling in my fishtail braid as he drove himself deeper. I gagged when he hit the back of my throat but moaned, encouraging him to continue. My other hand curled around his ass and the muscles shifted beneath my fingers as I pushed him further; let him fill me.

"Fates. You suck me so well," he growled.

I dribbled down his cock. A squelching sound filled the space between breaths as I devoured him.

My mate groaned; his wings splayed and flattened against the trunk. That sound was everything.

"Fuck," he rasped when I lightly grazed him with my teeth.

His hips thrust harder—driving his cock deeper.

"That's it, baby. Gods, yes. You're so good."

His praise and the sight of him coming undone was captivating. I pushed my hand between my legs. I was drenched. Desperate, I took care of myself as I took care of him.

Sucking hard and fast, I brought him to the brink.

Exekiel furiously fucked my mouth. His hands clamped around my head. His cock smeared with my lipstick. Sweat coated his chiseled abs. His mouth open; brow creased. Then, suddenly, he stiffened and his head kicked back as he roared loud enough to rival the music and poured himself down my throat.

With an appreciative moan that rippled through his cock, I drained him of every salty drop.

28

BEST LAID PLANS

One taste of Exekiel and I was hooked. I wanted—*needed*—more of him but the bastard pulled away. His pink eyes gleamed as he stared down at me with an expression of tortured longing. As if he felt something between us that he didn't want to face.

I felt it too; an attraction that went deeper than skin. Something that said I wanted to be near him for the rest of my life. But emotions couldn't get involved here. This had to be—could only be—about satisfying a carnal need. A physical attraction we couldn't seem to control.

Without a word, Exekiel scooped me into his arms and soared into the sky. Fueled by lust and Faerie-wine, I nibbled on his neck, licked his jawline—did anything I could to entice him, but he kept his gaze fixed ahead. His jaw clenched.

When we reached my balcony, he pushed open the doors that I'd left unlocked so I could sneak back in, and lowered me onto the bed. I locked my legs around him; pulling him down on top of me.

"Stay," I pleaded and rolled my hips.

Exekiel's fingers dug into my thigh.

"Fuck," he breathed.

I saw stars when he moved with me.

"Go to sleep," he whispered, even as friction built between us.

I arched into him; ached in a way I never had before. I grasped his shoulders and trailed my fingers down the length of his wing. A low sound rumbled in the back of his throat.

"Please," I panted. Our lips were close. Our breaths tangled. "I want you. Only you."

Exekiel groaned and continued to use his iron cock to grind me into the mattress. I widened my legs and met each one of his downward strokes—wished there were less clothes between us.

"Please."

He grunted and ran his tongue between my lips. I tried to catch it but it was fleeting.

"Please."

"No," he growled as he pressed into me. "I want you high on nothing but me; completely lucid when I fuck you."

He thrust his hips harder and I cried out. Damn these clothes. Unhooking my legs, I reached for him, but Exekiel was gone. Faster than I could blink, he'd moved to the door.

"Sweet dreams, little bud," he purred, then disappeared into the night.

My reflection scowled at me as the nymphs fitted me into a cream spaghetti-strap dress, for dance lessons. The second ball of the season was approaching and how well we danced would affect our rank. However, I didn't give a shit about dancing. All I wanted, was to throttle Exekiel. Partly for leaving me unsatisfied and partly because he was the only one, I wanted to satisfy me.

I'd almost run after him when he left last night but somehow found the will—the pride—to resist. I hated that he had this effect on me.

Soon he'll be gone. His barrier with him. No matter what I felt for the Shadow Saint, last night was all we could ever have. He wouldn't rest until he'd destroyed me and all those in the Outer Isles. And for that, I needed to destroy him first. My heart twisted but I squashed it down. Vladimir and Gwendoline had made it clear that seducing me was Exekiel's plan...that nothing he did or said, was real.

Now, I cursed the Faerie-wine. Yes, I'd wanted him and didn't regret a second of what I'd done but without the wine, I would've been stronger; would've denied myself what I really wanted.

"Thinking about the Protector?" Eudora smirked, knowingly.

His scent was on everything.

My scowl deepened. "I'm thinking about his barrier."

About the damage it caused and would continue to cause until I tore it down.

"I still can't understand how those werewolves got through." Eudora shook her head. "The Protector's questioning them but—"

"Questioning?" Cyrus snorted. "Is that what we're calling torture?"

I straightened. "Are there still werewolves here?"

Being tortured for an attack Loch instigated so he could get to me?

"Most were killed in the ambush, but those who survived…" Eudora shrugged. "Don't worry. The Protector will make sure they don't escape."

I gaped at her. How could she support Exekiel when he was a monster who oppressed innocents for standing up for themselves?

"There are many things wrong with the Five Isles but the Protector isn't one of them." Her eyes met mine in the mirror as if she knew what I was thinking. "He has a good heart and everything he does is to keep these Isles safe from those whose anger makes them crave war."

My mouth opened and shut. She wasn't wrong about the Outer Isles' thirst for revenge, but she was missing the justification behind it.

She threw me a shrewd look. "There are two sides to every story, Varialla. Remember that."

The worst thing about dance lessons were that they required a partner. All mated pairs from the first whipping Trial were put together and Vivienne's smirk was smug as she danced with Exekiel. Not that I cared. Last night had been a mistake. Now, I was thinking clearly.

The instructor paired together the remaining contestants. I got stuck with a handsy shifter who seemed to hate and desire me.

Catching my eye, Lucinda blew a taunting kiss from where she twirled with a stunning female elf. I flipped her off. Lucinda hooted.

Eventually, pairs were switched to mates of the second round. I braced myself as Exekiel approached. His taste was still on my tongue. He pulled me to him and I fought the urge to shiver. *Stupid body.*

The music started up. I counted the steps in my head but Exekiel moved with a fierce grace that took my breath away. Soon, I lost count and gave myself over to him and the command of his body. The call of the song.

His eyes glimmered. "Sleep well?"

"Never better."

I didn't mention that I'd had to take care of myself three times at the thought of him.

He chuckled as if he knew and pulled me closer—his hand pressed into the small of my back.

"Get all the sleep you can, little bud." His fingers trailed down my spine. "Soon this cock you crave will keep you up all night."

My breath hitched. Exekiel twirled me away then drew me back to his chest. His alluring scent surrounded me.

"I crave nothing from you."

Except the destruction of his barrier and an end to this infuriating attraction.

Exekiel chuckled then leaned in. His lips brushed my ear. "One thing, I don't understand about last night, is what you were doing so far from residence."

He pulled back to meet my stare which I kept blank.

"I was looking for the witch's party but got lost."

His eyes narrowed. "They were on the other side of the grounds."

"Like I said," I shrugged. "I got lost."

We continued to move to the music but the energy had shifted. Exekiel knew I was lying but I didn't care. Let him wonder and worry about what the sirens had planned. The shield on my mind had been strengthened and only what we wanted him to see could slip through.

"I hear you two had quite the evening."

We spun to find Goather behind us; camera-orbs at his back. Others drifted above the ballroom.

I flushed. I'd forgotten about the cameras when I'd gotten on my knees for Exekiel. I'd forgotten about everything. What would Adir think once he knew?

Something in Goather's expression darkened as if he sensed my train of thought.

"I must say, temptress, the last place I expected to see you was at a Fae party."

I half-smiled. "We all need to blow off steam sometimes."

"You definitely blew something."

I rounded on Exekiel. Did he seriously just say that? Laughter and challenge danced in his eyes. This was the Game—our chance to control the narrative. I could either be embarrassed giving them ammunition, or I could embrace it.

Choosing the latter, I rolled my eyes.

Goather cackled—only now I knew it was fake. "Indeed, she did," he purred then moved on.

I wasn't surprised to find the shell Loch had given me vibrating when I returned to my rooms.

His message was abrupt:

"Lagoon. Now." Fury rippled from each word.

I'd failed my first mission. Instead of meeting Danimous, our inside connection to Adir, I'd flung myself at Exekiel; our greatest threat. Now everything was at risk. My life and the lives of thousands. I was playing right into the Council's hands. Everyone knew that in war one should exploit their enemy's weakness and Exekiel was mine.

My pulse hammered in my throat as I rushed to Gargoyle's Lagoon. I wasn't used to having a chance to explain myself. Usually, people just left. Now, I had no idea what I'd say.

Loch was waiting within the trees; his tail now legs. Cherise, the little girl who'd asked for her mother's health, was with him.

Reaching them, I frowned. Had he brought her here to make me feel guiltier?

He seemed to read the question in my eyes and sneered. "Cherise has a mission of her own."

The girl looked up—her eyes wide. "You're still on our side, aren't you?"

I sighed, hating that I'd let them down and so soon after promising I wouldn't. I was never much of an over-indulger, but Exekiel awakened something inside me—something that had to die.

"Of course. I think every human just has to learn not to drink Faerie-wine."

A muscle ticked in Loch's jaw. "You're not human."

My old emotional shield slipped into place and I glared at him. Anger was always the best barrier. Sadness invited questions. Joy invited company. But anger kept people away.

Perhaps sensing the rising tension, Cherise dipped her head and took off.

"Danimous waited all night," Loch snapped.

My hands balled into fists. I didn't like being scolded. Not by social services and especially not by him. I made my own choices even if they weren't the wisest. Not having a family meant I didn't have to answer to anybody and I wasn't about to start. Not even if the sirens had started to feel like family—those memories and emotions imprinted on my skin.

"I get it. I screwed up."

Last night, Adir had sent Danimous to check on the proceedings of the ball. It'd been the perfect opportunity for me to slip him a note that invited the Primary to a private dinner. Instead, I'd had my mouth full of the Protector.

"But what now?"

I forced a shrug, as if guilt and regret weren't weighing on me. Adir was our only way into the Royal Court and it was unlikely he'd invite me anywhere now.

"What if we forget about the note and Danimous says it was a verbal invite?"

"No," Loch snarled. It was clear he still wanted to fight; his eyes like ice chips. "Adir could look into Danimous' mind and discover that wasn't true. We can't give him a reason to question anything." He spat, "Now that you've so publicly shown your affection for the Bravinore, it'll be next to impossible to convince the Primary that you're interested."

Affection...I didn't like that word. It tiptoed too close to the truth. Made me acknowledge that what I felt for Exekiel was staggering. Something I wasn't ready to name.

I stood taller. "We'll figure it out."

Loch looked me up and down. I tried not to squirm. I wasn't used to being relied on. To meeting people's expectations.

Doubt shadowed his eyes.

"I can do this."

Not only to save my life but because the Royal Court had to be stopped. They controlled everything. Who was blessed by the Conduit, my people's starvation, my mother's captivity. Rage burned in my chest and I didn't know if I was angrier at myself or the situation.

Either way, I would make it right.

Loch pursed his lips. "We'll discuss it over training. We have some time before Cherise returns." He headed for the lagoon. "Let's go."

"Now?"

He rounded on me. "Is there somewhere else you need to be?"

I hesitated. I'd told Max and Lucinda I'd meet them for lunch. If I kept blowing them off, they'd start asking questions. But Loch was on the edge. I could only push him so far.

Finally, I nodded. "Let's go."

29

THE BINDING CEREMONY

Training was brutal. Loch seemed to be using it as a form of punishment and the added resistance of the water made every move more difficult. I groaned; my limbs aching.

"Widen your stance," Loch barked, smacking the backs of my thighs. "Lift your chin. Lower your elbows."

Command after snarled command.

Eventually Colette and a male siren swam towards us. The male turned to Loch and I used the opportunity to pounce on my drink that had been enchanted to keep out seawater.

"Hooking up with the Protector and ignoring the mission," Colette swam over. "Ballsy move."

I sighed. "Are you going to lecture me too?"

"On the contrary." Colette scoffed. "I won't pretend I wasn't pissed but…I get it. The Protector is sex-on-legs. Enemy or not, I'd get on my knees for him any day."

Something twisted in my chest. A possessiveness that I hammered down. Exekiel wasn't mine.

"Besides, we've all botched a mission or two. Loch's just jealous that you give the Shadow Saint more attention than him." She leaned in. "From the day his egg hatched, Loch's been told that you're his and he's yours."

I snickered. "Possessive much?"

Collette shrugged. "You can't blame him. A vow was sworn at the Binding Ceremony almost two centuries ago and it only strengthens with time."

"What?"

"The Binding Ceremony; it's a ritual that creates a connection between two unmated souls—a knowing that they're Sworn. It makes the union more…effective."

I shook my head. "No. Go back to the century's thing? I'm twenty-five."

"Technically, you're one hundred and ninety-two but who's counting?"

The world stopped spinning.

"Excuse me?"

"When the Royal Court discovered you existed— born of the Blessed and the disgraced—they hunted you. However, your egg masked your scent, so, your mother delayed your hatching.

"It was only after she was captured that we realized we needed her magic to free you. So, we had to wait for the enchantment to wear off. It took one hundred and sixty-three years."

My mind reeled. *One hundred and sixty-three years? I was alive but not?*

"During that time, Loch was the one who cared for you and when you finally hatched, he continued to care for you, for four years." Colette grimaced. "We age slower here which is why you were still a baby when we hid you in the human realm."

My breath came out in a rush. Bubbles burst around me. I had so many questions, and questions within questions.

Loch bellowed, "Get up. Now."

With a reluctant snarl, I returned to the training ring. I'd find out more about this bond later.

As soon as I escaped Loch's training, I settled into the familiar comfort of being with the sirens. Ballroom dance practice was all I'd had scheduled for the day and I was in no rush to return to the surface. Instead, I savored the sirens' tales of my mother who they called, the Siren Savage. I learnt more about my time with them as a baby; sifted through the memories that darted across my mind. I'd been happy there once, and I'd be happy again.

Home—the word rang inside me. A place I'd wanted all my life but started to think I'd never have. It was here.

Somehow, through goading and laughter, I ended up teaching everyone how to twerk.

"You're a natural," I told Cherise as her tail whipped.

Her cheeks flushed; her smile wide enough to melt my heart. She reminded me of the one thing I'd liked about growing up in a group home—being a big sister to the younger children.

I was in the middle of teaching her, Beyoncé's *Single Ladies* routine when Loch came over to us.

"Come with me."

Wondering if I was about to get another bollocking, I followed him out of the glass hall and down a seaweed-covered passageway. As he swam, I couldn't help admiring his sculpted form. The ripple of his muscles. I drew in a breath. Was I really magically engineered to be attracted to Loch?

"Where are we going?"

"The transformation chamber. The sooner we encourage your shift into siren, the sooner your magic will blossom."

Blossom. The word, like most things, reminded me of Exekiel. He called me, little bud, because he said I hadn't opened—blossomed—yet.

We stopped outside a steel door. Loch turned its wheel and the gears cranked open.

"I'll meet you inside."

I nodded and entered a box-of-a-room. Water rushed in behind me before the door sealed shut and I was no longer submerged. I shivered and instantly missed the waters warmth.

Another door lay ahead. It beeped then slid open. Beyond was a large, and thankfully, heated chamber. The walls and floor were made from white coral. A small island was in the center, surrounded by seawater.

Loch emerged from beneath. His hair, dripping wet. "Come here."

He gestured and I took the bridge that led to the island.

His gaze followed me. "Take off your dress."

"What?"

"The best way to stimulate the transformation is increased blood flow and a transference of energy." Loch blew into his hands and rubbed them together. His palms glowed blue. "It works best skin-to-skin."

I snorted. "Of course, it does."

I peeled off my wet dress and sat down; letting my feet dangle in the water. Letting Loch's stare trail over my black lace underwear. A part of me basked in his attention.

Finally, he exhaled heavily and grasped my leg. I tensed as my skin hummed. His touch stimulated me in a way I didn't expect.

"Your scales are cold," I lied when he looked at me.

Loch grunted, "Get used to it."

He massaged my foot. His power pulsed into my aching limbs and I moaned.

"That feels good."

He only grunted again, then moved on to my other foot. Silence spread between us as Loch massaged my ankles, my calves, and caressed my thighs. His touch was slow and deliberate. Tingles rippled through my skin. I wasn't sure if it was the stirring of the transformation or this thing that he stirred in me.

When the silence and the heat between us, grew too much, I snapped, "Are you going to hate me forever?"

His jaw ticked. "I could never hate you. I've spent too long loving you."

I sucked in a breath. Stories over the last few hours, had made my memories of Loch resurface. In them, he looked the same as he did now—mid-to-late-thirties and rakish good looks. He'd cared for me, sung me lullabies and rocked me to sleep. He'd been more like a father than a mate.

His fingers grazed between my thighs as he moved up to my hips. My heart kicked. Fathers didn't do that. It was so swift I could've almost pretended it didn't happen.

Almost.

Our eyes met. His own burned with need.

"Do you feel it?" he rasped, as his enchanted hands stroked my waist and continued up my body. "The bind between us?"

I nodded, unable to speak. Loch took my breasts in his hands and kneaded them between his fingers. I squeaked. I should've told him to stop but the word wouldn't come. I was in the throes of conflicted desire. My thoughts ricocheted between Loch as my father and as my betrothed. It was sick and confusing.

His thumbs brushed my nipples and a current of desire crackled in my skin.

"It enhances our natural attraction," he growled.

His thumbs brushed the other way. My heart pounded.

"It guarantees our heirs." He grinned, and brought his lips to the nape of my neck—kissed the vein that throbbed there. "Ensures my seed will go deep when I fuck you."

His touch became primal. He roughly pinched my nipples. His breathing, shallow. My body sparked, awakened by the bind between us.

Loch's teeth nipped at my neck and I jerked into him.

He groaned. "I've waited for you for over a century."

His hands curved around my backside and he pressed me against him; into the hard ridge that bulged beneath his scales. He was half-*fish*. And yet, it didn't feel weird. As if, deep down I knew I was the same.

What was strange, was his desire. Loch had cared for me like a daughter. I'd been a baby and he a man when we'd met. He'd fed me and read me bedtime stories. Now, his finger trailed down and pushed between my ass cheeks. I panted. Struck by the hot sensation that pulsed in my core.

"Nearly two hundred fucking years waiting for you to grow; to return to me."

Loch's mouth fastened onto my neck and he sucked. My head tipped back and my fingers curled into his biceps as he continued to guide my ass and move me into him.

This is weird. My mind insisted.

Not because Loch had gills, a tail, and webbed fingers, but because he was the closest thing I had to a father and now he was climbing on top of me; driving his hips into mine. I fell back against the sand and moaned. A part of me wanted to stop this, but another part spurred me on.

I didn't know how long Loch could stay out of water in siren form, but as his lips travelled to the soft flesh of my breast, he dragged me into the sea. I braced my elbows on the sandbank to keep from going under as he thrust into me—blocked only by the thin lace of my panties.

Hot tendrils flared in my skin, leaving me tormented. For me, the memories of Loch were fresh, as if they'd happened only yesterday. The way he'd cradled me and kissed my forehead. When it came to father figures, he was the only one I had and I was currently grinding into his cock.

His hand reclaimed my breast and my body responded; arching into his familiar touch—but only familiar because he'd held me as a child.

"Wait," I panted.

His ice-blue eyes shot to mine and narrowed.

"It's too fast."

He bared his jagged teeth. It'd been a few weeks for me—a lifetime for him. But he let me uncoil my legs and climb back onto the island.

"I...need time."

He snarled, "Because of the Protector."

Yes.

"Because of everything. Trials, training, missions, ceremonial binds." I let out a breath. "It's a lot."

Loch's jaw clenched but he bowed his head; seeming to accept this. However, it was clear his patience wouldn't last much longer.

30

THE SIRENS SONG

The Fourth Trial came too fast.

The arena seats were packed. Rammed with roaring spectators and waving banners. Each was painted with a symbol for the cast they supported. A leafy tree with a braided trunk inside a circle of vines for the elves. A tribal eye with horns for the shifters. A crescent moon inside a star for the warlocks and witches. And crossing swords with a wing in place of their blades for the Fae.

"Varialla von Hastings," Vivienne called as she stepped up to the ring of powdered-chalk drawn in the sand. "I choose you."

I couldn't say I was surprised. If some girl had given the guy I liked a blowjob in the woods, I'd probably want to shoot her too. The Fourth Trial offered the perfect opportunity for Vivienne to do just that.

The audience drummed their feet on the ground and the contestants on the edge of the chalk-ring made 'ooh'-ing sounds as I made my way to the center of the ring where three large golden hoops stood in succession. In order to win, we had to shoot an arrow through each hoop and strike an apple off of the head of a fellow contestant. We got to choose who that contestant was.

I'd chosen Lucinda. My aim had been off and the witch had had to duck to avoid being impaled. But I'd, at least, shot the arrow through the hoops, which was more than I could say for a few of the other contestants.

Camera-orbs swooped closer and everyone cheered as I balanced the apple on my head and stood behind the third and smallest hoop. Their bloodlust was thick in the air.

Gossip had circulated about what I'd done to Exekiel at the party and the death stares and hate threats on Enchant-a-Gram had only intensified. The new trending hashtags were #StitchTheLips and #NoSongNoSuck

At the thought of Exekiel, I couldn't help scanning the crowd for him. He hadn't been around in a while. There were rumors that something beyond the barrier was keeping him occupied but no one revealed what. As Protector of the Realm, however, he'd be allowed to complete the Trial at another time.

"Vivienne versus Varialla," Goather boomed once we were in position. "A standoff the realm has been waiting for."

Vivienne sneered. This could go either way. So far, three contestants had ended up in the infirmary and two had narrowly avoided being blinded. Something told me that Vivienne wouldn't miss but whether she would aim for the apple or my head, remained to be seen.

As if she'd been told to create suspense, the white-winged Fae stared me down as orbs circled us.

"How's your knees, whore?" she finally snarled.

Those gathered snickered into their hands.

I smirked. "They're bruised. Though not as badly as my throat."

The stunned silence was broken by Lucinda's bawdy cackle and others who hooted in approval.

Vivienne's eyes darkened; her cheeks ruddy.

"Bitch!" She nocked her arrow and took aim. "Give me a reason why I shouldn't end you, right now."

I stood taller. An outright attack was prohibited in the Games but Vivienne could easily make this look like an accident.

"I still don't understand why you're here. Your very existence is a threat and yet the Court and Council keep you alive like they're afraid of what will happen if they don't." She scoffed. "They tell us that you're beneficial; a way to bait the enemy—more creatures like you."

"Vivienne," Goather warned.

"But who wants more?" she cried. The arrow didn't so much as tremble in her grip. "In fact, if you're watching, slayers, listen closely." She turned to a nearby orb. "If any of you try to infest these shores, we'll exterminate you, one by one." Vivienne swiveled to me and drew back the bow. "Starting with you."

She let the arrow fly. It shot through the hoops and straight for my heart. The audience gasped, in the same second, I lunged aside. My elbow smacked the packed earth as I hit the ground. Another arrow came. This one spiraled for my head. I rolled; sand scratching my skin. More arrows rained.

Bounding to my feet, I dodged one only to jump into the path of another. It found its mark. The arrowhead sliced my neck as a song burst from my lips. Three lilting words that I didn't understand with my ears but knew with my heart. The arrow halted its lethal blow.

Energy crackled around the chalk-ring and I locked eyes with the one who'd attacked me. Not Vivienne but Lola. The elven bitch who'd tried to kill me all those months ago.

Rage ripped through my chest. The song I'd sung in defense seconds ago, turned to something cruel. The notes sharpened; the words said in a bite. Quicker than I could blink, the arrow spun away from me and shot through Lola's skull. Blood sprayed as the elf fell. Her body twitching.

I was stunned but not horrified as the last of my song faded with her life.

Centaurs slammed into me and I was tackled to the ground. Once my arms were secured at my back, they marched me towards the Gaming Council to decide my fate. I tried to make eye-contact with them; figure out if any were on my side—as angry as the others at how badly the outlanders were treated—but they gave nothing away.

Soon, I sat on a cold metal chair in the Council's circular chamber as they discussed my future. Apparently, they had grounds to disqualify and detain me in Blacktomb Bay, but surprisingly, the audience had sent in arguments against it. They insisted that what I'd done was in self-defense; that Lola had been the one to violate the rules.

"She really is a fan-favorite," Vladimir spat and threw me a dark look.

I sneered around the gag they'd pressed into my mouth. Despite my hands being shackled, he faltered. My magic danced at the sight.

Come closer, sweet boy. It sang. *And your worries, you'll miss. Come closer, sweet boy; find salvation in my kiss.*

The lyrics and melody surged inside me; filled me with a savage hunger. Was this the song the sirens sang when they lured sailors to their deaths?

Something had shifted in me since using this siren song. I felt indestructible; whole in a way that I hadn't since they'd stolen my childhood and hunted me into exile. All so they could keep the power of the Conduit to themselves. For that, they butchered families, condemned them to lives of poverty, starvation and plague, and built enchanted barriers.

"What's there to think about?" the red-headed Fae, Gwendoline, screeched. "We should lock her up and throw away the fucking key."

"That would only fuel the rumors," Alexov grumbled and stroked his greying stubble. "Vivienne isn't the only one who thinks we keep Varialla alive out of fear. That we believe our shores are unsafe." He clenched his fist. "We must deny all claims to this; show them that we fear nothing."

But fear me, they did. Fear me, they should. For so long, I'd been asleep; locked away and lost because of them. Now, I'd been found. I belonged with those they called the enemy and nailed to stone. With the mother they tortured and imprisoned.

The next time Vladimir looked my way, I winked.

31

THE ETERNAL CELLS

Fists rained down like an avalanche. One staggering blow after another. I could barely catch my breath before another strike came; knocking the air from my lungs, bruising my gut.

I screamed around the gag shoved into my mouth.

This was justice? Being imprisoned for a week in the Eternal Cells where everyone, including the guards, despised me? The Council pretended it was mercy to pacify the #FreeVarialla supporters but there was nothing merciful in this.

My brain rattled in my skull as I hit the cold concrete. The chains around my wrists clanked. A guards booted foot struck me in the side. Sour chunks rose in my throat.

"No Protector to save you this time, savage," a winged-guard spat.

The other chuckled darkly and his beefy hand wrapped around my neck. He lifted me; my toes barely skimming the ground. I tried to kick the bastard but my body screamed in agony.

"No cameras without clearance or useless fans who think you deserve compassion." His grip tightened and I choked around the gag for air.

"We're going to have fun with you this week, Shifter-Slayer," growled the first guard with a sinister glint in his eye. "Some real fun, indeed."

He was Fae, but if wingspan was anything to go by, he didn't hold as much power as Exekiel or the other Fae-contestants in the Games.

I twisted; biting back a muffled cry as I tried to break free. Anger burned through me.

The man squeezed tighter. My vision spotted and my chest seized. Forget the week, he was going to kill me right now.

I reached for my magic but it was suppressed within the prison walls. A flutter that promptly flickered out.

Air evaded me as he brought his lips to my ear and hissed, "My wife...my son..." He shook with rage. "They were shifters."

Agony ruptured through my entire being as the guard slammed my head against the wall.

Stars burst across my eyes then darkness flooded in.

Most people's lives flashed before their eyes in moments like this but mine was a pitiful thing that took barely a second. So, for the next few days, I clung to the memories the mark on my side fed me. The four years I'd belonged—had a home.

The sweetest ones were of my sister. A girl who played peek-a-boo with me, cooked the best stew and kissed my cheeks. My sister had loved me but, in the four years we'd had together, I hadn't grown enough to tell her I'd loved her too but I had. I felt it.

My throat constricted; claimed by a familiar rush of grief. I mourned for a sister I never truly knew, a family I never had, a life I never lived, because it was stolen from me.

Each night, the guards returned to work out their aggression. I always fought back. Each blow fueled my rage. I'd get in a few kicks and scratches, but I was weak. I'd been surviving on nothing but scraps once a day. A show for the orb stationed to record my captivity. Although it never came close enough to see the bruises. It hovered mainly by the guards as they spoke of my remorse and how this time was doing me good.

Bullshit. Pretty words to please people like Eudora who remained willfully ignorant. Who accepted this pittance of peace and called it kindness.

However, I was glad the camera didn't come close or stay long. That meant it didn't see the endless hours I spent fiddling with the hook in the ground.

Maintenance of the prisoners wasn't the only thing that was neglected here. My chains were strong and freshly polished but the hook holding them in place was red with rust and the concrete around it cracked from previous prisoners desperate to break free.

On the fourth day, it came loose in my hand. When the guards arrived, I smiled. My strength was depleted but my rage was renewed. My gag hadn't been replaced since my last meal and I bared my teeth.

"Still a feral little shit," spat Kaiu; the guard who blamed me for his family's death. He nodded to the other two with him as he shirked off his armor. "Hold her."

I stepped back. The men advanced. I gripped the chains that swung from my wrists and lifted them. My arms shook with their weight.

Kaiu arched a brow. "The savage wants to play tonight."

He stalked closer; his stare murderous.

When he lunged, I drew on every shred of strength I had and lassoed my chains around his neck. His eyes widened as I pulled, slamming him down on the ground. His skull cracked against the concrete and blood spilled from somewhere I couldn't see. I didn't wait to check if he would rise.

I used the guards shock to race passed them and out into the torchlit corridor. I swayed on my feet but refused to fall. These assholes had taken too much from me already.

"Get her!"

Shifter and Fae bounded after me as I hurtled through the dark. Iron bars glinted in pale moonlight. Prisoners hunched behind them. The air was damp and reeked of feces and sweat.

Wildly, my eyes searched for a hint of glowing glass. I had no delusions of escape but I didn't need to. I just needed to find the camera stationed to broadcast my captivity. My sole connection to the outside.

I wouldn't—*couldn't*—take another night of being beaten to a bloody pulp whilst the Royal Court preached of mercy to avoid a civil war. The people were being lied to and it was time I opened their eyes. The Council had considered me a threat before but they had no idea how destructive I could be when I really put my mind to it.

A glass-like sphere bobbed around a corner. *The camera.*

"Oi!" I bellowed, waving my arms. The guards were gaining on me; their grunts fierce and breaths hot on my neck.

"Over here!"

My shouts must have alerted whoever controlled the orb. It swiveled in my direction.

Just as I hoped, the guards screeched to a halt and flung themselves into the shadows.

"It's all a lie!" I bellowed.

The camera swooped close enough to see my swollen eye and busted lip.

"They say they want peace but then they do this." I yanked the collar of my tatty robe down to reveal the ring of bruises around my neck. "And I am not the only one."

The glow of the orb died. My transmission had been cut but my message had gone through.

The guards pounced and hauled me back to my cell, cursing my name. I didn't fight them. I was untouchable now.

There were three things waiting for me when I was finally released and escorted to my rooms in Residence Manor: Maximus, Lucinda and a bath of seawater. My heart swelled with emotion and I fell into my friends' embrace. I wasn't entirely sure I could trust them but I didn't care. They were here when nobody else was. And that was a first.

Loch had confirmed that Lucinda did smuggle fragments of magic to the Outer Isles but said that her loyalty was with the giants and those she felt were unfairly punished for what the sirens had done. She'd never extended kindness to the sirens directly. However, as the witch and warlock eased me out of my blood-stained prison clothes, I could have wept with gratitude.

Lucinda took in the mess of bruises, welts and gashes along my body and made a sickened sound in the back of her throat. "Bastards."

I croaked, "Agreed."

With Maximus's help, they slipped me into the ocean bath.

"Seawater helps heal…your kind." Lucinda met my gaze.

We shared a silent understanding that I knew what I was, even if neither of us would voice it.

Whilst I soaked, Maximus told me about attacks taking place beyond the Eternal City—the Outer Isles growing brave or more desperate. Not only that, but my onscreen outburst had been viewed by enough people to cause riots between those who thought me being in the Games would lead to change, and those who feared what change would bring.

Lucinda swore. She just wanted peace. But I knew peace, like a rainbow after a storm, would only come after the war.

The last thing I wanted was to go to a ball but it was ironically what I needed. I'd been out of the Games for a week and my rank had plummeted. If I didn't change it before the next Trial, I'd end up in the Blood Battles.

I wasn't sure how people would respond to me since my onscreen outburst but Goather kept gushing about ratings gold. I could tell from his expression that I'd done my people proud. Not only had I protected myself, but I'd turned the Court's attention to the chaos within their own borders and away from the Outer Isles.

Eudora stepped back and I studied my reflection in the mirror. My hair was pulled up into a chignon and I wore a blue sheer dress that plunged at my bustline and slitted up past my thigh. It shimmered silvery glitter when it caught the light as if I was draped in a shard of star-flecked night. The straps were braided and silver chains tied around my waist.

I thanked the girls then headed out and hauled myself into a Pegasus-drawn-chariot. Thankfully, the worst of my injuries were almost healed after the seawater bath and salves Maximus had applied, but it still hurt to hold onto the handrail as I was whisked away to Infinity Hall.

Celebrations were in full swing by the time we arrived. Noblemen and women flocked around us, eager to get a glimpse of the players they'd only seen on orb-vision. They watched me closest. Some with awe or fear; others with blatant disgust.

Then I felt him. An electric current that pulsed at my back. Slowly, I turned and found Exekiel towering over me. He was sheathed in fitted black breeches with a white buttonless shirt tucked in at the waist. It hung open at his chest and gave him the look of a pirate. On his feet, he wore hefty black boots.

My stomach tightened. It'd been a fortnight since I'd seen him but it felt like *years*. I fought the urge to throw my arms around his neck. How could I miss him and despise him at the same time?

His sun-bronzed skin was darker, making his pink eyes more luminous. His black hair was disheveled and a light layer of stubble shadowed his chin. Every eye was on him but his gaze held mine. A vice that wrapped around my soul.

"Little bud," he murmured.

My heart skipped. Despite everything, I still wanted him. Even though I knew he was the poisoned apple; a serpent's kiss. And I couldn't forget the memory revealed to me in the prison...

He eyed my throat as if he could still see the ring of bruises.

"Who hurt you?" he snarled with a ferocity that made my heart race. Made me want to run to him and be wrapped up in his arms. It was where I felt happiest...safest. But his embrace was the most dangerous place I could be. Because it made me forget myself. Forget the monster he was and the things he'd done.

"Varialla..." His voice was low and edged with lethal calm.

When I said nothing; his fingers brushed mine. My entire arm tingled.

"Who?"

"It doesn't matter." I took a step back.

I couldn't do this; couldn't be around him. A week of beatings made a girl fragile and I needed to keep a clear head.

Exekiel bared his teeth; cloaked in an aura of cold fury.

"Shadow Saint," Goather called as he approached. "How are things beyond the barrier?"

With that, Exekiel was swarmed and I silently slipped away.

32

SLEEPING WITH THE ENEMY

Adir beelined towards me. There was determination in his stride and a false smile on his lips. The realm was watching; waiting for him to reveal his prejudice. To confess that the barrier wasn't for the benefit of the people but for the Royal Court. That the Outer Isles were suffering and he knew it.

"Glad to see you in one piece, Varialla," he bowed. "You're looking lovely, as always."

I matched his tight-lipped smile and curtseyed. I still needed him on my side; my way into the Court. A way to find out what they knew about the sirens and what they had planned for us.

"You're too kind, Primary."

"I must say I was horrified to see the injustice you faced in the Eternal cells."

I arched a brow but said nothing. Everything in politics was a game and it was his move. My stunt had highlighted serious issues with the regime. Now the question on everyone's mind was, what was he going to do about it?

We meandered through the crowd and he made sure we were captured on the cameras. His hand rested on the small of my back, but it was rigid; more controlling than kind.

"Believe it or not," he said through his smile, "I don't want bloodshed any more than you do." His tone said otherwise. "The Conduit chose you and I respect that."

Because he had no choice. To go against the Fates could lead to greater chaos.

"Unfortunately, not everyone feels the same." I walked faster, forcing him to lower his hand from my spine. "Certain casts of people are being mistreated under your reign and riots are raging." I tried not to sound smug. "The people are scared, Primary." I folded my arms around myself; playing my part. "*I'm* scared."

We stopped walking and I lowered my gaze. I could practically hear his need to dominate, rising. If I played my cards right, he'd see me as a damsel in distress right up until the day, I demanded his head. He would invite me into the heart of the Court and I'd rip it out. And whilst the Courts attention was on me; my people were free to move their pieces into place.

"Perhaps, we can come to some sort of…arrangement."

He trailed his finger down my spine and over my ass.

Disguising my disgust, I looked up at him with hopeful eyes. "What kind of arrangement?"

His grin was wolfish. He thought he had me right where he wanted me.

"My status brings power, Varialla." He took my hands in his, turning me to face him. "A certain level of protection that only I can offer."

He drew me closer. I braced my hands on his chest as his own slid down my arms and over to my waist.

"Wouldn't you like to be protected?" He moved in, soaking me in his scent of sweet liqueur. "Associating with me could lead to others seeing certain casts in a more favorable light." He rocked us to the music. "It could save your life and the lives of millions. Wouldn't you like that?"

I whispered, "Yes." Pushing childlike longing into that breathless gasp.

Adir stroked a hand down my cheek. "Then let us use each other."

I swallowed. "In what way?"

Orbs panned around us, broadcasting every sultry graze.

"Let me use your body for my pleasure and I will give you the perks of my title."

Sick bastard.

I forced a smile. "Okay."

"But," he waggled a finger at me. "If we do this, you're mine. No more Shadow Saint. No more rendezvous in the woods. I won't be made a fool of. Do you understand?"

I wrestled my instinct to lash out.

"Yes."

The Primary grinned and pulled me against him.

"Then we have a deal, my pet."

We danced for longer than I wanted. Adir's touches grew hungry. Thankfully, court etiquette prevented him from doing anything *too* risqué but he was definitely pushing the boundaries. His breath on my neck. His hands on the slope of my ass and cradled beneath my breasts.

Eventually, I excused myself and headed for the restroom. I needed to wipe his stink off my skin.

A figure cut me off in the corridor. I teetered back and peered up into a pair of punishing pink eyes.

"I've just returned from the cells." Exekiel's fists were clenched; his knuckles bloody. "Had a little talk with your guards."

My heart stuttered. He'd left the ball? Confronted—*tortured*—the men who'd hurt me?

"Kaiu is dead. Apparently, you're responsible."

"What?" I snorted and sauntered past; like I hadn't yanked the sadistic guard down with my chains.

Exekiel growled, "Blades up."

I spun as a dagger flew towards me. Without thinking, I caught the blade between my fingers, mere inches from my face.

"What the fuck?"

Exekiel prowled closer; his gaze sharp. "The guards said you showed impressive skill."

I flung the weapon on the ground. "You're insane."

Exekiel swung his fist at my face. Stunned, I blocked his attack. His grin sharpened. I was only proving his point.

"Who are you working with?"

"Get lost," I snapped but he kept swinging and I kept blocking.

I considered letting him hit me to prove him wrong. But every time he came close; self-preservation kicked in and I countered his blows.

Exekiel dropped low; attempting to kick my legs from under me.

I saw it coming and leapt into a spinning kick. There was no hiding my training now. I almost struck the side of his head but he grabbed my ankle and I went down, hard.

He pounced; crushing me beneath him. My wrists gripped in his hands.

"Do you really think you can win against us?" His breath beat across my lips. "Against me?"

I bucked, trying to throw him off. He pressed closer. His scent was overpowering. Despite all logic, my body tightened with need.

"Get off me!"

I headbutted the bastard. Exekiel blinked; surprised, and I flipped over; rolling him underneath me. Something sharp and cold pressed into my side. His dagger.

"You're going to get yourself killed."

I snatched my own blade from my garter and pressed it to his throat. The air crackled between us with something heady and toxic.

"You'll kill me either way."

We glared at each other; breathless. Hearts pounding. Blood thrumming.

Exekiel growled and his lips found mine. I froze, but within seconds, drowned in his kiss. It was intoxicating; maddening—addictive.

He moved his hips and I responded. God, what was I doing? I tried to pull back but he curved his hands over my ass and rocked me into his hardening cock. I whimpered.

"Fates, I want you," Exekiel breathed when our lips parted, "before the Kingdom crashes and you force my hand."

My laugh was hoarse as I grinded into him. "Force it in what way, exactly?"

Exekiel wrapped his hand around my throat and stole another kiss. It was rough and demanding. My heart slammed into my chest.

"Before you force me to kill you."

"What?"

Exekiel flipped us over; bearing down on me—forcing me to feel the full pressure of him. I moaned then pressed my lips together. Fuck. Any minute now, someone could hear us—*see* us.

Adir had just explicitly told me to stay away from him.

"Tell me you haven't thought about killing me," he whispered as he unhooked the clasps of my dress and licked my cleavage.

I panted, "I haven't."

Exekiel grinned. "Liar."

His hand pushed inside my dress and palmed my breast. I arched into him. My core hot and dripping.

Camera-orbs drifted overhead. A jolt ran through me. We *had* to stop. But gods, I couldn't. With every press of Exekiel's rigid length between my thighs; with every graze of his lips, I was consumed.

"I want to be inside you." His fingers travelled lower and hitched up my dress. "I want you stretched over my cock."

He pushed his hand between my legs. My body shook.

"W-we c-can't," I stammered, trying to cling to my sanity.

Exekiel kissed me again—drawing the air from my lungs and the fight from my body. I melted into him. He stroked me harder.

"I wasn't asking."

In one fluid motion, he yanked me up and pulled me into an alcove. Fragrant water trickled down the dimly-lit wall. The stone worn and rough. He pressed me against it. Icy water bit into my too hot flesh. Then he buried his face in the nape of my neck and sucked. I trembled.

I couldn't do this. Not again. But my body ignored my mind. It craved Exekiel and he craved me. His hands were claiming as he peeled down my dress and licked my nipple.

Struck, I gripped his shoulders. My breaths ragged. My cells on fire. Every touch was a preview of the passion he promised—unbridled, unburdened and brutal. I wanted all of it. I wanted him.

Push him away; my mind screamed but I pulled him closer. My fingers fumbled with the ties of his breeches as his own fisted my panties and tore them off.

I squeaked. "I liked those."

He chuckled. 'Then let this be a lesson not to wear underwear around me.'

His teeth captured the lobe of my ear. White hot ecstasy shot down to my toes.

Exekiel was ravenous and he hungered only for me. He lifted me up and I coiled my legs around him—toed off his trousers. When they fell below his ass; his cock surged free and prodded my aching entry.

I didn't know which one of us moaned the loudest.

Fuck, this had to stop. One night with him and I might spill our secrets. Might betray all those in the Outer Isles—my *family*. The only ones to ever love me; want me. For an orphaned girl with no home, there was nothing more valuable. But the way Exekiel moved his hips had every argument flying from my head.

He grasped my waist, holding me steady as he positioned his cock. My heart flipped.

"Wait," I gasped, searching for an excuse to end this. "Someone might hear us."

"Moan quietly." Exekiel clamped his hand over my mouth, forcing my head back into the stone.

"You once asked me why I called you, little bud," he rasped as he nudged my wet entrance. My nerve-endings sparked. "I told you it was because you hadn't opened yet." He grinned, and widened me on his pulsing head. "What I didn't say, was that I was the one who would open you." His eyes flashed. "Open wide, little bud." His ass clenched and Exekiel drove his cock deep inside me.

I screamed into his hand—tasting the salt of his palm. *Holy shit!*

He was power and pleasure brought to life and both blasted through my body with each bruising thrust. There was nothing gentle in his motions. Teeth gritted, Exekiel plunged into my silken depths and shattered my soul.

"Fuck," he groaned. "You're unbelievable."

I clawed at his shoulders—brushed his wings.

He thickened and thrust harder, faster. My back arched as he slammed into the deepest reaches of my being. I moaned hotly.

Shit. His cock was made for fucking. His body made for mine. I'd never felt so full; so complete.

"That's it, little bud," he growled. "You like that?"

I nodded, unable to speak.

"Fuck, you take my cock so well."

I bucked and moaned deeply; clinging to his shoulders like a life raft in a storming sea. He was lightning and fire and sin. Everything deadly and delicious; captivating and catastrophic.

This was so wrong. I was supposed to be his executioner. Now, I was the predator fucking the prey.

He lowered his hand from my mouth and ran his tongue across my lips. "Say you're mine."

I didn't think before I breathed, "I'm yours."

Exekiel grinned but I cupped his face. Our eyes met. The realm held its breath.

"And you're mine."

His eyes flickered. "Always."

Exekiel fucked me like a beast, taking what he wanted and, at the same time, giving me everything I never knew I needed, and now, could never live without. I was his and he was mine. Every moment in my life had been leading up to this.

He bit down on my breast and I came undone. A puddle on the end of his willful strokes. Exekiel beat into me. His hips were a vicious slap against my own. I cried out—aching…falling…drowning.

33

MISGUIDED WRETCH

Someone said my name. Their voice drifting through the cracks of my orgasmic haze. Slowly, I reentered my body; rejoined the outside world. Exekiel groaned as he emptied the last of himself inside me; his still rigid cock twitching. Breathless, I rested my head on his shoulder. His wings splayed around us.

"Where did she go?" a familiar voice huffed but it took me a moment to realize it was Adir.

Icy dread coursed through me; dousing the fire Exekiel had ignited.

I moved to pull away but Exekiel rowed his hips. My body tightened and I bit my lip to keep from moaning.

"I'm sure she's here somewhere," Lucinda replied.

I tapped Exekiel's shoulder, signaling him to stop. He grinned as he withdrew to the tip, then plunged back in. I squeaked and shot the bastard a glare. We needed to stop but he seemed determined to go another round, and fuck, I wanted to. He did it again—one slow receding motion before driving back inside me.

Holy shit. My hands slipped on the slick wall as I tried to scramble away from the building pressure. I was still wracked with the aftershock of my last release but I was about to erupt again.

Exekiel cupped my backside, forcing me to move on his cock. I panted. Sweet, tortuous desire pulsed inside me.

Footsteps clopped towards the alcove. Exekiel's rhythm intensified. I moved with him. He was undeniable. Incredible.

Adir snarled, "Find her. Now."

I bit my upper lip as Exekiel unraveled me. Wet heat throbbed between my thighs. We had to stop.

"Fuck," a voice whispered.

My heart leapt and I turned my head to see Lucinda. Exekiel didn't slow. He continued to plough into me, sparking pleasure through my entire being.

Lucinda swiveled and said loudly, "Maybe she went to explore the gardens."

She stayed in front of the alcove; blocking us from sight.

Frantic, I uncoiled my legs and slipped to my feet. Exekiel looked like he might reach for me. I glared at him. Maybe this was his plan; to ruin any chance I had of getting close to Adir.

I wanted to put distance between us but the alcove was small. Even when I turned away, my back was pressed against him. His hardness dug into my spine.

"Poor, misguided wretch," Adir grumbled as he stormed past. His shadow briefly darkened the alcove.

"Doesn't she realize I'm her savior? As long as she keeps me well-fucked, I'll keep her safe."

He spoke as if he was doing me a favor—a kindness. I almost went out there and punched him in the face.

When the garden doors slammed shut, Lucinda spun back to face us; her arms folded. "Can't you two stay away from each other for five minutes?"

Exekiel's arms curled around my waist. "That's four minutes and fifty-nine seconds too long."

I shivered. The heat of his breath beat across the tip of my ear. My body responded to him as it always did and I wrenched away.

"I need to get back."

I rushed from the alcove but Lucinda grabbed my arm. "And how will you explain why you smell like sex—like him?"

She threw Exekiel a pointed glance. He grinned in a way that made me ache.

"Okay…Tell Adir I felt sick and left but to send word when he wants to meet."

Lucinda wrinkled her nose. "There are kinder ways to save your life than giving yourself to that male."

I hesitated. I couldn't confess that it was only a ruse. That I planned to string Adir along until I was welcomed into the Royal Court. A blade in the belly of the beast.

Exekiel murmured, "I'll come with you."

"No," I snapped, almost falling backwards in my rush to get away. "You've done enough."

I didn't know if it was the intensity of our bond but I had to get away from him. For the mission, for my sanity…for my heart.

Loch hit the seabed. The sirens cheered. I smirked down at him. Over the last few weeks, my skills had sharpened. My muscles harder and more pronounced. My stamina and strength increased beyond anyone's expectations.

Training was what had helped me beat Vivienne in the Seventh Trial. Hand-to-hand combat with an opponent of the audiences choosing. We'd both put up a hell of a fight but when the horn sounded the end of the Trial, only I'd been left standing.

Respect shone in Loch's eyes and I beamed like a little girl who'd made her father proud. A part of me still saw him that way. Even though the bind corrupted that. Made me attracted to the man who'd partly raised me and made him want me in ways a father shouldn't want a daughter.

But I couldn't focus on that right now. It'd been weeks since the ball and footage of Exekiel and I, making out on the floor before sneaking into that alcove was trending. I'd had one public dinner with Adir since then and kept waiting for him to bring it up; to end our tentative alliance, but he said nothing. His silence was more unnerving.

I couldn't shake the feeling that the Primary was up to something. That he was using me as more than a way to quell the unrest in his kingdom.

After training, I decided to stay for dinner. I usually refused. They didn't have much food to spare. But tonight, I didn't want to leave.

The meal was nothing like the feasts in the Five Isles. A meagre spread of sea grapes, kelp and aquatic insects.

"Just put it in your mouth," Loch drawled as I eyed a red worm on my plate. Apparently, the creatures were popular near the lagoon.

Colette cackled. "That's what he said."

Everyone but me laughed. I prodded the dead insect.

Cherise giggled. "They're delicious."

I wasn't convinced. I wanted to embrace their customs but *worms*?

"Some savage, you are," Loch goaded.

He scooped up the insect and held it to my lips. I squealed and wriggled, trying to get away but his strong arm wrapped around my waist; holding me in place.

"Say, "Ahh"", he cooed, the same way he had when I was a child.

I screeched.

Loch laughed. "Such a baby."

He swallowed the worm himself but didn't immediately release me. For a moment, our gazes held. My skin heated and I felt a pull in my chest.

Algeron, the elderly man who'd embraced me that first night and every night since, cleared his throat. I flushed and turned to the others seated at the stone table. They smiled at us; their eyes warm and hopeful. Believing they stared at their new leaders—A new day.

Loch let his hand rest on my leg as he returned to his meal.

"At least, try the larvae," Collette urged.

I snorted. "I'll stick to sea grapes."

I popped one in my mouth but almost choked when Loch's fingers slipped through the slit of my dress and grazed my thigh. My gut clenched.

Loch isn't my dad, I told myself. Though in every memory, he fit the bill for the father I'd always wanted.

Loch isn't my dad.

His fingers slid higher. I swallowed thickly; aroused yet equally disgusted. This was...twisted. On top of that, I couldn't stop thinking about Exekiel. I'd managed to avoid him the last few weeks. Outside of doing what was mandatory for the Games, I spent most of my time in the Coral Court. And Exekiel was kept busy with business beyond the barrier; attacks in the isles.

"What was he?" I blurted—trying to distract myself as Loch stroked my inner thigh. "My father."

No one had mentioned it and I assumed they didn't know but now, I needed this conversation, to remember that Loch wasn't him. To know who was and where he was now.

Algeron grimaced. "Your mother was quite secretive about him. All we know, is he was a shifter who vowed to rally his kind into accepting the sirens as their own but went back on his word."

Loch added, "Whoever he was, your mother loved him very much. It was his betrayal that ultimately started the Brutal War."

"What do you mean?"

Loch's thumb drew idle circles on my skin. "After he rejected her, your mother used her abilities on the most powerful shifters of all—the dragons."

I lurched; momentarily distracted from the pull of Loch's touch. "Dragons?"

Algeron nodded. "They were the ones in power who kept us out, so she compelled them to destroy themselves and any who tried to stop them from doing so."

"That's why they call her the Siren Savage," Cherise said in awe. "She was strong, powerful and wicked. Would do anything for her people."

I shook my head. No wonder sirens were feared.

"If they were the most powerful, how was my mother able to control them?" I couldn't imagine the strength it took to manipulate the minds of beasts.

"She used us," Loch said casually, as he pushed my thighs apart and lightly brushed my core. I tensed. "It was our power combined that ultimately wiped out the dragons."

"We were almost crowned the new rulers of Shifter Springs until the Shadow Saint stepped in," Collette snarled.

The air in the chamber shifted.

"Apparently we could conquer an army of dragons but were no match for the commander of the Fates."

I didn't know much about Exekiel's magic but knew it allowed him to speak to the Fates—the Gods of this realm—to wield their power as his own.

Loch palmed my sex. I almost shot out of my seat. I gripped his wrist, trying to stop him as he stroked me. But he knew a part of me wanted this—wanted the male I saw as my father to finger me beneath the table. Thus was the dysfunctional crux of the bind.

He was also doing it because he didn't want me thinking about Exekiel or his immense power. How the Protector called to me in a different way; one that wasn't manipulated by magic but designed by destiny. What Loch didn't know, was that I was always thinking about Exekiel.

He pressed the heel of his hand down and I gasped. My eyes darted around us. If anyone looked beneath the table, they'd see what he was doing to me. I dug my nails into the back of his hand. He chuckled lowly.

"Your Grace, I'd like to show you something before you leave," Cherise said.

"Yes." I almost fell off my seat as I scrambled to get away from Loch.

I was relieved when he didn't try to stop, or worse, follow us. But his cold blue eyes trailed me as Cherise and I left the dining hall.

34

SECRETS & SHELLS

Together, Cherise and I swam to the far reaches of the Coral Court. The press of water was exhilarating. Its strokes playful and imbued with power. When we finally broke the surface; I was invigorated. My mind and soul revived. I studied the cave we'd arrived in. Its water, a luminous blue and the walls, alight with glowing algae.

Awestruck, I swam to the bank and pulled myself up on the craggy stone. "What is this place?"

Cherise, who remained in the sea, smiled. "I found it when I was looking for a way into the Five Isles a few years ago, before Sir Loch finally gave me a mission."

It was a mission he didn't expect to succeed. However, Cherise had wanted to feel like she was doing something to help her mother and she was small enough to fit through the barrier with him. So, Loch had tasked her with exploring the moat around the Gaming Council to try and find a way in.

I took in the damp cave; the hum of transcendent power in the air. "It's…beautiful."

Cherise beamed. "I wanted to bring you here because it's special to me and so are you." Her eyes were bright. "You're the Princess I've been praying for and the sister I wish I had."

I swallowed around the knot in my throat. Tears rimmed my eyes. Cherise didn't know how much her words meant to me. How many nights I'd cried myself to sleep; wished I had a sister, a brother…a *friend*. But I never fit in in the human realm. It was like everyone could sense something other about me and it didn't take them long to run. Clearing my throat, I pulled her into a tight hug.

"I'm the sister you *do* have." I kissed the crown of her head. Cherise snuggled closer.

We stayed like this a while, then she murmured, "There's another reason I brought you here." She looked up; her eyes wary. "This place has a secret I think you should see."

She slid back beneath the water and beckoned for me to follow. Obeying, I hissed at the cold bite of the ocean, but my body soon warmed to it and I was, once again, overcome with that glorious thrill of savagery and seduction.

We swam further back into the cave where the walls were no longer lit but the water still glowed. Little luminescent fish skittered below. At last, Cherise slowed and climbed out of the sea; her peach tail draped over the rock. She ran her fingers across the rough stone wall.

"It looks like a face."

"What does?"

Cherise didn't reply as her hands continued to explore the stone. I silently watched, burning with curiosity.

Finally, she curled her fingers around the edge of a rock that, from a certain angle, did look like it had a face carved into it. When it came loose, Cherise reached inside and pulled out half of an eggshell that was almost the size of her head. The outside was black and scaled; each one scored with threads of scarlet and turquoise, and the smooth inside shimmered like liquid gold.

The thrum of power grew sharper in the cave. Cherise held the egg out to me and I couldn't say why I recoiled, as if touching it would somehow alter the world.

"What is it?"

She leaned in, almost like she feared the shadows would hear. "A dragon's egg."

The words rattled through me. "How?"

According to the others, my mother and her army had destroyed the dragons—or rather, had made the dragons destroy themselves and countless others. That was what led to the Brutal War, the construction of the barrier; the exile of the outer isles. So how was there a dragon's egg here, of all places?

Cherise inhaled. "You asked about your father."

I frowned.

"I think this egg might be yours."

I rocked back. Hilarity swept through me. "Mine?"

"Your mother, sister and Sir Loch, were the only ones who saw your egg. They said it was to keep you safe, in case a Fae ever got inside a sirens mind in search of you. We all assumed you were born in a fish egg like us but...what if you weren't?" Her gaze dropped back to the eggshell. "What if your father was a dragon shifter?"

Laughter and confusion bubbled up inside me. "As awesome as that would be, I'm pretty sure there would have been signs by now." Wings. Fire breath.

I'd often dreamt of being as free and wild as a dragon, but the chances of me actually transforming into one, were slim.

Cherise made a noncommittal sound. "My mother said the same. That surely if you were part-dragon, you'd somehow know. But..." She scowled. "Why else would this be hidden down here?"

I shook my head. "The ocean has a way of moving things with its tide. Maybe this got carried in."

Cherise's shoulders slumped. "Maybe."

Resting my hand on hers, I asked, "Do you wish the dragons still existed?"

Cherise tucked her tight curls behind her ear; the water reflected on her pale brown skin.

"I wish the Brutal War never happened, and it started because of their deaths." She swallowed. "People had equally loved and feared the dragon shifters. In human form, they were fiercely kind. As dragons; they were simply fierce. No one went against them and those who did, didn't get very far."

I cocked my head. "Until my mother."

At dinner, they'd made it sound like my mother's savagery had been a good thing—a way to defend her people and bring about a necessary change.

"The Siren Savage," Cherise said with the same awe as earlier. "The stories are incredible. And if she'd been successful, everything would be different. But now...on the days my mother hears about our plans to revolt, her condition gets worse. She doesn't want to live only to die a gory death in battle, and she doesn't want me to grow up in a world of destruction."

She looked up at me; her eyes brimmed with tears. "If you were a dragon, you'd be as powerful as the Protector himself. You'd be able to demand he tear down his barrier without bloodshed. Demand peace. You'd be a big enough threat that they'd have to listen to you."

I hated how much that idea appealed to me. How, after everything, I still wanted to save *him*...wanted to believe that Exekiel and I could somehow ride off into the sunset together. But it was the foolish dreams of a foolish girl who should have known by now, that dreams don't come true. Although finding the sirens— a possible home. That had once been a dream too.

I sighed and squeezed Cherise's hand. "You heard Loch tonight. He doesn't know anything about my father which must mean I was born in an ordinary fish egg." I paused. "There's something I never thought I'd say."

Cherise's lip trembled.

"But I promise you, Cherise, your mother will get better. The Outer Isles will be freed. Once again, blessed by the Conduit, and this war will be the last."

Back in the black dress I'd left in the shrubs on the shore of the lagoon, I darted through Creature's Copse towards Residence Manor. Most of the players had gone to their rooms, though a few lounged in the gardens and practiced their powers. They didn't seem to notice or care as I passed, but, just in case, I stayed in the shadows.

Thoughts of sirens, revolutions, assassinations and dragons swirled through my head.

When I neared my room, my steps faltered. The door was ajar. Was someone inside? My pulse pounded as I crept closer and felt the press of foreign magic; a dark crackle down my spine. I drew on my own gifts. The taste of sugared-honey sizzled on my tongue.

Loch had recently taught me how to push my power into my strikes, to enhance their force. I let it travel down my arm and morph around my clenched fists, then kicked the door open.

My stomach lurched. My bedroom had been ransacked. The dresser toppled, clothes scattered, pillows shredded, linen torn. The bed was halfway across the room; its canopy in tatters; one leg busted.

Sensing no immediate danger, I rushed further into the room. What happened here? Was it another messed-up threat? Or something deeper; more menacing? It sure as hell felt like it.

My eyes shot back to the bed and my blood ran cold. What if the intruders hadn't been searching for anything in particular…but they'd found something anyway? I ran to my bed and threw up the sheets; searched the pillowcases; shoved my hands beneath the mattress. It was gone. My connection to the Coral Court; evidence that I was working with them.

The shell was gone.

35

RUTHLESS RAKE

At the sound of my name, I swiveled; my heart racing. The shell was gone. Now, two burly centaurs stood in my doorway. They each wore brass breastplates, golden horseshoes and grim expressions.

Neither seemed surprised by the state of my room, which made me wonder if they'd caused it.

"The First Primary requests your company."

I gestured around my chamber. "Now's not a good time."

The larger centaur trotted forwards. "Now is the only time you have."

Goosebumps prickled along my flesh. What did that mean? Had Adir ordered this raid? Did he have the shell? And if so…what then?

Death was the punishment for treason and I had no intention of dying. I finally had something to live for. Family, friends; a home. A revolution.

Contestants murmured excitedly and whipped out their phones as I was marched passed. The fact that the centaurs didn't stop them, made it clear, the Court wanted this public. However, the camera-orbs that broadcasted beyond the barrier were nowhere in sight.

The centaurs led me outside, towards a black carriage drawn by two blue-winged Pegasus. A shifter; half-transformed into a bear—pulled open the door. Once I was shoved in, he followed and claimed the seat on the opposite side. Through the window, I spied the centaurs flank the carriage. The larger one barked a command and they were off. Their hooves thudded in time with the clack of the wheels.

My gaze landed on the window latch and the bolts the bear shifter had pulled across the door. Until then, I might have convinced myself that Adir had summoned me as part of our arrangement, but this was no romantic rendezvous.

For ages, we charged down cobbled streets, past towering trees and over rickety bridges.

"Where are we going?" I asked but was met by silence.

Eventually we came to a cliff. At the base, warm light shimmered like fireflies. A village. The carriage careened down the narrow path and the centaurs pulled back, chasing at the rear; as the Pegasus spread their wings for balance.

"We've left the Eternal City," I breathed, gaping at the world outside the walls of the Game.

The bear shifter grunted; his clawed fingers drumming on his muscled thigh.

"Why?"

Contestants were forbidden to leave the confines of the Games—to know anything of the outside. Why was I now allowed to leave and where were we going?

The shifter said nothing.

My power stirred. Thin filaments of pink that only I could see, slithered from between my lips and I directed them at him.

"Answer me."

His fist—now a bear's paw—shot out and knocked me back. I slammed into the door. My ears ringing.

"I work at Blacktomb Bay," he snarled; his voice as coarse as gravel. "I've been dealing with the likes of you and your corrupt gifts for longer than you could walk."

Eyes watering, I eased back into my seat.

"You're a pup compared to the savage I guard."

Savage…*The Siren Savage.*

Was this man my mother's warden? Had he delivered the punishment of thirty lashes for thirty months and doled out centuries of endless torture?

The carriage slowed; stealing my attention. My heart beat in my throat.

The shifter sneered before he unbolted the door, grabbed my wrist and yanked me outside. There, a great crowd was gathered. Some cheered. Others hissed.

I was pulled through the throng towards a wooden stage. On it, was what looked like a medieval torture device—the rack; used to stretch its victims and tear them limb from limb. It stood vertical with shackles dangling from each corner.

Terror struck and I heaved against the shifter— desperate to get free—but he only transformed more, and wrenched me forwards.

Hooded figures stood still beside the contraption, except one with great brown wings who paced like a caged beast. Though his face was shadowed, I knew, with every fiber of my being, that it was Adir.

His grin sharpened when I was shoved up the steps. Before I could speak, the cloaked figures descended. My arms and legs stretched wide as they wrestled me onto the rack.

"Get off!" I pushed my power into my words, but the men didn't yield.

I swung with my free arm, catching a man's hood only to reveal that his ears had been cleaved clean off. I gaped at each figure that moved around me and guessed they'd experienced the same treatment. Was this how they'd once defended themselves against the sirens?

The final manacle snapped shut with a clang that reverberated through my body. I set my sights on the audience. If I could coerce them to fight on my behalf, I could escape. Could find a way to the ocean—to my home.

As if he anticipated this, Adir sneered and held up a leather muzzle with bronze buckles. "Can't have the bitch yapping."

Feeling my chance slipping away, I yelled, "Help me." My limbs shook as I pulled against the restraints; tried to steady my nerves enough to command the audience. "Help me!"

"Stand down," Adir barked as he prowled towards me, "by order of Your Primary."

Still, drawn by my gift, one woman stepped forward. A sword punched through her gut. The people screeched and stumbled back—my connection to them severed. I'd learnt to use my abilities against powerful opponents but never on more than one at a time. Now, my head throbbed.

"Anyone who interferes will meet the same end," Adir roared.

Rage emanated from him. The pulse of his power in the earth. In that moment, I understood how he'd become Primary.

He fastened the muzzle over my mouth, buckling it behind my head. I gnashed my teeth; almost catching his finger but he was fast.

Finally, he stepped back. Dark delight was stark across his shadowed features.

"I believed we could work together. That you would learn the crimes of your people and want to atone for them. I believed you wanted mercy; protection." He trailed his hand down my body, travelling between my breasts. I stiffened. "I believed we had a deal. Then I found this."

From his robes, he withdrew the shell. But the triumph in his eyes said this was about more than that. This was because of what I'd done with Exekiel at the ball.

"Imagine my surprise when a voice inside told me to meet them at first light. They didn't say where but a simple tracking spell will help us retrace your steps."

Ice flooded my system. He'd intercepted a message and now my family were in danger. How long had he been plotting this? How long had I felt like I was in control but had lost it the second I left the ballroom?

"Imagine their surprise when instead of you, they find me and my entire army waiting."

I yanked against the shackles.

Adir laughed, raised the shell's freshly sharpened edge and slashed through my dress. The garment pooled to the ground and the crowd roared.

The bastard drank in my curves; the swell of my full-breasts inside my bra. "I told you I'd get you out of your clothes one day."

I snarled behind the muzzle and tugged against the restraints, but it was hopeless. There was no way out.

His fingers slid into my hair, almost lovingly, but then he pulled; wrenching out a fistful of strands. My gut lurched.

"For the tracking," he grinned, then turned back to the hollering crowd. "Let this show, that I tried to be merciful. To work as allies against the enemy but she has chosen to join them!" He gritted his teeth. "Now she will suffer the consequence."

He gripped the crank that bound my right wrist and pulled. I screamed as my arm was wrenched upwards and pain lanced through my shoulder.

"What a beautiful sound," he breathed. "Let's see how well you sing, siren."

My eyes shot to his. It was the first time he'd said aloud what I was. On top of that, he didn't explode. Did that mean he hadn't sworn the Blood Oath or that it was no longer valid since I knew the truth?

He looked to the cloaked figures. "Altogether now."

As one, they turned the cranks; stretching me—pulling me apart. Agony speared down my spine and bit into my bones.

My muffled cries ricocheted through the now silent square. Everything burned. It was torture beyond anything I'd ever known. The tugging and tearing of muscle, bone, and sinew.

A vicious pop sounded as my shoulder was ripped from the socket. I howled. Sour chunks filled my mouth but with the muzzle I had no choice but to swallow them.

Tears stung my eyes. Cold sweat drenched my skin that was feverish in the balmy night. I'd lost the support of the people. When I was an unfairly treated outlander, they'd been on my side. But now I was a conspirator, working with the enemy that had commanded dragons to their deaths. That would bring war to their doors.

"You're a detestable little creature," Adir snarled into my ear. His breath cold against my neck. "Your cast are an infestation on our Isles."

Another turn of the crank forced my back to arch. He hungrily watched the heave of my breasts; the ragged rhythm of my breathing.

"We create a fair system and your cast destroy it. For your own selfish gain, you slaughtered thousands." His body shook and he turned the crank with extra vigor. My head kicked back. A strangled scream torn from my throat only to slam into the muzzle. "We build a barrier and you seek to tear it down."

I groaned, claimed by another bout of nausea.

"How many lives will be enough?" Adir's rough fingers trailed my damp skin and dragged over my stomach. "Though, I suppose the lure of death is in your blood. In the very essence of your soul."

The cranks pulled again. I choked back a sob; fought the surge of tears that threatened to spill down my cheeks.

"Some say your kind thrive off it. That your song of death gives you a temporary high—a magical boost. But it doesn't last. Nothing born of evil ever lasts." He leaned so close; I scented his ale-soaked breath through the leather. "And neither will you."

My other shoulder popped. Piss trickled down my leg. I'd wet myself and the men cackled, cruelly.

"And now I've made you wet." Adir's laughter was cold. "Told you, I was a man of my word."

36

BURN WITH ME

I slipped in and out of consciousness as the hours ticked by. The crowd was long gone. My wrists were sticky with blood. The flesh rubbed raw from where I'd tried to pull free. My lips were dry and cracked where the muzzle chafed, and the piss that coated my legs did nothing to temper the evening cold.

Biting back a shiver, I struggled to focus. I had to get to the lagoon before dawn. Had to warn Loch and Cherise before they walked into a trap.

My gaze fell on the key Adir had intentionally dumped on the ground just out of reach. The tarnished silver glinted in the pale moonlight. It was his attempt to appease the Fates and, at the same time, taunt me with the possibility of escape, knowing I had no way of reaching it. He declared that if the Fates wanted me to survive this, then I would somehow reach the key. If not, my death was their blessing.

I gulped down a breath. Mentally prepared myself for what I had to do. Now or never. I heaved on the shackles. The steel cut into my skin but I kept going. Bit down on my bottom lip so hard, it bled. That smart of pain was nothing compared to the gut-wrenching snap of my thumb as my knuckle popped out of place.

Vomit rose in my throat and I ripped off the muzzle in time for the chunks to spill down my front. Tears, I couldn't control, rolled down my cheeks. Sweat and blood; bitter and metallic on my tongue. Not daring to stop, I dislocated the thumb on my other hand, unleashing an anguished cry.

My hands slid free and I collapsed; my knees giving out. I huddled there, fighting the lure of unconsciousness. Pain consumed every facet of my being. But the memory of Cherise's embrace; the promise I'd made the outcasts, forced me to drag myself up and slam against the rack. My eyes watered and the world spun as my shoulder was rammed back into place.

Time splintered. I lay there trembling for too long and not long enough. Finally, I mustered the courage to yank my thumbs back into their sockets. Everything hurt but I grabbed the key, made quick work of freeing my ankles, staggered to my feet and ran.

I'd taken note of the route we'd travelled and, if my memory was correct, the woods that loomed ahead were a part of Creature's Copse. That meant somewhere within that mass was Gargoyle's lagoon.

I hurtled towards it and tore through the trees; allowing twigs to tug at my hair and slash my skin. More times than I could count, I fell and retched or wept, but I hadn't come this far only to come this far.

Dawn light crept in and desperation spurred me on. Right now, Adir could be forcing Loch to his knees; slapping Cherise in irons…or worse.

At last, shouts filled the woodland. Guards roaring to one another.

"He went that way!"

"Find him!"

I screeched to a halt. It was Adir; the sound of his voice inflicted a jolt of fear and cold fury.

Nostrils flared, I followed the commotion. Then a girl screamed.

"Silence sea-rat!" There was the thump of a fist striking flesh.

My blood ran cold. Through the trees, I spied Cherise thrashing in a guard's grip but she no longer screamed. Her mouth now swollen and blooded. He'd hit her—a *child*. My power burned—not a sweet aftertaste but a fire in my throat.

A hand clamped over my mouth and I was wrenched backwards into a muscled chest.

"Be still," a voice whispered. Loch.

I gaped at him over my shoulder, willing him to let go. Using my eyes to tell him: *They have Cherise*. But Loch's dark expression suggested he knew.

"Go out there, and you give them a reason to slit your throat," he murmured.

Something smashed as Cherise, still fighting, was thrown onto the back of a chariot.

"The Conduit chose you, Varialla, and, though they may wish it, the Court cannot defy the Fates—the Conduit's master."

Loch lowered his hand as the chariot swept into the sky, pulled by a hulking black Pegasus. However,

countless guards remained behind in search of him—
the true prize.

He stepped back and I spun to face him. He was
bruised and bleeding but relatively whole. "They won't
risk the wrath of the Fates by killing you without cause.
But if you attack, they'll be within their holy rights to
offer you up to the gods."

Frustration tightened in my chest. Cherise had been
captured and taken who knew where to suffer who
knew what.

"We'll get her back," he snarled; his words echoing
what I'd already decided.

More soldiers bellowed; closer now.

"Don't let them find you," Loch hissed. 'Return to
your rooms and play the Game. Win it, so we can take
the crown and put an end to this—so we can drive the
shitheads into their graves." He brushed his bloodied
lips across mine and then was gone.

I was starting to think the Games were stripping away
my humanity. I never really cared for people—all they
did was leave—but I didn't think I'd ever become numb
to their suffering. That I'd watch with detachment as
one impaled another under the guise of glory. But after
all the death and pain I'd seen—*caused*—lately, the
Blood Battles didn't bother me like they once did.

I was just glad I wasn't in them. Grateful for a day
of mourning. No tests or Life Token challenges. Just a
day for the contestants to recover between Blood
Battles and Trials. And time for me to recover from my
ordeal on the rack. Eudora had summoned the best

medical aid the Residence had and ointments sent from Lucinda's source, had healed the worst of my wounds.

Now, I laid in bed; restless. Too tightly wound to sleep. My thoughts spinning and emotions undone. Front and center, was rage. I was angry at Adir, the Court, and myself. I needed to get out; to exercise my power and make sure that I was never in this position again. That the next time guards came for me, I'd be powerful enough to stop them. To save Cherise.

Sprinting to the garden's training grounds, I unleashed myself on the practice dummies. When physical exertion was no longer enough, I plunged into my magic. Manipulated its honeyed threads to wrap around every animal in the vicinity and drew in as many of them as I could.

The trees rustled as the creatures approached, eliciting a kernel of triumph. It would take more to control a group of people with ever-changing emotions, but it was a start.

"Care to try a real opponent?"

I spun; chest heaving and sweat dripping into my eyes. My blood chilled.

Exekiel stood a few feet away. His pink eyes gleamed. His hands were in his pockets; a grin on his unfairly handsome face. His dark hair was disheveled, as if he'd just run his fingers through it, the way I had the night we'd…I wrenched away from the memory and scowled at the bastard.

It'd been weeks since we'd been alone together, but the distance hadn't distanced him from my mind—from my heart.

Using my tank top to wipe sweat from my brow, I huffed, "Back from torturing children, so soon?"

His eyes flashed. "Excuse me?"

"You're the Protector, aren't you?" My rage returned, tenfold. "Apparently you people think a little girl is a threat."

"I'm not in the habit of butchering children."

"Your barrier would beg to differ."

Too late, I realized what I'd revealed. That I'd been out far enough to see the bodies strung up in warning.

Exekiel stalked towards me. "So quick to point the finger but never at yourself."

I stepped back, afraid of what I might do if he got too close. Of the things he always made me want to do—enemy or not. I was no longer under the illusion I could resist him. The best I could hope for, was to get away.

"You're the one who got caught up in things you don't understand. Who thought a pillow was a good hiding place." His tone dripped with derision.

He moved closer. His wood-smoke scent slithered over me. "You're the one who couldn't save her. And now you're mad she belongs to the realm; to me."

"Fuck you!"

He sneered. "The truth hurts, doesn't it?" The bite in his tone made me wonder if he was referring to my comment about the bodies on his barrier.

I shoved him hard in the chest. Instead of stumbling back, the bastard stepped forward.

"Do you want to fight me, little bud?" he snarled as if he needed a release as much as I did.

Remembering what happened the last time we sparred, I spat, "No."

"No?" The growl of his voice was like a stroke down my spine.

I pushed past him, needing to get away.

Exekiel grabbed my wrist. "Then what do you want to do to me?"

The heat of his touch made my pulse race. His gaze a rough caress.

I whispered, "Nothing."

We both sensed the lie.

"I have a confession, little bud." A muscle ticked in his jaw. "I watched the footage of you on that rack more times than I can count. The sight of you stretched out, sweat-soaked and screaming, had my cock in a chokehold.'

Desire pulsed at the juncture between my thighs. Suddenly the image of him turning the crank, bringing me to the brink of pain before soothing it with sweet, agonizing pleasure, filled my mind. What was wrong with me?

"You're sick," I hissed.

Exekiel smirked. "I'm honest." He dragged me against him. His grip tight on my jaw as he tilted my head back. "And right now, I honestly want you on all-fours, panting my fucking name."

His mouth captured mine; shrouded me in a blaze of rage and endless longing.

Instinctively, my fingers curled into his shirt and I drew him closer—as if kissing him could chase away the shadows, pain, and uncertainty. He growled against my lips and heat scorched through my veins.

"Sleep with me," he breathed, almost like a prayer, but there was nothing holy or pure about all the ways I was going to let this Fae defile me.

It was wrong, stupid and a betrayal to our people, but the fire that raged between us was undeniable. As

282

hot as if it surged straight from the gates of hell. And gods, I wanted to burn…burn with him.

37

PUNISHING PASSIONS

The kiss was the beginning and end of everything. Of my deliverance and my damnation. With one stroke of his tongue, Exekiel consumed me.

My knees buckled. My earlier anger and hatred forgotten as his touch sparked a hunger that thundered in my soul. A need for my mate—for him; Exekiel V'alin. The Fae-bastard that had imprisoned my mother, murdered my sister and forced me from the realm when I was just a child.

Logic told me to punch him in the face. But the way I felt about him defied all logic; all reason.

Exekiel took my ass in his hands and hoisted me up. I coiled my legs around him. Every argument I had was obliterated by the hard press of his cock between my thighs. I moaned, hotly.

"That sound," Exekiel groaned as he rowed his hips. "That sound has possessed my every thought."

I clung to him; once again stunned at how much he affected me.

"I can't stop thinking about you," he murmured against my lips.

My chest squeezed. I could taste the truth of his words as sharp as the sweet berries of his breath.

I swallowed thickly, terrified of this man. I didn't let people in. They always hurt me, always left, and he would do the same. But, somehow, he evaded my walls and struck my heart. Every. Single. Time.

Shaking, I whispered, "I missed you."

Exekiel held me closer. "And I you."

He claimed my mouth again. As he did, his wings splayed; casting a shadow over the setting sun.

My eyes fluttered open and my heart lurched when he shot into the sky. The force of it, thrust him against me; tore a moan from my throat. My mind spun.

We were airborne; circling the distant stars as his length stroked me. My eyes rolled back in my head. My body overawed by the sensation of flying and the feel of him. I slid my hand beneath his shirt. My delicate fingers skimming the hard planes of his abs.

Lust rocketed through me. "Will I ever stop wanting you?"

"Not even on pain of death."

His words were a reminder that death was the only way this would end for one of us. Somehow, I was supposed to make sure it was him. To save my people and myself, Exekiel had to die. But the thought left me cold; gripped my heart in a vice.

His wings slashed downwards then back up. With every stroke, his thighs flexed, his ass clenched and his thick erection dug into me. I squeaked softly. We needed less clothes—no clothes.

The wind howled around us but did nothing to cool the heat of my skin.

Desperate, I undid his ties and pushed my hand down the front of his breeches, tugging him relentlessly. Exekiel roared at the sky. If the camera-orbs hadn't noticed us already, they would now. But I didn't care. All I cared about was him—tasting him, pleasing him.

He was my weakness; my drug. The threat to our entire plan. Yet nothing could tear me away.

Our lips collided. I grasped fistfuls of his dark hair and continued to jerk him off; felt him thicken in my hand. His scent of woodsmoke, warm apples, and something unmistakably masculine surrounded me. I moaned and brushed my thumb over the head of his shaft.

Exekiel swore. "Keep that up and I'll fuck you right here above the arena."

My blood heated. "Promise?"

He chuckled. Neither of us cared that if someone looked up, they'd see us.

I stroked him again and he rasped, "Behave. I swore the next time I had you, I'd take my time with you. That I'd fuck you endlessly in a bed so I could hold you after."

My laugh was breathless but my heart fluttered at his words. "Then for fuck's sake, get me to a bed."

Exekiel descended, whizzing us between trees. The wind shifted and we slammed into a trunk, both roaring as our centers met. For a moment, Exekiel grinded into me and I gripped the branches above my head to keep from falling.

"Not here," he grunted, branding my mouth with a searing kiss.

It took more effort than it should, but we managed to pull away and Exekiel hurtled us through the trees. He didn't slow until we reached a room of the tallest tower. His room; the Protector of the Realm.

Reality sunk in. What the hell was I doing? There was no happy ending to this story. Either he would kill me or I, him. For either side to be victorious, one of us had to die.

The barrier was a death-sentence to thousands of people and only Exekiel's end would destroy it. I was the bridge between both realms; a threat to the Five Isles, and for that, the Court would never let me live. It was Exekiel's life, or mine and countless others.

Exekiel lay me down on his massive bed with an iron headboard shaped like wings, and climbed on top of me.

"Stop thinking," he growled as if he sensed the direction of my thoughts. "Focus on me; on how hard I'm about to fuck you."

Propped on his elbows, Exekiel used his hips to drive me into the mattress. His dark hair falling into his deep-red eyes.

"Ahh," I panted and bucked against him. A moan stuck in my throat. Desperately, I unbuttoned his shirt.

"Fuck," he breathed as he slid his hand down the front of my leggings and felt the wet awaiting him.

I ground into his fingers. Pleasure blazed through me.

"How much do you like these leggings?" he growled.

Sensing he was about to rip them off, I lifted my hips and let him peel down the garment. At the same time, I toed off his breeches and pulled off my top.

Now, in nothing but my bra and him in his open shirt, I palmed his cock.

"I want this."

His fingers pumped a wicked rhythm inside me, but I didn't want his hand. Pushing up, I pressed on his chest until he rolled onto his back.

His eyes met mine as I straddled him; flesh on flesh. We both moaned. I moved with unchecked hunger. Exekiel held my ass and guided me; rubbed me over his length.

"You ready, little bud?"

It was like he knew I needed to prepare for the fullness of his weighted cock. I nodded, no longer able to form words, and lifted up until he was positioned at my dripping entrance.

His hands tightening on my ass was the only warning I had before he yanked me down on top of his hard, throbbing shaft.

Reckless, we writhed together. My walls rippling to adjust to his rough intrusion. My nails bit into the fine hairs on his chest and he brought one hand up to cup my breast. I spasmed, drowning in the feel of him.

"That's it, little bud." He panted; stroking the pad of his thumb over my nipple. "Use me. Take what you need."

I did. I arched back, gripping his thighs, and rode him.

Exekiel met my thrusts and pressed down on my clit. My body tightened.

He groaned, "Look at you." His calloused hands slid over my soft, plump breasts. "You hate me and yet, here you are, riding my cock like a good little girl." He grasped my neck and pulled me down; pressing my lips to his as he thrust upwards, over and over again. I aggressively shook.

"Such a good fucking girl."

I shrieked as he drove himself deeper. Striking parts of me that I hadn't known existed. Spots that welled up and leaked. That burned and racked my body with blinding bliss. That forced me to fist the sheets until I violently coated his cock with my sticky release.

Exekiel thrust again; his head tipping back.

"Fuuuck." He held my ass, forcing me to keep moving through the throes of my orgasm. "Don't stop…That's it…"

Feral, I rode him like my life depended on it. My walls clamped tight around him and he groaned with every pull.

His body juddered. "Fates…You're perfect."

I almost climaxed again. His words were a fire to my furnace. I bounced on his cock, faster and faster; desperately wanting him to chase my high, to feel as good as he made me feel.

Exekiel barked out and pushed his thumb into my mouth. I sucked…hard. His eyes widened and his muscles bunched.

He gritted his teeth. The veins in his neck bulging and his body strained, then he erupted.

I came again; crashing like a wave against the shore.

But Exekiel barely gave me a second to catch my breath. Almost immediately after he came, he rolled me onto my back and plunged inside me. I moaned hotly; my pulse pounding.

"My turn," he snarled.

I gasped; burning from the inside out as he sucked on my breast and fucked me into oblivion.

The walk back to my room was difficult. Every part of me ached. Particularly the point where my mate had railed into me more times than I could count—had forced me to climax repeatedly on his cock, his fingers, his tongue. But I'd refused to spend the night in his chambers. It was bad enough that I'd gone there at all and the camera-orbs had definitely caught it.

He'd offered to fly me to my rooms but I needed this time to clear my head; to process the ramifications of what we just did.

My mind was no less muddled when I stepped into my room.

"About time!"

I yelped, stunned to find Lucinda sprawled on my bed.

The witch shrugged. "Eudora let me in."

Slamming the door, I kicked off my shoes. "And why are you here?"

Not that I wasn't happy to see her but it was the middle of the night.

"Call me crazy, but when your friend recently spent a night on the rack, you tend to check on them. But of course, you weren't here. You were with him."

I frowned as I undressed. "What?"

"The Shadow Saint—your mate. That's where you were, isn't it? There's always a glow about you after seeing him."

My chest tightened and I stalked into the bathing chamber so she wouldn't read the truth in my reaction. I hesitated at the edge of the water. A part of me didn't want to wash Exekiel off my skin. God, I needed help. Shaking my head, I climbed in.

Lucinda padded after me. "There's just one thing I don't understand; how will you live with yourself after you kill him?"

38

THE TENTH TRIAL

Lucinda's question hung in the air between us, partly because I didn't have an answer and partly because she'd figured it out. Knew that I planned to kill Exekiel and break the barrier.

"Don't look so surprised." She strode into the bathing chamber. "Working with the outliers means I often hear things, and recently, I heard a rumor that the Sea-Queen is going to slay the Shadow Saint." She rolled up the legs of her black lace harem pants and settled at the edge of the pool. "But they don't know that the Sea-Queen is also sleeping with him. *Mated* to him." Her lips pursed. "Care to explain?"

Words lingered on my tongue. How much could I say? How much did she already know? I was relieved to finally have someone to talk to, but it was risky. Loch warned me that Lucinda sympathized with the Outer Isles but not necessarily with the sirens, which meant she couldn't be trusted. And yet, she'd trusted me with her secret of smuggling magic beyond the barrier, and she'd been there for me when no one else was.

Finally, I said, 'Remember the visitor I had, the night of the werewolf attack?"

"The messenger who gave you the blade that gave you that scar." Lucinda indicated the faint slash on my upper arm.

"He was more than a messenger." I braced myself then said, "He's been ruling the Coral Court in my absence. He discovered that if Exekiel dies, the barrier dies with him and we even the playing field."

"And start a war." Lucinda's stare hardened. "I agree that the barrier has to come down, Varialla, but slay the Shadow Saint and you damn us all."

"Loch has a plan so it doesn't come to that."

For me to win the Games, become the rightful Primary and use that title to execute anyone who stands against us.

Lucinda scoffed.

"If I don't do this, the Court will kill me and then go after my family."

"Those people aren't your family," she spat.

I flinched. "You're right. My family was killed and imprisoned by the Royal Court. By my precious fucking mate that you're so desperate for me to spare."

"Open your eyes!" Lucinda barked. "Of all the people in all the realm, you're mated to the one male who could put an end to this."

"And?"

"And the Conduit doesn't make mistakes. You're here for a reason." Lucinda's tone was steel. "What if that's to join forces with your mate? I told you, you had incredible power, matched only by his. If the two of you worked together..." She shook her head. "You'd be unstoppable."

My laugh was bitter. I still hadn't tapped into this wealth of power people claimed I had, and the Court were out for my blood.

"The Protector would actually have to want peace for that to work," I snarled, remembering what he'd said about Cherise. That she belonged to the realm...to *him*. "Instead, he's currently using a little girl as bait to lure in my people."

"And your people are using you!"

"They're n—"

"They are!" Lucinda hopped to her feet. "But you're so desperate for a family; to be accepted, that you refuse to see it. You'll do anything even if you don't agree."

The words struck a chord. I bared my teeth.

"You're nothing more than their weapon. The Five Isles have the Shadow Saint and they have you. Two mates divided...for what?"

My nostrils flared; fists clenched. It was easy for Lucinda to preach of honor and peace when she'd been born in an honorable household, not hunted and cast out. Alone and unloved. Abandoned.

Lucinda grimaced, her rage simmering. "I'm sorry but it's true. They may care about you but only because of what you can do for them."

"As opposed to you?" I seethed. "You also want to use my power for your own gain."

"With one significant difference," she snapped. "I want you to be happy. Killing your mate won't make you happy."

My lungs tightened; ached at the thought of being without Exekiel.

"Which makes me wonder, is this plan that you've agreed to, what you want or what they want?"

Before I could respond, Lucinda strode out of the chamber.

"I've left you some pippy-root tea," she called. "Can't have you birthing your mate's child on top of everything else."

We'd made it. Endured mental, emotional and physical warfare to get to this point—the tenth and final Trial. After today, the finalists would be decided and after a short break with their families, all players would return and the real Games would begin.

Today, we were gathered at the denser end of Creature's Copse. Sixty-seven players from the one hundred we'd started with. Each carrying an air of grim determination. We'd suffered losses but had as much to gain.

Goather waited on a raised platform. His shoulders slumped and mouth downturned. Something was wrong.

I glanced at Maximus and Lucinda who stood a few paces away. Max shared my look of unease but Lucinda kept her gaze ahead. She may have left me the contraceptive tea but we were apparently still in a fight.

She couldn't see that she was wrong. Yes, the sirens needed me to reach their goal but they loved me because I was one of them. And they looked out for their own. Which was why, once I made it through the Tenth Trial, I was going to somehow contact the others and together, we would find a way to save Cherise.

As if my thoughts summoned her, a hulking Fae descended with Cherise in his arms. She was bound in chains. Her hair wet—suggesting she'd been kept in water, though her tail was now legs. Her face bruised and wrist bound in bloody bandages.

Cold fury slid through my veins. I could barely concentrate on Goather as he held the microphone to his mouth.

"Initiates!" His voice was as commanding as always but carried an undercurrent of despair.

My unease deepened. The Fae dumped Cherise on the ground. I fought the urge to run to her.

Loch's words came rushing back: *Play the Game. Win it, so we can put an end to this…*

"As many of you know, the Hunting Trial is often done with wild beasts from beyond the barrier." Goather swallowed; cleared his throat. "However, in this season of Fit for the Throne, the Council thought it was fitting that the beast be one of the savages who broke through our barrier and tried to infiltrate the Crown."

His haunted gaze flickered to something over our heads. Looking behind me, I spied Alexov and the others on the edge of the group. Their stares were dark and brimmed with cruelty. Ice trilled down my spine. This was about more than me. It was about Goather. Had he somehow implicated himself? Revealed that he may be working with their enemies?

The satyr drew in a weighted breath and tipped his chin high. "That is why, for your final Trial of Ten, you are tasked with hunting and killing this traitor."

My heart plummeted like lead in the pit of my stomach. White noise filled my ears.

A few of the other contestants looked equally repulsed though some grinned wildly.

My gut roiled. Were they serious? They wanted the contestants to hunt and slaughter a little girl?

"As added incentive," Goather's voice cracked and again, he cleared his throat. "Whoever wins this Trial will automatically be placed in the top ten regardless of their current rank."

The air sharpened with determination. Excited chatter filtered through the contestants. Those who, moments ago, had been horrified, were now ecstatic. What was the life of one girl; one exiled savage, for the sake of the Throne? That's what the Trials were about after all. Testing if they could do what needed to be done for their Kingdom.

There was a dull thunk as Cherise's chains hit the ground.

"Of course, since we ourselves are not barbarians," Vladimir prowled between us; his grin slanted. "We will give the traitor a head start." He swiveled to Cherise, his black cape billowing. "Run."

Cherise threw one desperate glance at me then took off, disappearing between the trees.

My thoughts stumbled over each other. This had to be a mistake. They couldn't really be asking the contestants to do this. But the Council were closing in and their glares were directed at me and Goather. This was personal—punishment for outwitting them; for my outburst in the prison. This was murder; sick…and unforgivable. Rage took root in my bones.

Lucinda could say what she wanted about peace but this was proof that these bastards craved war. Wanted blood spilled along their shores and I would make sure it was theirs.

"I think that's long enough," Vladimir drawled in his icy tone.

"Agreed," Alexov called. "Good luck, Initiates. May you go with the brave and the blessed."

Goather brought a shell-horn to his lips and blew. The sound reverberated through the gardens and the contestant's raced forwards with warrior cries. Lucinda turned as if she meant to say something but I overtook her in a frantic race to get to Cherise first. To find a way to free her.

Slender fingers grabbed my arm. I reeled around and faced Vladimir. His pale green eyes traveled up my body.

"You've been a bad girl, Varialla."

I tried to tug free but his grip only tightened as he leaned in and ran his nose up my cheek.

"I have a special way of dealing with bad girls." His breath was cold on my neck. I shuddered. "And I've been told that if you continue to misbehave, the Court and Council will give you to me, to punish as I please." The elf drew back. When he grinned, I swore I saw fangs. "Unlike my brethren, I do not cow to the Conduit when justice must be served."

"Let go of me, asshole." I uselessly tried to pull away.

"That's it," he hissed and stroked his thumb over my lips. I recoiled "Cling to that fire, sea-witch. Do something stupid." He made a sound that made my skin crawl. "I'll be waiting for you."

39

HUNTING HER

Shaking off Vladimir's words, I charged into Creature's Copse. The air was thick with scents of moss and earth, and echoed with cries of bloodlust. Grown men and women were hunting down a child for sport—for glory.

There was no glory in this.

I called on my magic. My mouth filled with a sweetness that slithered from my lips as I hummed a song only known in my soul. It rippled through the trees until it, finally, latched onto Cherise and pulled. It was like it was lassoed around her and I held the other end. When I tried to take another path, I felt the tug to turn back.

Satisfied, I ran in the direction the song beckoned. My heart pounded. Wet leaves slipped beneath my feet. I had to find her.

The harsh grunts of a beast rumbled at my back. I swiveled but no one was there. Yet the sounds were unmistakable. Another contestant—a shifter—must have scented Cherise, and was closing in.

Pushing my power into my limbs, I raced harder than I ever had before. My palms sliced on rough tree bark as I stumbled over raised roots and broken branches.

At last, I burst into a clearing and my song faded.

"Cherise?" I whispered, eyes wide and searching. "Cherise!"

A shrub at the base of a tree shuddered, then Cherise emerged. Relief almost dropped me to my knees but the shifter wasn't far behind.

I rushed towards her, gripped her arm and gasped, "Run."

Together, we charged deeper into the woodland.

I summoned my song to find the lagoon but the Council had brought us somewhere too far to reach it through magic. We were on our own.

Cursing, I raced one way only to skid to a halt when we heard the shouts of witches and elves. Twisting, we thundered another way and were met with more bellows for blood. Again, and again; we circled, frantic for an escape, until, finally Cherise stopped running.

"What are you doing?" I shrieked between my teeth. The other contestants were close—too close.

"Whoever kills me will be entered into the Top Ten regardless of their current rank."

Voices drew nearer. Adrenaline shot through my veins.

"Run!" I reached for Cherise but she stepped back.

"I'm not getting out of this alive but I can choose how I die."

"What?" I hissed, afraid that I knew what she was about to say.

"You have to kill me."

"No."

"Kill me."

"No!" The word tore from my throat; burned in my chest.

"I wanted to do something to help my people," Cherise said; her voice surprisingly steady. "Let me do this. Let me help you win the Games so you can change the world."

My chest tightened. I wouldn't do it. I couldn't. There had to be another way...if Cherise would just *run*.

"They're not going to let me live. And if they catch me," she jerked her head towards the contestants whose hollers grew closer. "They'll make me suffer." Her eyes settled on me. "You can make it quick."

"We'll find another way."

"There isn't time!" Cherise's voice cracked, betraying her emotion, before she smoothed her hands down her front. "Let me help save my mother. Let me die with dignity."

She seemed wise beyond her years, reminding me that even though Cherise was a seven-year-old girl, she had been alive for far longer; aging slow in this world that denied time.

Cherise plucked the blade belted at my waist and forced it into my hand. It was the same dagger we'd used for the Illusion Trial and were told to bring today. I hadn't expected this.

"In war there are always sacrifices."

"Not this. Not your life."

Cherise straightened. "Your mother would not hesitate."

Shouts of the other contestants grew too near to ignore, accompanied by the snarls and grunts of hungry beasts.

"I'm going to skin her before I let her die," someone bellowed.

My gut lurched. This wasn't right. Wasn't fair. All Cherise had wanted was a future where she was free. Granted passage into the Five Isles without invitation or toll. A world where her mother could get the care she needed and where they were once again blessed by the Conduit. Able to siphon its magic and aid their lands. She hadn't wanted war and she deserved better than this. But there wasn't time to do anything else.

I turned to Cherise; blade poised to carve across her neck.

"Do it," she urged. "Do it."

Magic wrapped around my fist and my eyes went wide as I felt the command in my bones. I tried to resist but my hand shifted, angling the blade.

"I can't," I cried, fighting the pull.

"You forget, sister. You may be royal but I've been practicing my magic for much longer than you." Cherise half smiled. "Take care of my mother."

Her eyes glowed and her magic did the rest. Like a puppet on a string, my hand twisted and slashed Cherise's throat.

The world stopped spinning. Cherise's body fell. I went with her.

"Cherise!" My voice broke as I uselessly pressed a hand to the gushing wound. "Cherise."

She didn't move; would never move again. A harrowing cry ripped from my being as contestants burst through the thicket. The force of it sent them hurtling backwards. Their bodies cracked against trees.

A savage song of sorrow spilled from my lips in a language I'd never learnt but couldn't hold back.

Through a blur of tears, and choked song, I heard the yelps of the contestants and felt the rising wind.

Everything is shattered. My heart, you did break. My mind translated the words I sang. *In time, this I promise, your souls I will take.*

A bruising force slammed into me, knocked me onto my back and cut off my song. Blinking, I found Exekiel standing over me. His eyes a blazing red as he snatched me up and tore into the sky.

I thrashed, wildly. Needing to get back to Cherise's side. Needing to be far away from him. He had to have known what they'd planned for Cherise. Heck, he'd probably planned it.

"Get off me," I roared, shoving at his arms.

Exekiel snarled and soared higher as if that would deter me. I kept fighting. I'd rather plummet to my death than spend another second in his arms.

He flew like a beast on a hunt. In no time, we reached his balcony. Exekiel kicked open the doors, stalked into his room and dumped me on the bed.

"What are you doing?" I sat up even as exhaustion weighed me down.

"Containing a threat." Exekiel undid the top few buttons of his shirt and went to stoke the fire. "You were losing control out there."

"I lost much more than that." I shot him a glare. "Did you know that's what they planned?"

Of course, he knew. He was the Protector of the Realm but I had to hear him say it. Some part of me still foolishly hoped.

His jaw clenched; his face half shadowed by the flames. He said nothing.

My heart twisted. They'd warned me not to trust him, told me he was the enemy but I didn't listen. I hadn't wanted to. My stomach turned.

Convinced I was about to be sick, I hurtled from his bed and staggered towards the door. Every step was an effort as if the amount of magic I'd used had sapped my strength.

"What are you doing?"

"Leaving."

Exekiel's eyes flashed. "Get back in bed."

"No," I gritted out and forced myself to keep moving.

"Varialla."

"No!"

In a blink, he was before me.

"I can't let you leave."

"Tough shit." I shoved him but he didn't move. "Get out of the way!" I struck again and again, unleashing my wrath.

"Stop!" he snapped.

I didn't. I couldn't. Every hurt, every horror carved up my insides.

"Let me go," I shouted, my fists pounding on his chest.

Exekiel grabbed my wrists and wrenched me against him. "Stop!"

Rage rattled through me. If I had the strength, I would have gouged out his eyes; eyes that made me yearn—that I'd let distract me for too long. But no more.

"You knew!" I screamed; bringing my face close to his. "You knew!"

"I didn't!" Exekiel bellowed, "I didn't know!" His breaths were ragged. "I knew they wouldn't let her go but…" His voice trailed off and he heavily exhaled. He hadn't known they'd do this.

I blinked up into his violent pink eyes and all I saw was the truth. He looked like he wanted to say more but after a pause, he shook his head and stepped back.

"Get some rest."

He returned to tend to the fire. Shaken, I slumped onto the bed and hugged my knees to my chest.

When he was done, Exekiel grunted, "Sleep."

He strode towards the door.

"Wait." The word left my mouth before I could stop it.

He halted. Waited.

I didn't know why I'd stopped him, only knew that I didn't want him to leave. That with just one declaration, I believed him about Cherise.

"I…don't want to be alone." The confession cost me, but grief and exhaustion weighed heavily on my bones and only his embrace could soothe it.

Exekiel studied me in a way that made me feel exposed. Like he could see every crack in my façade.

"Always trying to get me into bed," he finally uttered, but there was no spark of laughter in his eyes.

I flinched. Of course, he assumed that I wanted him physically. That was the only connection we had—could have. Blind passion or burning rage. Nothing more; nothing deeper.

To hide the conflicted anguish in my eyes, I rolled onto my side.

"Never mind," I whispered. "Goodnight, Shadow Saint."

Barely a heartbeat later, the door slammed. I sucked in a breath then let the tears fall. The horrors of the day raced through my mind. I wept through the pounding in my head and the tightening of my lungs.

Suddenly, the bed dipped as someone climbed in beside me and curled their body behind mine. I tensed. Exekiel. He brushed his lips along the back of my neck soothing some of my sobs.

"Can't I go take a piss without you falling to pieces?"

I half laughed through my tears.

He drew me closer and whispered, "Cry, little bud. I won't tell anyone."

40

Sing For Me

Memories of the final Trial plagued me through the night. I woke gasping; tears tracking my cheeks. I was quick to wipe them away. I was tired of crying—of feeling weak. The pillowcase was soaked with my tears. My throat hoarse and eyes puffy. My world was officially breaking but I couldn't crumble with it. There was still so much to do—people to save, to make sure that Cherise's sacrifice hadn't been for nothing.

As the last dregs of restless sleep faded, I registered the press of a hard body behind me. Inhaled the warm scent of woodsmoke and apples. Everything after the Trial came screaming back: Exekiel carrying me to his room. His arms around me as I wept. They were still around me now.

I risked a glance at him over my shoulder. My breath stilled. He was beautiful. His dark hair fell onto his brow. His thick lashes casted shadows on his well-cut cheekbones, and sunlight haloed his tanned skin and the peaks of his wings that were folded behind him.

I hated the pang of longing I felt. After everything he'd done, I still wanted him. Still believed he was the only one who could hold my broken heart together.

I jolted when something thick and hard prodded my backside. My thoughts scattered. I'd heard of morning wood but this felt like a whole damn tree. I tried to steady my heartrate and ignore the current of desire that shot through me.

Exekiel was a problem. He could distract me from my grief, and the fact that he could, was the very reason I couldn't let him. The very reason I had to leave…but something held me in place.

Slowly, I pushed back into the bulge in his pants. Once. Twice. My eyes rolled and I let my head fall back on his shoulder when he began to move with me. It was wrong and stupid. I should be pulling away. Should be getting the hell out of there but I welcomed his gentle motions. The heat of his body.

His hand tightened on my waist and my eyes flickered open to find his own peering down at me—a vibrant pink.

I couldn't breathe. Exekiel wrapped his other hand around my throat, forcing me to hold his depthless stare as he rowed his hips harder.

My heart galloped in my chest. Now that he was awake, the air shifted with a promise of things to come. Things I shouldn't—couldn't have.

"Helping yourself to my cock, sea-witch?"

I flushed, knowing I should feel ashamed. That was exactly what I'd been doing. It was probably why he'd woken up. But I couldn't find an apology beneath my hunger and my pain. All I wanted was him and the power he held over me to take it away.

"I think I preferred you calling me, little bud," I panted as I continued to rock into him.

Exekiel chuckled. "And I prefer you riding me when I'm awake."

His other hand slid between my legs. I jerked. Since my clothes had been covered in blood and gore, at some point during the night, I'd removed them. Now his fingers easily pushed inside my panties and teased my clit.

"Not that I mind waking up to you leaking for me." He dragged his finger along my slit and made a low appreciative sound. "So wet, little bud."

His words were a whisper that rippled over my skin and settled deep in my belly.

"How wet will you get for me?" Exekiel pressed his thumb down then thrust a finger inside me.

Sparks lit up every cell in my body. The pressure of his hand, the thump of his cock meeting my ass; it was all too much. Too overwhelming—intense.

We should stop. We had to stop. But my need for him was crippling. It consumed me in a way that made me forget everything else. A blissful moment of distraction, where I was wholly his and he was mine.

Exekiel sank another finger inside me. I moaned. My nails bit into his forearm. My muscles coiled tight.

Exekiel's hot breath shuddered across my ear.

"Who will you make that sound for after you kill me, little bud?"

My eyes flared open. "What?"

Exekiel continued to wet his fingers inside me; slow, leisurely movements as if he wasn't unravelling my very soul.

I tried to concentrate; to focus on what he'd said.

"The only thing your kind has wanted since I erected the barrier is to tear it down and continue their senseless war."

His fingers pumped faster. I tensed; conflicted by his words and my urge to come.

"I'm not so naïve as to believe you haven't figured out how to do that by now."

"Ask you nicely?" I breathed.

His low laughter didn't reach his eyes. "Or carve out my heart."

Exekiel slid his fingers in harder. I cried out; shaking.

The heel of his hand pressed down on my swollen clit and his fingers pulsed an erratic beat inside me that matched the wild thrashing of my heart.

"Since you're the only one, I'd ever let close enough, I'm guessing you're the one who's supposed to do it."

My mouth fell open but no words came out; only strangled squeaks and breathless gasps as he conquered me.

My face creased; eyes falling closed.

Exekiel's grip tightened around my neck. "Look at me."

The timber of his voice rattled through me. Aching; so desperately close to the edge, I forced my eyes open and was undone by his. I came, violently. As I did, he brought his mouth to mine and kissed me. The angle was odd but I welcomed it. Welcomed all of him.

Then I was on my back and Exekiel was upon me; his wings splayed. As he kicked off his plaid pajama bottoms, I made myself focus.

"You think I plan to kill you, but you brought me to your bed?"

He moved down my body; peeled off my panties.

"Maybe I'm a sucker for punishment." Exekiel let my knickers fall from the ends of my toes and grasped my ankles. "Maybe a part of me wants to believe you'll never do it."

His eyes met mine and the air grew taut between us. I swallowed thickly. Sorrow and longing hollowed my heart. All I wanted was to be with him. To chase away the fear, the future, and the despair that lay beyond these walls. But the cost was too high.

I whispered, "What if I do?"

With my ankles in his grip, Exekiel spread my legs. His gaze sank to the spot between my thighs that was now exposed to him. Every part of me burned.

He kissed my ankle then continued up my leg. My pulse spiked when he reached the silken flesh at the back of my knee. A blaze of desire followed the path of his lips.

"Then I would die happy, knowing I have had you in my bed." His teeth scraped my inner thigh. The soft strands of his hair tickled my flesh. "Knowing I have kissed your lips." Only he kissed the lips between my legs. I trembled. "Knowing I have sucked on your supple breasts."

His hands came up; grasping my tits. I arched into him, pushing my center closer to his mouth.

"Knowing I have tasted your skin. Eaten this cunt."

311

Exekiel gripped the backs of my thighs and dragged me towards his waiting mouth. His rough tongue circled my clit. I panted. Pleasure spearing through me.

His wings rose above his head, scored with threads of violet. Exekiel watched me as he teased me with his tongue and alternated with his fingers. His breath was hot on my fevered skin. He closed his mouth over my clit and pulled. I gasped—shaking.

Exekiel purred, "Fucking...delicious."

The Shadow Saint devoured me, until he had me dripping down his pulsing fingers and jerking on his tongue.

My knees locked around his head but he pried my legs apart.

"I want you to feel everything," Exekiel growled then plunged back in.

I didn't recognize the sounds I made; the living embodiment of need that I became.

He groaned. "You taste like my cock's salvation."

I rolled my hips and eagerly fucked his mouth; entirely lost.

When I inevitably came, Exekiel's grin was savage. His lips glistened with my wetness. Slowly, he licked it off and slid up my body. Before I could fully recover from the aftershocks, Exekiel sheathed his cock inside me. No warning. No time to prepare.

We both moaned; an endless tortured sound. Then we moved. Not rough and wild but deep and exploring. Our gazes held; breaths shared. I smelt myself on his tongue and it excited me.

He had one elbow braced beside my head. His other hand pressed down on my hip; pinning me in place as he watched his cock enter me—down to the root and withdraw.

"You're beautiful," he whispered.

Tears filled my eyes, brought on by pleasure more acute than anything I'd ever felt, and sorrow because it couldn't last. Neither of us was safe whilst the other lived. And my people were depending on me, just as his own were depending on him. All we had was now, and I wanted to savor every second.

I gripped his shoulders and didn't look away as he fucked—no, *claimed*—me. Bound me to him more than I had already been which I didn't think was possible.

With every downward stroke, Exekiel filled me in immeasurable ways. He made my heart swell, my body tighten and my soul soar. And when he withdrew, he took some of my grief with him.

In—pleasure. Out—freedom. In. Out. In. Out.

The rhythm of his hips was hypnotic and I was mesmerized; suspended on his hard length. Exekiel thrust deeper and my hips bowed off the bed, my fingers slipping on the soft sheets. My breaths came out thick and fast as pressure built inside me.

"E-Exekiel," I stammered.

He groaned and his paced increased.

"Aahhhh-yes!" I cried. "*Yes!*"

Exekiel doubled his thrusts, and purred, "That's it, siren. Sing for me."

41

WEAK AT THE WELL

Walking away from Exekiel wasn't easy. We'd spent the day entangled with each other. Teasing, exploring and seeing what made the other moan loudest. After our last time, we held each other close. Neither one of us wanted to let go. As if we knew it was the last chance we'd have together before duty pulled us apart.

I was a siren who had a genuine claim to the Eternal Throne and for that, the Court and Council wanted me dead. They didn't realize that it was their determination to destroy me and my people that was leading to the very outcome they feared. That forced me to follow in my mother's footsteps and challenge their reign. Forced me to carve out Exekiel's heart and in turn, my own.

Eudora didn't question my disheveled state and puffy eyes as the nymphs ushered me into the bathing pool to prepare for the final ball of the season.

After tonight, the contestants would go home and spend time with their families before they returned for the official Games and perhaps never made it home again. I didn't have a home to go to, but now, that familiar sadness, came with a bittersweet aftertaste. Soon, I would have the family I'd always wanted…but at the cost of Exekiel's life.

Eudora tutted. "Stop crying, you're ruining your makeup."

I snorted as she dabbed at my eyes. "Apologies. I'll do my best to hide my suffering."

"You must," Eudora pressed. "One sign of weakness and the Court will pounce. They'll peer inside your mind; use your mate's connection to get you to turn on your own."

She was right. I didn't have time for grief or wishing things were different. The Trial of Ten had ended and I was ranked among the highest. Though this increased my chances of winning the Games, it also increased the target on my back. No one wanted to see a siren on the throne. It didn't matter that my father—whoever he was—was one of them. He'd sullied their blessed bloodline with my mother and for that, I would never be accepted. If I wanted a place in this world, I would have to fight for it.

As I descended the steps into the great ballroom of Infinity Hall, I didn't blame the heads that turned in my direction or the way eyes widened or narrowed as they watched me. The nymphs had done an incredible job.

I wore a stunning sapphire lace and tulle ballgown that spilled out from my hips. The ribbed-bodice that framed my breasts was encrusted with flecks of silver, and from its back flowed a cerulean cape. On my head, I wore a white-gold tiara dotted with sapphires.

Adir met me at the foot of the stairs. I hated the thread of fear that unfurled in my gut.

"A crown on your head doesn't make you a queen," he hissed quietly.

Rage emanated from him like a physical blow. It seemed the rumors were true. The Primary was furious that I'd managed to escape the rack. That the Fates had spared me again.

Spine straight, I met his frosty glare. "No, but being a queen, makes me a queen."

And that's what I was. Queen of the Coral Court and soon the entire Five Isles if that's what it took to be free.

Adir's lips thinned and he roughly gripped my arm. "Don't forget your place, wretch, or I'll remind you."

Camera-orbs panned around us and with a withering glower, he stalked away.

Sometime later, Vivienne approached. Her white wings were dusted with silver glitter; her pink lips pursed into a false smile.

"I get it now," she purred. "It doesn't make sense for us to kill your kind, when it's so much more satisfying to watch you kill them for us."

Her words struck like a blade to the heart. It took all I had in me not to rip her throat out. But royals battled with words as well as power, and if I wanted the throne, I had to play the game.

"Only a monster could find it satisfying to watch the murder of a child." Fury roiled inside me. "So, what does that make you?"

Before Vivienne could answer, I strode off leaving the bitch with her mouth flapping. Even her doting lackeys seemed to take a step back from her but I didn't feel triumphant. I felt sick. Vivienne wasn't the only one who'd celebrated Cherise's death. Who'd found it poetic that it was done by my hand.

Needing some air, I stalked towards the open doors that led out into a lantern-lit courtyard. A fountain stood in its center, surrounded by white gravel, stretches of grass and grand arches that veered off into other parts of the gardens.

I stormed towards a well with a spired roof at the far end of the yard. It was slightly enclosed by a hedge wall and I ducked behind it; welcoming the solitude.

There, I steadied my racing heart. Soaked in the balmy night air and inhaled the scents of wildflowers.

"Missing me, already?"

I spun; my heart in my throat, as Exekiel stepped out from under a nearby tree. He looked unfairly gorgeous in a black trench coat adorned with silver filigree, and a shirt and fitted slacks beneath. I took a step back as he approached.

"What are you doing here?" I snapped; arms folded across my chest.

We'd agreed to stay away from each other. That what had happened earlier couldn't happen again. It'd been a moment of weakness that we'd both willingly succumbed to but soon, the survival of our loved ones would come down to my life or his. Him, sworn to protect the barrier, and me, determined to destroy it.

Exekiel moved closer. "Same as you, I imagine."

"Wishing you could ram a fork into Vivienne's eye?"

His grin was a slash of white in the silver light of the moon.

"Wishing things were different."

My heart twisted. I continued to move back as he advanced. "Different in what way?"

"Every way."

Exekiel was so close, I could feel the thrum of his power that seemed to reach out for mine. I wanted to retreat from its familiar caress but my legs hit the rough stone wall of the well.

"Although, if I could only change one thing, I'd change the fact that the Fates made you; the greatest threat to the Five Isles, my mate."

His eyes glittered. He seemed angry. As if this was my fault. As if I'd asked him to abduct me and bring me to this world where everything I wanted existed but was out of reach. Where I was forced to choose between my love and my life.

No, not love. I didn't love Exekiel…did I?

Clinging to anger, I snarled, "Of course. It would be much easier to kill me if I was just another nameless siren."

I prodded him in the chest, forcing him back a step.

"They weren't all nameless," he growled. "Some were my closest friends."

"That's worse," I spat. "You called them your friends then slaughtered them. You strung them up on your barrier as a fucking warning to the rest."

Exekiel bared his teeth. "You hear one side of the story and think you know everything."

"I know enough."

"You know nothing." He pushed forwards, forcing me to sit on the well's wall. "You don't know what your people did. What they took from me."

His magic rumbled through the earth and his hand shot up around my neck. My pulse pounded against his palm.

"I should kill you."

In a flash, Exekiel had me hanging over the well—my feet swinging. My stomach lurched and I grabbed onto the rusted chain in one hand and the pulley above my head, in the other.

"What are you doing?"

Exekiel's grip tightened; not hard enough to choke me, but enough to make my body ache for him in ways it shouldn't.

"You threaten everything I've managed to save," he bit out. "I should kill you. Instead, I'm the one dying because I cannot have you."

I swallowed. "You can't have everything you want, Shadow Saint."

"Not want. *Need*." Exekiel pressed closer. "I am addicted to you, little bud. Not infatuated. Not in love." He slid his hand down my throat and over my breast. My breath hitched. "But something achingly more profound."

I wanted to run. His words were undoing me. The graze of his palm across my breast made my blood thrum. I needed to get away, but he had me trapped; suspended over the well with only a deadly drop below.

"I am entirely and irrevocably obsessed with every breath you take." Exekiel fisted the frills of my dress and drew them up over my knees.

My flesh pimpled when the cold air stroked my skin. My heart hammered against my ribs. Exekiel grabbed the backs of my knees and opened my legs so he could step between them.

My eyes frantically searched for an escape. I couldn't do this again. Couldn't lose myself to him again. Each time it was harder to walk away.

"What are you doing?"

Exekiel dragged a finger along my sex. My eyelids fluttered.

"I'm pleasuring my mate," he purred as he bent over me.

I heaved on the pulley, trying to wrench myself up, but Exekiel brought his mouth to mine and the world stopped spinning. I craved him. My pulse pounded as his tongue slid across mine.

This was wrong, but all I did was hang there, poised over the well, as Exekiel tugged my underwear to the side. Without preamble, he thrust his stiff cock inside me.

My head kicked back; my breath strained. I shook with the effort of holding myself up and the pressure of my mate pumping between my thighs. His strokes were deep and endless, drawing out every part of me and setting it alight.

I moaned. I wanted this. Needed this. But giving into Exekiel was the very thing that would get me killed.

A low voice snarled, "What the fuck?"

42

BLOOD & SEA

I thought I heard someone—a low growl; a whisper of rage. But when Exekiel groaned and slammed into me harder, I thought of nothing but him. This was everything I shouldn't be doing and yet nothing had ever felt more right.

The rough well wall scraped the backs of my legs as Exekiel rammed into me. The cold chain bit into my palm. My shoulders ached. But I was entirely consumed by the feel of my mate, claiming me—undoing me.

He brought his mouth to mine and we came together in a clash of teeth and tongues. A feral hunger neither of us could tame.

"Exekiel," I whimpered as he hiked up my leg and penetrated deeper. My body sparked.

"*Fuck*," he breathed, drowning in the feel of me. His eyes falling closed as he pumped faster.

The chain clanked, hitting the wall. Overhead, the pulley groaned.

"And here I was, thinking you might need to be rescued."

Exekiel swiveled in one graceful motion, pulling up his trousers as he did. For a second, I mourned the loss of him inside me, but my gaze snagged on Loch and the three large sirens with him. Konch, Viktor and Reed. I recognized them from nights in the Coral Court. My mind spun. What were they doing here? How much had they seen? Although judging by their glares, they'd seen enough.

Loch snarled; his teeth gritted, "Perhaps I need to remind you, that you are sworn to me!" He waved his hand and icy water shot up from the well. It slammed into me and I yelped as I was thrown back. Losing my grip on the pulley, I tumbled down into the abyss.

Overhead, Exekiel grunted and the shadow of his wings thrashed.

Fingers slipping, I fumbled to grab onto the rusty chain as water continued to batter me. Through the deluge, I saw two menacing blue eyes. There and then gone.

Loch.

At last, I caught the chain. My shoulder screamed. I struck the wall and pain exploded through my skull. It was hard to breathe, to see, to think. Teeth clenched; I heaved on the chain. All lust I'd felt seconds ago, now doused and undone by fear.

I'd been caught with Exekiel. The Fae responsible for the sirens—and so many others—suffering. He was the worst of their enemies and the one male they'd told me to stay away from. But I couldn't stay away. Why couldn't I stay away?

A wave of power rocked through the earth and I recognized its deep rumble as Exekiel. Light flared overhead.

Loch boomed, "We've got him now."

I braced my feet on the wall and clung to the chain as I climbed higher; terror thick in my throat. Exekiel may have been the Protector of the Realm, but he was outnumbered and caught with his pants down; literally.

I shouldn't care. In order to free my people and save myself, I was supposed to kill him for fuck's sake. But that didn't stop my desperation to get to him—to save him.

Reaching the top, I scrambled out of the well and landed with a thump on the sodden earth—shivering from cold. My head thudded wildly.

Exekiel was a few feet away, on his knees as the three hulking sirens held him down, and Loch sang a song that conjured pain. Each note carried a weight that seemed to slam into the Shadow Saint and strangle his power. Symbols of the Fates bloomed on his skin but every time his magic rose, he bellowed in agony; his head thrown back.

"Stop!" I stumbled to my feet.

A syringe lay discarded on the ground and my gut lurched. They'd injected him with something but what? Exekiel was the most powerful being of the realm. How were four sirens overpowering him?

I turned to Loch. "Let him go."

Magic burned at my fingertips but before I could unleash it, Loch snarled, "Freeze."

I froze. My entire body was paralyzed by his command. His magic bitter on my tongue.

I gaped at him; wide-eyed as he plucked an obsidian dagger from inside his sleeveless tailcoat and prowled towards Exekiel.

"I've let this continue too long."

He crouched before the Protector and stroked the blade down his throat. Exekiel snarled and spat blood from his busted mouth. His eyes were unfocused; his breathing labored. Loch's power still somehow choked his own.

"I understand that mates have their urges—a suck here, a lick there, but now you've gone too far." Loch pressed the blade down and blood trickled from the line he carved. "Now you've fucked my wife."

His wife? Incredulity rocked through me. I wasn't his wife. I wasn't anything to him except bound by a bond forged before I hatched. Rage rattled inside me and I heaved on my magic. But trying to defy Loch's command was like trying to wade through tar. My head screamed. Tongue fuzzy. What was going on?

Noticing my struggle, Loch grinned and sent another roiling wave of pain through Exekiel. The Protector bucked; jaw clenched and brow creased.

"You know what's another great thing about this bond between us?" Loch mused. "It allows me to siphon your power and wield it as my own." He chuckled. "The only power of equal match to the Shadow Saint, himself."

My mind swayed—my headache intensifying. Of course, there was more to this Ceremonial Bind than us being compatible as Mate-Sworn. It was to give him access to my power. A guarantee that if I failed, he would not. Loch drained more magic from inside me and slammed it into Exekiel. I somehow felt each blow to his lungs—felt his insides rupture.

"Stop," I croaked, barely able to move my mouth.

Loch tutted. "I thought you were stronger than this. That you cared about your people enough to not fuck their oppressor." His upper lip curled. "I thought you cared about me."

Fury darkened Loch's heedless gaze and he bounded towards me.

"Instead, you beg me to spare him." His hand clamped around my neck, choking the air from my lungs as he lifted. "He is the enemy!" He roared; his breath as cold as his blood. "You cannot save him. You're supposed to destroy him!"

His hold on my magic snapped as he released me. My knees struck the ground. Loch went with me.

Before I could rise, he pushed me down into the earth and sat across my legs. My cold, wet dress clung to my skin as I writhed to get free. My pulse beat an erratic pace.

"When will you get it, Princess? You belong to me."

Loch's lips met mine. An electric current crackled between us. A bond forged long ago and growing stronger. I recoiled but he pressed closer. Urging his tongue passed the seam of my lips, he stroked it across my own.

Dirt caked beneath my fingernails as I drove them into the ground; tearing up tufts of grass and fighting the desire to grab onto him—to pull him closer.

"Kiss me," he growled.

I didn't know if he meant to use his siren gifts, but the order crashed into me—enhanced by our bind.

Loch groaned as I opened my mouth for him and kissed him back. It was sick; a violation of my body and being. My insides at war. Part of me screamed to break free—to find a way to Exekiel. But the oath that bound me to Loch had my fingers curling into his waist. My legs parting as his hand pushed between them.

Finally, he pulled back and breathed, "I'm doing this for you. For us."

I swallowed; my lips swollen and mind fuzzy as he slid off of me. It was like waking from a trance.

Immediately, I looked to Exekiel. He was hunched over. His eyes glazed and face blooded. Apparently, whilst I'd been kissing Loch, Exekiel was being beaten by the others. My heart cracked and chunks rose in my throat. How did this happen?

"I see now," Loch drawled as he sauntered over to Exekiel, "that you're more connected to the Shadow Saint than I first realized."

He gripped Exekiel's hair, yanking him up. The Protector's magic flared—six symbols across his face and arms but the drug and the press of my power made his aim sloppy and weak.

I scrambled to my knees. My tongue turned sugar-sweet.

"I now believe that the key to fully unlocking your magic is connected to the very outcome we need."

Dread pooled in my gut as Loch once again brandished his obsidian dagger.

"The death of Exekiel V'alin." He grinned. "We won't need to win the Throne to take it. All we'll need is you and that well of power his death will unleash."

My heart lurched as he drew back his hand and plunged the blade into Exekiel's heart.

Something shattered inside me. A chink in the chain around my chasm of raw power, snapped. Exekiel slumped forwards. Blood pooling from the gash.

I screamed.

Power billowed around me in waves of teal. Heat blazed through my skin and a melody burst from my lips. It was not a song but a symphony. As the rush of magic rose, my body violently shook. Inhuman growls rattled in the base of my throat and somehow, I knew— *knew*—that my eyes had once again returned to those reptilian slits. Every sight sharper.

But when my skin hardened with black scales, heat slickened my throat, and midnight horns curved from the crown of my head, I knew I wasn't transforming into a snake…but a dragon.

Agony shot down my spine. Sprawling wings as red as blood, with sharp edges and thick veins of cartilage, ruptured from my shoulder blades. I howled. It was both song and shadow—a blend of melody and thunder.

I rounded on those around Exekiel's prone form and hissed in a voice I didn't recognize, "Get away from my mate."

My mouth yawned wide. Heat rushed me from within. And I unleashed a spray of deadly fire; the color of blood and sea.

43

IT ALL FALLS DOWN

My fire fell in waves. The sirens tried to outrun it, but my power arced and shifted around benches and shrubbery that obscured my path. It didn't stop until it wrapped around them. They were incinerated in seconds. Their faces frozen in agony before their bodies plumed to ash.

The scent of Exekiel's blood stung the back of my throat. The lingering stench of smoke on my skin. Grief and rage bloomed in my chest and I swiveled to Loch—the monster who'd plunged a blade into my mate's heart.

He's not dead. He couldn't be. Although wasn't that what I needed if I wanted to live, to free the Outer Isles and save my people? Exekiel had to fall and his barrier with him. But right now, nothing was worth his life. Nothing.

I raised a flame-ringed hand; swirls of red and teal at my fingertips.

Loch sneered. "There she is."

His tone brimmed with pride. He didn't see me as a threat. Not even as I stood before him with murder in my eyes and his comrades' decimated bodies at my feet. I tried not to think about them…the howl of their screams.

I stepped forward, ignoring the hammering in my skull as the bastard siphoned more of my power and drew it into himself. He was strong, skilled and had wielded his gifts for longer than me, but I clung to what I could. My magic was bottomless—a crash of sea and fire that thundered in my bones.

I searched his face for some sign of remorse, but all I saw in Loch was a rage that matched my own.

My gaze fell on Exekiel. Maybe someone inside the ballroom could staunch the bleeding—had healing powers that could save the Shadow Saint's life.

"No one's coming to save him, Princess," Loch purred. "They've been instructed to continue their celebrations no matter what." He chuckled darkly. "They may even dance themselves to death."

I tensed. All it'd taken was one uttered command from a siren and the people of the Five Isles were at his mercy. Suddenly their fear seemed justified.

"You lied to me," I hissed through teeth that felt sharper than usual.

He'd told me he had no idea who or what my father was, but here I stood; half-woman, half-dragon. Outside of my mother and sister, Loch was the only one who'd seen the egg I was born in. Who'd cared for it—for *me*— once my sister was slain and my mother captured. The one who'd probably hidden the eggshell in the cave

Cherise had found. He knew what I could be and yet he'd hidden if from me.

Now, he shrugged. "I had to make sure our bond was activated. Couldn't have you thinking you could do this on your own."

Anger churned in my chest. The unfamiliar weight of my wings made my steps unsteady as I moved towards the Guardian of the Siren Sea. Him, I wanted to take my time with. Him, I wanted to suffer.

"Not so fast."

Loch ripped more magic from inside me. I doubled over. Spots streaked across my vision.

"Do you think anyone in the Outer Isles will accept you if you harm me?" He stalked closer. "I am their hero and here, you weep for their executioner."

Rage rolled from him, turning my magic bitter on my tongue. I gritted my teeth. Agony held me in a vice.

"You need me to save the unblessed. To free Colette, Algeron and the others. You still care about them, don't you? Still care that Cherise died for this?"

My heart cracked. Of course, I cared. The Coral Court had become my family—my home. And I'd vowed to help Cherise's mother and all those unfairly exiled. But there had to be another way.

I wasn't sure of much, but I was certain that I couldn't let Exekiel die—if he wasn't already dead—anymore than I could abandon my people. I needed time to think, regroup and make my own decisions.

Lucinda had been right. In my desperation to be accepted, I'd willingly overlooked the red flags and flaws in Loch's plan. I'd overlooked the beast inside him.

He grasped my hair and yanked me upright. His breath was like ice on the back of my neck. "You were always a means to an end," he hissed. "It's why your mother chose to seduce the Dragon Prince."

I struggled to get free but he wrenched me against him; my back pinned to his chest, squeezing my sensitive wings. My arms trapped at my sides.

Furious, I reached for my magic. But every time it rose, Loch pulled it tight in his grasp. A tether to my very being that he seemed to coil around his fist.

"Give up, Princess," he pushed me against the nearest wall; face first. Rough stone cut into my cheek.

"Your mother falling for the prince was a happy bonus, and for a while, we actually believed he would save us. That he'd convince the shifters to accept us as their own. That we could use the Conduit and aid the unblessed." He snarled and stepped closer. Used his body to force mine into the wall.

"But on the night, he was supposed to defy his father and support us, the prince announced his betrothal to another."

Loch pushed his hand down the front of my dress and palmed my breast. Disgust and desire pooled in my gut.

He was a bastard. A maniac. But his hold on my gifts—this bond between us—kept me paralyzed.

"Luckily, by then," he went on as if his finger wasn't circling my nipple. "Your mother had secured us you. A blessed-unblessed with a rightful claim to the Eternal Throne. A creature with the power of land, sea and sky."

His fingers pinched my nipple and ecstasy blazed through my core.

"A power that we couldn't risk losing."

I shrank from the sensations he elicited inside me. I needed to break free. My mind was warped—twisted by whatever they'd done to me at birth. I wasn't thinking clearly. I still saw Loch as my protector; my *father*...my lover.

He grasped my hands and braced my palms flat against the wall. My breath hitched as I felt him harden behind me. I hated him. *Hated* him.

"Stop fighting, princess," he murmured, as he grasped my hips and moved into me. "The sooner you accept that you're mine," his sharp teeth trailed down the back of my neck. I stifled a moan. "The happier we'll both be."

"No." I tried to twist free but my body only responded to him; completely at the mercy of his will and the bond between us.

Was this how the dragons had felt during the Brutal War? Their minds their own but their body's controlled by someone else? Forced to slaughter their loved ones? To stain their hands with the blood of their kin and be powerless to stop it? All because the Dragon Prince had defied my mother?

Loch moaned as he used his hips to press me harder into the wall. I gasped—fighting within myself. My thoughts a blur.

My soul screamed for Exekiel but rationality or Loch was taking hold. Was Loch right?

Being with Exekiel wouldn't protect me from the Court, wouldn't free my people and all those exiled in the Outer Isles. But being with Loch would. It could dawn a new day; of equality and peace...but only after a war. And was Loch any less of a tyrant than those already upon the throne?

Too many fragmented thoughts tangled in my mind. I didn't know which ones were mine and which ones were Lochs. I could follow the Guardian of the Siren Sea and his path to freedom—but at a cost I wasn't prepared to pay. Or I could find some other way…

Loch lifted up my dress.

I flinched. "No."

This wasn't what I wanted.

"You're mine."

I wasn't. He was a monster. A mad man. Fists clenched, I heaved on my power. With a bone-shattering cry, I wrenched it from Loch's control. I was finally free.

Dizzy, I dropped to my knees and crawled towards Exekiel. He was deathly pale. His eyes closed and skin clammy. Turning him onto his back, I pressed my hands over the wound. Desperately praying for the flutter of a heartbeat.

Behind me, Loch growled. "You're too late, Princess. Your mate is dead. It's time you let your bond die with him."

I choked back a sob. My heart splitting. He couldn't be dead. He couldn't be. A mournful cry ripped from my chest as I hunched over him.

"Exekiel," I pleaded. "Exekiel."

Loch huffed, "Who's side are you on?"

"Mine!" I roared.

My eyes blazed. Rage hot in my throat; ready to be unleashed. I'd always been on my side—fighting in my corner when nobody else was.

My wings splayed—a stretch of scarlet. Fangs jutted from my mouth. Right now, I was all dragon; death and destruction. Loch must have seen it, for he stepped back—his jaw clenched and nostrils flared.

"Soon you will see that we are on the same side," he snarled. "For now, say your goodbyes and meet me at the barrier. It's finally going to fall and we need to be there to welcome in our army."

44

BONDS IN BLOOD

Loch's departing words barely registered as I poured my power into Exekiel. The blood flow slowed but not enough. *Not enough.* His skin was ghostly white, his head hung to the side and there was no whisper of a heartbeat. No rasping of breath. No indication that his vibrant pink eyes would ever open again.

My soul splintered. Exekiel was dead.

The dragon within me roared and I bowed my head to his; cradled his face in my hands.

"Wake up," I begged.

But it was too late. He was already gone.

"What happened?"

I swiveled at the sound of Lucinda's voice. Her lipstick was smeared; her hair disheveled. Her lavender skirts askew. She took in my horns and wings. The slight widening of her mouth was the only indication that she was surprised, though not entirely, as if a part of her had known.

The words; "you were right", hung on the edge of my tongue.

Instead, I whispered, "Save him."

Lucinda shook her head. "I can't."

I crumpled. That final breath of hope I hadn't realized I was holding, released.

"But you might." Lucinda added, kneeling beside me. "There's a window between life and death. A moment where the soul crosses between planes and in that sliver of time, it's believed that one might revive their mate...but it requires a blood-enchantment." She grimaced. "One that will bind your life to his."

I froze. "You mean—? If I die..."

Lucinda nodded. "And if he dies...you die."

The ground rocked. This was big; could change everything but I didn't hesitate before saying, "Okay."

Lucinda looked like she might argue; force me to truly think about what I was agreeing to, but there wasn't time.

"Unbutton his shirt," she said briskly.

We worked fast. Following Lucinda's instructions, I slashed open the palm of my hand and used my blood to draw a symbol on Exekiel's chest. I did my best to avoid the stab wound forged with an obsidian dagger. The only weapon powerful enough to slay a Bravinore Fae, especially when handled by someone of equal power. Though Loch wasn't of equal power. He'd used poison and his ability to wield my magic as his own. I shuddered. Hurt and rage crawled up my spine.

A song—a spell—spilled from my lips and I let it pour as my magic flowed into Exekiel. They were the words Lucinda gave me, but, in a tune, neither of us created. The mark on Exekiel's chest glowed a vibrant teal; the edges shimmered scarlet.

"Now," Lucinda urged.

I pressed my lips to his. They were still warm, yet lacked the fire they usually held. Tears slid down my cheeks. I tasted their salt. But I refused to crumble; to lose hope. I would bring him back. I didn't know what would happen after, but Exekiel had to come back to me.

The song echoed through the courtyard as my lips stroked the Shadow's Saints. The earth trembled and something inside me cracked.

"Blood!"

I bit down on Exekiel's bottom lip and tasted the salt and iron of his blood. As soon as it touched my tongue, the last of my magical restraints snapped and my power bloomed like a phoenix from the ashes. My wingspan doubled. The scales on my skin hardened. Every sound, every sight was intensified. I poured myself—my soul—into Exekiel, binding my life with his.

Beneath my palm, pressed to his chest, his heart fluttered. My own skipped a beat. Then Exekiel groaned and I leapt back as the Shadow Saint rolled over and retched. A sour scent filled the air. The poison they'd injected him with that had thrown off his aim and distorted his power fizzled on the ground.

Lucinda staggered forwards, seeming as shaken by Exekiel's return as she was by the toxin dripping down his chin.

"They created a poison to overpower *him?*" she whispered; her face pale. "Fates unhappy fortune. I'll be back."

With that, Lucinda took off. I turned to Exekiel who was pulling himself up to rest his back against the well.

I moved to help him but he grabbed my wrists, stopping me.

"What have you done?" he rasped. His chest rattled and his skin was clammy.

"What I had to."

Exekiel snarled, his teeth gritted. "Why?"

"Because." I tried to pull away but his grip tightened.

"Why?"

"It doesn't matter!"

"Why?" he bellowed despite his pallor.

"Because I love you!" I shouted; breathless and skin flushed. "As stupid as that is."

Exekiel bared his teeth; the pink of his eyes sinking to deep red. He tugged me towards him with more strength than anyone who'd almost died should have and pressed his mouth to mine. He tasted of wine and bile but that couldn't slake the heat that flooded my core.

Our kiss was hungry, endless and unforgiving. Hands desperately groping; fisting in each other's hair. Our hearts pounded, beating with the fury of a war drum.

With a groan, Exekiel pulled me onto his lap. Fevered, I ground into him. The Shadow Saint responded like a beast unhinged. He grasped my backside, rocking me into the hardening ridge beneath his slacks. The mark on his chest still glowed. My power still swirled around us; pulling tight and wrenching us closer. My heart punched in my chest.

This was unreal. A moment like no other—of pure powerful ecstasy. One graze of his finger and I almost came.

"You're a fool," Exekiel growled, moving to trail kisses down my breast.

My skin tingled—over sensitized by his touch.

"Tonight, your people started a war, and you have bound yourself to me."

Freeing my breast, Exekiel sucked my nipple into his mouth. I bucked. My arms wrapped around his head, holding him in place. My insides tightened. My body flushed with desperation. I needed him urgently. Our connection stronger; amplified. Limitless. I could drown in an ocean of Exekiel and never come up for air.

"We are on opposing sides," he grunted as he slid his hand beneath my dress and stroked between my thighs. "And now your life is in my hands."

He pushed a finger inside me. I moaned; clinging to his shoulders as desire and fear shot through my core.

"The survival of the bastards who attacked me, depends on you."

Exekiel's power gathered around us like a swell of shadows. I tensed. Suddenly I understood his title: Shadow Saint. Every symbol of the Fates bloomed on his skin and danced with the smoke of his ability that plumed and arced as if seeking an enemy…seeking me. The girl straddled across his lap. My hands fisted in his shirt and my lips swollen from his kiss as his fingers pumped inside me. His arm fastened around my waist, restraining me on top of him.

Exekiel's tone sharpened, "Do you really expect me to believe it was a coincidence that you came out here?" He fingered me faster.

My eyes scrunched closed. My heart thrashed and mind raced.

"That you didn't plan to seduce me so that your people could attack?"

"I-I didn't—" I panted as I jerked on his hand.

His answering laugh was callous. "Bullshit. I bet you expected me to thank you. Thought I'd help you destroy the Isles." His shadows thickened, obscuring his features until all I saw was the red of his eyes and all I felt was the rough thrust of his fingers.

"When I find a way to break this connection, which I will, little bud." His breath was hot against my neck. "I will make you regret being born."

I bit my lip—fighting the need to come. His fingers moved as if he was taking out all his rage between my legs. I moaned hotly. I didn't know what I'd expected after saving the Shadow Saint but him finger-fucking me whilst threatening my life, wasn't it.

He pressed down on my clit and I cried out. My body spasming as I came. Heat blazed through my entire being. My head thrown back and limbs tight. In that same instant, Exekiel unsheathed his cock—unable to deny the pull of the bond between us that seemed heightened in this moment. Whether by the fear of almost losing each other or by the blood bond, I didn't know.

Despite his threats, I willingly widened my legs and Exekiel pushed inside me. My soul cried in ecstasy but his words swirled through my mind. He blamed me for what happened. He believed I'd set a trap for him and was going to make me pay for it. But not just me. Every siren and every innocent in the Outer Isles.

My magic took hold. Before I knew it, another song filled my mind and I sang. The melody seemed to fuse us together and our centers met more aggressively. Exekiel groaned; his fingers digging into my sides.

His head tipped back in pleasure, but he rasped, "What are you doing?"

I panted, "Protecting my people."

I kissed him hard even as he tried to pull away, and bit down on his lower lip. I let a whisper of my power in, which was sacrilege. A violation of our bond. He'd told me the night of the werewolf attack that to use my power to coerce him would tarnish our connection. I didn't know in what way. But nothing between mates should be forced. However, I didn't have a choice. I couldn't let him or the Court hurt anyone else. So, I forced my will upon him.

The melody compelled Exekiel to keep what happened a secret. To give me time to figure out my next move without the threat of death or the devastation of the Outer Isles.

My mind bellowed and my body ached as if I was severing a part of myself but I sang on as Exekiel bucked beneath me.

Then it was done. We both came with a visceral cry. I shuddered on top of him, eventually, meeting his dark stare. I flinched from the hatred that shone in his eyes.

45

BITTER ENDS

Two weeks had passed since the ball, but my nerves were still frazzled; my magic depleted. How had so much happened in one night? And why, despite everything, was Exekiel's hatred what bothered me the most? Not Loch's betrayal or the fact that I was part-dragon or that I'd violated my mating bond and had no idea what that meant, but the fact that Exekiel was mad at me.

I groaned and raked my fingers through my tight ringlet-curls which, since my transformation into part-dragon, had changed from black to turquoise. My nails were also sharper, thicker. But no wings, scales or horns remained. They'd faded when I'd used the last of my strength to undo the enchantment Loch had put on those in the ballroom.

It had been a small mercy that Lucinda hadn't been in there at the time. She'd been with her source. Her secret lover who'd warned us about the potions Trial, and sent first-rate ointments to aid our recovery. If it hadn't been for Lucinda, Exekiel would have died and the realm would have descended into war.

Although, I couldn't prevent the inevitable much longer. Not now that Loch could wield my power, and Exekiel was out for blood.

I shuddered and slumped onto my bed. The waiting was the worst part. Endless days without distraction. The Trials were over and the contestants had all returned home to spend time with their families before risking their lives in a deadly game. But I had nowhere to go.

Both Lucinda and Max had invited me to join them but just me being in the Eternal City for the Games caused riots in the streets. There was no telling what the people would do if I, a siren, was actually walking amongst them.

A knock sounded on the door and I scowled. Only the nymphs, camera crew and Resident staff had remained behind and I'd told them to leave me alone. I needed time with my thoughts. To process Loch's deception, Exekiel's hatred and what the hell I was going to do about both—whilst also trying to stay alive and find some way to win the Games.

The knock came again.

"Go away!"

"Open the door, Varialla."

My blood ran cold. "Danimous?"

The centaur who'd given me the communication shell and brought Loch into my life. At the time, it'd seemed like a blessing, but it was only more manipulation—more lies.

"That's right," he said from behind the door. "Let me in."

I scoffed. If Danimous was here, he'd been sent by Loch or the Primary, and I had no desire to hear from either.

"That's not happening," I grumbled.

There was the distinct click of the lock turning. I bolted upright as the door swung open and Danimous trotted in.

"What the hell?"

He shrugged. "You have a visitor."

Like the last time, a swathe of fabric was draped over his quarters. My skin leeched of color when a figure dropped to the ground beneath him. Danimous stepped back to reveal Loch crouched with a cruel grin on his face.

"Hello, Princess."

Overcome with rage, I lunged. I slashed at Loch's face. My sharp nails catching his cheek before he grabbed my wrists. I brought my knee up to drive it into his groin, but he dodged my attempt.

"Get out." I seethed.

Uselessly, I fought to pry my wrists free but his grip was unyielding. He watched me with mild amusement— his ice-blue eyes shimmering—which only enraged me more.

"Give us a moment, Danimous," Loch drawled. "Stand watch."

The centaur bowed his head and panic speared through me as he strode out of the room. Not that I was any safer with the centaur here but he seemed to be kinder than the monster before me.

Refusing to let my fear show, I stepped forward, getting right up in Loch's face.

"What the fuck are you doing here?"

My body was hot with hatred. All this time he'd been molding me for his own gain. Using me. Deceiving me.

"I've come to take you home."

"I have no home," I spat.

He'd taken that from me. Taken the only place I'd felt safe and truly wanted, and turned it into a lie.

His brow lifted. "Nothing's changed, Princess. You're still an enemy of the Five Isles and they still want you dead. And I'm still your only chance of survival, of saving those you care for in the Coral Court. Of avenging the fallen."

Cherise's face filled my mind, along with the vow I'd sworn to protect her mother. I thought of Colette, Algeron and all the others I'd befriended over the last few months. Loch had betrayed me but they hadn't. Like Cherise, they genuinely didn't know what I was or how severe the Ceremonial Bind had been. But Loch...

My hands balled into fists. "Everything's changed because of you."

He sighed. "In that case, pack your things, and you can yell at me on the way home."

Anger burned through me at his nonchalance; his arrogance. Did he care at all?

"I'm not going anywhere with you." He opened his mouth but I shouted, "Get out!"

Loch stilled. Someone might have heard that. Though the cameras were no longer running, security was in full force; patrolling the grounds and guarding the Conduit. Knowing I was there, Exekiel and the

Council had also taken it upon themselves to frequently return unannounced.

Loch bared his fangs and his power wrapped around me.

My limbs locked up as the bastard growled, "Get on the bed."

My eyes shot wide and I wrestled inside my skin as my legs turned and marched towards the bed. I sat, rigid; clawing from the inside to break through his command.

"How are you doing this?" I gritted out. I'd spent the last week working on my Mind-Shield; protecting myself from coercion, or so I thought.

Loch chuckled darkly. "I'm the one who put that Shield there, Princess. Do you really think I don't know a way around it?"

My chest tightened. Anguish and rage rose within me. How had I been so blind? So stupid? I'd trusted Loch; given him access to my mind, my power...my body.

I snarled, "You'll have to release me at some point, asshole."

"True." Loch took a menacing step closer. "But think of all the things I can do to you before then."

His lips slanted into a grin. My heartrate tripled.

"Lay down." He ordered.

Powerless, I obeyed.

"Open your legs."

Fear spiked through me. All I wore was a large T-shirt. Nothing beneath. I gaped at him in horror as my legs fell open. Loch groaned when I was revealed to him.

"Bastard," I hissed.

He didn't seem to hear me. "Touch yourself," Loch whispered, his gaze fixed between my thighs.

My stomach turned.

"You've made your point," I grunted, fisting the sheets and denying his command. It pounded inside me—yanked on my tendons.

"Touch yourself," he growled.

I glared; jaw clenched. But eventually, I trailed my fingers along my leg. I knew what he'd meant but his command gave me room to interpret it my own way. He'd told me to touch myself but he didn't specify where.

I sneered when he realized his mistake.

Loch's stare darkened. "Clever."

Quicker than I could blink, he grabbed my hand and pushed it between my legs.

"Here," he ordered, guiding my hand. "Touch yourself here."

Heat swept through me. I barely suppressed a moan. My body was still inexplicably drawn to him. Hopelessly turned on as he pumped my fingers inside me. My head kicked back—my back arching off the bed.

"That's it," he panted, stepping back to watch me with hunger in his eyes.

"You're an asshole," I cried.

Like before, he ignored me. His deranged eyes danced, waiting for me to fall off the edge.

"I won't do it," I spat, though all I had were my words to wield.

Loch purred, "Then allow me."

In seconds, he was upon me and his scent slid down my throat. I gasped when he withdrew my fingers and sank his own inside me, picking up where I'd left off.

I bucked; my face scrunched with pleasure and revulsion. His fingers plunged deeper; curling to strike a point that made me leak.

"Yes," he rasped, stroking his thumb across my clit. I almost combusted. Rattling on the edge of his hand.

What was worse was that his magic no longer controlled me. I was responding to him because I wanted to. Because I couldn't help it. Because the bond between us—forged when I was just an egg—drew me to him like lightning to a storm.

"Do as I say willingly," he growled, "Or I will compel you to do so much more. Got that, Princess?"

I nodded; shamelessly grinding into his hand. Right now, I would have said yes to anything. I reached the precipice of lust but before I could tumble off the edge, Loch pulled away.

My eyes sprang open. I glared as he smirked down at me. I didn't know if I was angrier that he'd denied me my release, or that he'd made me want it in the first place.

Loch greedily sucked on the fingers he'd had inside me and moaned. "So sweet."

I trembled with loathing and desire.

"Now pack up your things, Princess. We have a lot to do before the official Games begin."

DID YOU ENJOY

FIT FOR THE THRONE?

If you enjoyed this book, please leave an honest review on Amazon, Bookbub and/or Goodreads.

Reviews and ratings are extremely valuable for indie authors like myself. It helps new readers decide if this book is something they would enjoy, and it enables me, the author, to get some invaluable feedback and keep writing the books you love.

I cannot wait to hear what you think and I truly thank you for taking the time to read this story.

More from S. Mcpherson:

A Court of Echoes
New Adult Fantasy Romance Trilogy

Witches of the Damned (The Scarlet Court)
New Adult Fantasy Romance Trilogy

Dark Saints Academy
Upper YA Fantasy Romance Trilogy

The Last Elentrice
Young Adult 6-book series

The Emerald Eye
FREE with Newsletter Sign Up

Transform Your Life 365 Degrees
A self-development handbook to help you revolutionise your life.

S. McPherson

S. McPherson is a young British-Jamaican expat living in Dubai. She works as a kindergarten teacher and when she is not at work immersed in a world of imagination and fantasy created by the children, she is immersed in her own worlds of imagination and fantasy at home, dreaming up tales and writing them down.

As well as writing, S. McPherson loves spending time with her friends, spoiling her cat and dancing and singing around the house, usually to the latest song that's gotten stuck in her head. Or she can be found reading a deliciously delightful fantasy. Her TBR is extensive.

The Trial of Ten is the first book in S. McPherson's fourth series, *Fit for the Throne*.

(Dark Saints Academy Book 1)

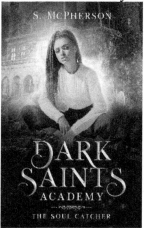

A fallen angel. A dark Queen. An age-old prophecy.

As heir to the shadow throne, Ryleigh De La Cruz is the world's greatest threat. Whisked off to Dark Saints Academy, she must learn to control her shadow magic or become the greatest evil ever known.

There is only one who can stop her—save her—Danté Ramirez, a dark angel with a mysterious past, and a connection to Ryleigh that is as brutal as it is beautiful.

But time's running out. With Ryleigh's powers rising and her father, Sovereign of the underworld, on the move, Danté must find a way to bring Ryleigh into the Light before she surrenders to her shadows and destroys them all.

Fans of Sarah J Maas and Jaymin Eve are addicted to this heart-pounding, medium burn, paranormal romance from Bestselling author, S. McPherson.

Printed in Great Britain
by Amazon